KAZAKH
PEN CLUB

КАЗАК
ПЕН КЛУБЫ

SAIN MURATBEKOV

The Crossing and Other Stories

Published by The Kazakh Pen Club, © 2020

Translation copyright © Simon Hollingsworth, 2020

Sain Muratbekov
The Crossing and Other Stories

KAZAKH
PEN CLUB

KA3AK
ПЕН КЛУБЫ

SAIN MURATBEKOV

The Crossing and Other Stories

Translated into English by Simon Hollingsworth

Edited by Simon Geoghegan

Published under the supervision of
President of the Kazakh PEN Club
Bigeldy Gabdullin

Cover design by Madina Niyazbayeva

Printed in the United Kingdom

ACKNOWLEDGEMENTS

The publishers would like to thank the Kazakh PEN Club for their continual support on this project. The project was initiated by Kazakh PEN Club President **Bigeldy Gabdullin**, designed to expose the best works of classic Kazakh writers to the global literary stage through their translation into the English language. Through the tireless efforts of Mr Gabdullin, the project gained the financial and logistical support needed from influential Kazakh state organisations and private companies. The translation of this collection of stories and novellas of Sain Muratbekov was possible thanks to the generous support of the **Akimat of Almaty**.

TABLE OF CONTENTS

SHORT STORIES

THE NIGHT RAIN

Assiya looked at her father and smiled. She had never seen him look so angry and this made her want to giggle. He was frowning, waving his arms about and screaming. And his moustaches! They had transformed into camel's bristles. Could you imagine ever kissing those?!

However, the more Otar raged, the more serious his daughter became. Assiya's smile slid from her face, her cheeks became flushed and she bit her lip to stop herself from crying.

'Love? Don't love? What do these words mean anyway? No one ever asked your mother and me if we loved each other or not. Our fathers were wiser. We were matched and that was the end of the matter and our hearth has been burning forty years now. And, thanks to Allah, we have been living harmoniously all this time. We've had children... Meaning you. And we never asked one another whether there was love or not. They're nothing but empty words.'

Old Zhakup, who had bestowed them with a visit, looked askance at the girl.

He seems a decent enough man and he was chairman of the collective farm, Assiya thought, looking at him. *But his son... Such an idler and a shirker. He knows full well that I have no time for him, so he's sent his father instead.*

Assiya recalled how that summer, old Zhakup had come over and talked at length with Otar. Back then, Otar had only one thing to say in response:

'Let her decide. Young people are like gazelles; you can't tell them what to do...'

But now?

Otar fell silent for a moment and looked at his daughter. *So, what's her objection? It's not as if I'm giving her away to some old man. The lad's young and he's good-looking. Zhakup is decent enough and she's not marrying into a poor home. So, what's the problem?*

It seemed as if Assiya had heard these unspoken words. She lifted her face and her eyes flashed a decisive *no!*

Otar could stand it no longer and screamed like the lash of a whip:

'So, you'll be leeching off me until you're an old maid, I see!'

And this was her own father talking! The girl's face flushed and she ran outside in nothing but her flimsy dress and light *ichigi* boots[1], almost falling in the snow. She hid behind the shed and waited until Zhakup had gone. She didn't feel the frost; only her feet were cold, while her face burned.

Spring had come unexpectedly and with it the southerly wind had ripped away the hammered armour from the surface of the earth. The soil had melted and was breathing freely and happily. Caravans of birds stretched over the steppe. Noise levels had picked up in the village and it was boisterous and merry.

---

[1] *Soft, leather boots, often decorated with leather inlay and stitching*

It had woken from its winter slumber and was clattering about, stretching its sleep-filled limbs. The tractor operators fussed around their machines, checking ploughs and seeders, and dispersed over the fields. The scale operators hustled and the husbandrymen bustled. One tractor, like an unbroken horse, suddenly turned into a narrow street and came to a halt by Otar's house. The tractor driver revved the engine, making all the windows rattle. Old Rash poked her head out of the window, looking frightened and wondering if it was Zhakup's son who had driven up. However, the driver who killed the engine and jumped down from the cab was a large-headed, wheat-skinned man. Naturally, he had his cap at a jaunty angle, as all dashing drivers do.

'Hey, people of the house! Come and receive your guest! Is there anyone alive in there?!'

It seemed to old Rash that an entire crowd had gathered at her door. She came out to the gate, but there was only one person there. Just one, but he was making such a din. The man was already approaching her; he smiled and offered his hand.

'My name is Noyan. I'm from the central estate. The foreman sent me over to live with you. Just temporarily, mind, while they're finishing off the hostel.'

Otar frowned as he looked at the man from behind the wattle fence and he muttered through his whiskers:

'Could they not have sent a more suitable person? He chatters like a magpie and there's no stopping him.'

Noyan threw off his boilersuit, shook it out and nimbly threw it onto the fence.

'You'd better keep an eye out, son, you don't want anything chewing through your clothes. The animals around here really aren't picky about what they eat...'

'Let them eat their fill, I say! Who knows? Perhaps they'll get a taste for fuel oil.'

'Oh no, they'd get poisoned! Best, you hang it up further away and higher up.'

Noyan burst out laughing with a wave of his hand. He walked calmly and confidently into the house as if he'd been living there a good while already. He sat in the seat of honour, as befits a guest.

Assiya was standing by the window. Hearing footsteps, she turned around. Although it was not particularly bright in the room, Noyan could still make out her large eyes, full of surprise. He felt awkward but collected himself. He screwed up his eyes a little and asked jokingly,

'You're not Bizbeke² by any chance, are you?'

'No, I'm Assiya and why are you speaking to me in that way?'

Again, Noyan felt rather awkward.

'Oh, just because. Don't go thinking I believe Otar-*aga* is a *Shygaibai*, although, to be honest, there are some people who think that... Well, not exactly, to be honest... But that's why I asked,' he said, now completely at sixes and sevens. 'Well, anyway, I won't be staying for long; it's just until the hostel is finished.'

---

² *The daughter of the greedy Shygaibai from the Kazakh folk tale*

12

'I see. So, not for long...'

Assiya first plaited, then unplaited her hair with her slender fingers.

'Oh,' the driver sighed, 'I had no intention of causing offence. I was only joking, but now look what I've gone and done.'

He whipped off his crumpled cap and flattened down his dishevelled hair. He wanted to retrieve his comb but remembered he had left it in his boilersuit. He looked at the girl apologetically.

Having hurriedly herded the animals into the barn, Otar entered the house. He continued to behave as if their guest was not there. He sat down on his blanket, spat on his fingers and took to turning his moustaches that were sticking out like twisted wires.

'Otar-*aga*, have you been cultivating your moustaches long?' Noyan asked, as if out of the blue.

Laughter appeared in his eyes. Otar looked at his guest with a frown; he turned away and lay down on his pillow. Assiya snorted and ran to the other room. Otar grunted and was on the verge of crying out, *Shut up, you shameless devil*, but he thought better of it. The only way to get this insolent smart-alec off his back was to remain silent.

Otar had heard of Noyan's antics; he was well-known throughout the collective farm for his barbed tongue and his love of tricks.

Noyan also sat in silence, although Otar was the last thing on his mind.

The next morning, Otar rose earlier than everyone else, as is fitting for the master of the house. He took a

13

long time dressing, groaning as he did so. Then he went out to let the cattle out of the shed.

At that early hour, the steppe was both majestic and taciturn. It was also on the cool side and this was to Otar's liking. He stopped and screwed up his eyes. The sun's first, slender rays were cutting through the darkness as the fiery sphere rolled slowly into view. The tractor was shedding its frosty, white sheen from the night before, drops of water splashing down into little puddles.

Otar returned to the house. Of course! Noyan was still snoring with his head nestled into the pillow.

'Hey, smart arse! Do you think you've come here just to sleep?' Otar snapped.

Noyan rose from the bed in a single leap, rubbed his eyes and quickly dressed. He then rattled about in the sink on the terrace. As he walked past the room where Assiya was sleeping, he happened to look into her window and stopped. He pressed his forehead against the glass.

When Otar emerged onto the terrace, Noyan hurriedly stepped back from the window and began wiping his face with a dry towel.

What's that devil looking at? Otar thought and went to the window. Assiya was sleeping serenely at the back of the room, her black hair strewn over the pillow. The blanket had slipped down, revealing a bare shoulder.

Otar struck a furious fist down on the frame. Assiya shuddered, woke up and, not understanding what was going on, she took fright and pulled up the blanket.

The springtime tilling was in full swing. Machinery hummed day and night, rattling all the windows in the village. Being the nearest dwelling to the field, Otar's entire house shook. The crockery rattled on the shelves and it seemed as if the house was teetering on the edge of an abyss, about to fall at any moment. Otar was unable to get to asleep from the constant noise and his many thoughts. He jumped up, dressed and for a long time paced about the yard.

Assiya worked the night shift on the seeding machine and barely saw her father. She would return from work when Otar was taking the cattle out early in the morning. She would be covered in dust with only her eyes sparkling. Sometimes, she wouldn't touch her food and would just wash and go to bed. Cannons might have roared and she would have slept just as deeply. By the time her father would return, she would be out in the fields once more.

Otar cursed to himself, in a fit of temper: *Serves her right for refusing to marry that lad.* He had become unsettled and was often angry. Rash came up to him with tears in her eyes.

'And what's the matter with you?'

'She says, she's going to leave us. The sowing will end, and she's going to leave.'

'Eh? Well, I never. But where's she going to go?'

'She didn't say... She has already started packing her clothes in her suitcase.'

15

'Good riddance is all I can say,' Otar said as indifferently as he could. 'Let's just get some dinner.'

However, he didn't want to eat. When he picked up his bowl, there was nothing he could do with his shaking hands.

That night, he could stand it no longer. He dressed up warm and stepped out into the dark.

Tractors could be seen in the distance, their headlamps shining. One of them had stopped and a cart with seeds approached it, its wheels rattling as it went. The sowing women jumped down and began to drag the sacks off. He heard a familiar man's voice:

'Wait, Assiya, wait! I'll get it.'

Yes, it was Noyan. The vehicle hummed and lurched forward. Spots of rain began to fall, becoming steadily heavier. The rumbling of a tractor could be heard. Otar became worried.

Why ever is he not stopping? If that scoundrel mixes seeds with dirt, what damage will he do to all the good work the farm has done?!

The tractor crept to the edge of the field and the engine stopped. The rain, clearly delighted at its victory, transformed triumphantly into a heavy downfall.

'What a clot!' Otar said, losing his temper. 'He could have come and sat here with us while it was raining. Perhaps Assiya will have more sense.'

He stomped about, waiting for his daughter, but she never materialised. Otar returned home, threw on a canvas raincoat, took a coat for Assiya and headed out for the field.

It was hard-going across the wet, ploughed earth. He made his way onto the fringe and walked on. The tractor could barely be seen; it was standing by a rick of last year's straw.

Calls himself an agriculturalist?! Otar scoffed to himself with a shake of the head. *These things need to be set alight at the right time.*

He had already reached into his pocket for some matches when he heard a girl's laughter and a man's whisper he couldn't make out.

'What wonderful rain! Noyan, trying sticking your face out!'

Without really knowing why, Otar threw back his unshaken face to the rain. Cold streams trickled over his moustaches and down his neck.

'That rain really is something!' the tractor driver replied.

Otar winced and wiped his face with a rough hand.

How daft they are, the pair of them! It's just like any old rain.

'What if your father finds out? He can't stand me.'

Too right, I simply can't stomach the lad.

'You told me yourself that nothing in the world can stand against love,' Assiya said quietly.

They both fell silent for a moment.

'Noyan, Noyan! You've really turned my head. When you first entered our home, I felt my heart miss a beat; it was as if I sensed it. And then I had a dream and that dream was just like things are now. Do you remember how you tried not to look me in the eye?'

17

'My darling...'

Otar stood by the rick, his head drooped. Then he slowly walked away across the ploughed field.

Nothing in the world can stand against love.

He could not get these words out of his head. *No, people only sing about this; but not in real life, surely? Or is it that our children have come to know more than we do? Are they happier?*

Otar brushed these questions away and tried to think about something else. He looked up at the stars and recalled the argument he'd had with the stock breeder. And yet, he kept hearing that magical phrase.

Nothing in the world can stand against love.

He simply couldn't believe that his Assiya could say such a thing.

He remembered one episode and his recollection was rekindled just like a hot coal in the wind. But when was it? He had even stopped walking. Yes, a lot of water had passed under the bridge... He had turned nineteen and his first son Basar had just been born. Yes, that was right, when the labourers had arranged a cooperative and he had become a member.

That same year, a doctor had come to the village. She was a Kazakh girl and that had been a rarity back then. Makira was her name; Otar had taken a liking to her the first moment he saw her and he had really wanted to find an excuse to see her. The only thing was that he hadn't been unwell.

That summer, which had been swelteringly hot, he drank a large amount of cold water and his throat became sore. Otar had set off for the hospital.

18

He could still remember how beautiful she was, standing there, a picture of seriousness in her white coat. She had listened attentively to her patient and had touched his cheek. There could have been no better medicine. Otar had long since recovered but he had been continually drawn to the hospital. 'It's my throat again,' he had said, trying to portray suffering as best he could.

One day, Makira had quietly said to him:

'But my dear, you have a family. There is no need for all this.'

A year later, the girl had left for the city. How many years had gone by since then? How wonderful she was!

He cast up his head. Then, he darted off to one side and then back again, as if he had lost something dear and was looking for it in the spring night.

So, there is love in this life?

Streams of rain rolled down his raincoat, which had grown stiff from the frost, and viscous mud stuck to his boots. Otar walked off in no particular direction, clutching his daughter's coat tightly in his hand.

THE WINDING PATHS OF AUTUMN

The day had slipped beyond midday, stretching the necks of our shadows and making our heads look like pumpkins. There were three of us: Grisha, Kanatay and I. We were sitting on a flat rock near the mill, chatting idly for wont of anything else to do. Kanatay was the youngest of us; he was a pale-faced, scrawny little lad. He was two years younger than me, but you could have shaved another couple off of him, given his appearance. Grisha was thick-lipped and ginger. He was past thirty and that made him the centre of attention in our hotch-potch little company. Moreover, he occupied what we believed to be a very high, official position, for he managed the mill in these parts. The flour dust that covered him from head to toe always reminded us of his standing.

A narrow but pretty boisterous stream gurgled at our feet. The current, raging and hissing, broke onto the indulgently patient stones beneath in a show of resentment at the lack of respect and seriousness that people showed it. The waters gave off a pleasant coolness that tempted and drew one closer.

Grisha and I maintained a dignified appearance, as befits grown men, and we wiped the sweat from our brows as if unintentionally. Kanatay, however, behaved like a child. Extending a leg in trousers rolled-up to the knee, he immersed a bare foot into the bubbling stream. Each time he did this, he registered a look of pure bliss.

Grisha looked askance at Kanatay and then got down from the rock, rolled up the sleeves of his sateen shirt, scooped up an entire lake of water in his enormous hands, splashed it on his freckled face and snorted with pleasure like a horse.

'Show us, Uncle Grisha! They're so cool!' Kanatay cried out.

I couldn't take my eyes off Grisha's powerful arms either. They were decorated with intricate patterns, like the skin of a snake. There was so much going on there: an anchor, a heart, pierced by a dagger, a boa constrictor and all manner of other wonders.

'Where did you get all these, Uncle Grisha?' Kanatay persisted.

'Back when I was a kid. When I was just a lad,' Grisha told him, while also admiring his tattoos.

'And you drew them all yourself?'

'Of course not. This is the work of a specialist. That said, it's not that hard to do. I'll tattoo your date of birth if you want. Here, give me your arm.'

'Won't it hurt?'

'Of course, it will. But you're not a little child, now, are you? How old are you?'

'Sixteen'

'So, all grown up then. Don't be afraid, lad. You'll have an arm like a real man, too.'

Grisha pulled a stubby indelible pencil from his pocket, which he had only just used to sign delivery notes. Then he drew out a needle with coarse thread from a torn old bag.

'The bag can wait. I'll get round to sewing it up later. Right then, roll up your sleeve,' he commanded. Kanatay turned paler still, pulled his sleeve up to the elbow and thrust out his arm decisively.

'You think I'm scared, eh? There, do your worst!'

'Well, aren't you the brave one,' Grisha said and spat on the pencil. 'Hey, you're dad's not going to have a go at you, is he? Because that means I'll get it in the neck too, you see.'

'I don't have a dad,' Kanatay objected.

'Well, then let's get going.'

Grisha spat once more on the pencil and drew Kanatay's name on his arm.

'What was your dad's name?'

'Zhansultan.'

'Excellent! We'll add the letter *Zh*... There, that's come out nicely! And now we'll poke it.'

Grisha wiped the needle on his trousers and began to prick at the image. Kanatay turned away and gritted his teeth. Catching my eye, he forced a grin.

'So where's your father? What happened to him?' Grisha asked, either from curiosity or in an attempt to strike up a conversation and divert his client's attention.

'Papa died in the war,' Kanatay replied through his teeth, afraid of moaning from the pain.

'There, the name's done,' Grisha said, admiring his handiwork. 'That's top drawer, that is! And now for the date of birth. What year were you born?'

'Forty-seven.'

23

'Forty-seven. Hey, wait a minute. Are you pulling one over on me? How could your father have died in the war, if you were born in forty-seven?'

'Papa died in the war. The Second World War!' Kanatay repeated stubbornly.

'There's something not right there, lad. I think you're talking rot,' and Grisha shook his head.

'I'm telling the truth! My Papa died in the war! The Second World War!' Kanatay screamed.

Tears appeared in his eyes and he clenched his fists. We realised that another word and Kanatay would start a fight. Grisha gathered his wits and peaceably changed his tone:

'Alright, alright! I'm kidding, can't you see that? Let's get this thing finished, shall we?'

Kanatay scowled and extended his arm once more. Soon, we were admiring Grisha's latest work of art. The skin around the fresh tattoo was red and swollen, and droplets of blood emerged here and there.

'Not a bad image, if I say so myself,' Grisha said, although his boast didn't contain any enthusiasm.

We agreed for decency's sake, but the conversation wouldn't get going after that. Kanatay continually touched his arm and narrowed his little nostrils. Grisha became bored and began to yawn. I looked at the stream that raged and frothed before disappearing beneath the mill. It emerged into the open on the other side and flowed serenely along the ravine. Here, it was no more than ankle-deep while elsewhere one could even clearly see the shingle on the river bed.

The noise of the water deafened out the sound of the millstones but, if you looked closely, you could see that the mill, made of heavy logs, shuddered slightly from their turning.

The slopes of the ravine, overgrown with elm, honeysuckle and purple willow, drew in from both sides of the mill. Autumn had already scorched the leaves, but they still held firm on the branches. A path ran through the clumps of purple willow, winding up the hill from the stream. For those who came from the hilltop, this path led down to the stream.

It went down for me when I had come here an hour before with Kanatay and his mother Bibi. Their dappled horse, harnessed to the cart, was now standing in the shade, while Bibi herself was filling sacks with flour at the mill.

Hooves clopped on the path behind us and we all turned in unison. The muzzle of a horse and the fur cap of the man on a cart flashed from beyond the willow bushes. When he made the last turn and emerged at the mill, we saw a man dozing, his head drooped down onto his chest. The horses came to their customary stop but the man sat motionless for a while thereafter. Then he stirred, brushed away the flies and raised his head.

'Hey, Grisha! Get out here, Grisha!' he cried out groggily.

'That's my kinsman Shintemir,' Grisha informed us with a smile and rose to address the new arrival: 'What's with all the shouting? I'm right here, Shintemir!'

'Ah, you're here!' Shintemir said, brightening up. 'Is the flour ready, Grish?'

'Yes, and it's been waiting for you since this morning, Shintemir,' Grisha said animatedly.

At this point, Bibi appeared and I saw Shintemir's eyebrows shoot up in surprise and then his mouth spread in a broad smile.

'Bibi, is that you? How come you're here, sweetheart?' Shintemir exclaimed.

Bibi smiled through the flour dust that covered her face, revealing large white teeth. She glanced at Kanatay and me in passing and then asked in a ringing voice,

'No, you tell me how come you're here?'

'Well, our auls do neighbour one another,' Shintemir explained, narrowing his eyes slyly, before bursting out in laughter. Bibi laughed with him.

Shintemir got down from the cart and walked over to us. Only then did I notice that he had an artificial leg. He also seemed oddly familiar to me. However, this was the first time we had met; I knew that for sure. However, he had a frightening resemblance to someone I had lived with pretty much side by side.

Meanwhile, Shintemir shook hands in greeting with Bibi and Grisha. Bibi proudly told him,

'And this is my son Kanatay.'

Shintemir looked at Kanatay.

'My, how he's grown. He's almost an adult now.'

I imagined I heard a certain sadness in his voice.

'Son, come and say hello! Come on, sunshine, give the man your hand,' Bibi said to Kanatay.

26

There was something Kanatay didn't like in Shintemir, for he extended his hand with some reluctance. However, Shintemir squeezed it tightly and held it in his hand until Kanatay drew it back.

Grisha was by now fed up with being out of the limelight and, clearing his throat, he spoke up, pointing to the tightly filled, striped sacks, which were stacked up by the mill entrance:

'Well, Shintemir, there's your flour. These young'uns,' he said, nodding in our direction, 'will load it onto your cart in no time. In the meantime, we'll go inside for a cup of tea. Why don't you join us, Bibi?'

'Well, if it's just for one cup,' Bibi said, as if indecisively, but I couldn't help noticing that Grisha's invitation was to her liking.

The three of them disappeared into the crooked little house on the side of the mill with the one window, while we had to load the sacks onto Shintemir's cart.

'Who's he, an old acquaintance of yours?' I asked, unable to hold back.

'First time I've seen him,' Kanatay blurted.

The first of the three to emerge was Grisha. His face was red and perspiring from the hot tea. Their get-together had evidently been accompanied by some vodka, too. Grisha's eyes shimmered with an oily sheen.

'So, lads, an excellent grind that, isn't it?' he enquired merrily and gave a sack a slap. 'And I'm happy to turn the millstones for a decent chap, as well.

People like Shintemir, there, deserve to live to a ripe old age.'

With that, Grisha, took to showering his friend with compliments. Then he gave me a wink as if to beckon me over. We stepped to one side and sat down on one of the boulders that were so generously scattered around the mill.

'Well, did you twig?' he asked in animated fashion. 'It turns out that Kanatay is my old mate's son. How d'you like that, eh?'

'Shintemir's, you mean?' I almost swallowed my tongue in surprise.

I was prepared to assume anything but that.

'Shh! Keep your voice down! Well, I guess from the way they were chatting. Shintemir and Bibi, I mean,' Grisha explained ostentatiously. 'Just compare the two of them if you don't believe me: Kanatay is the spitting image of Shintemir. Like two peas in a pod, right?'

How could I not have seen it myself?! After all, Kanatay and I lived pretty much in each other's pockets and yet I never made the connection.

'There's Bibi and Shintemir for you!' Grisha said with a shake of the head.

Soon, Bibi and Shintemir came out of the house. Bibi's cambric scarf had slipped a little from her head, revealing black locks without a grey hair in sight. Looking at Bibi, with her slender, yet firm frame, you would never have imagined she was in her forties. Shintemir appeared shorter. He was hobbling about

28

next to her and was trying to convince her of something.

'So that was what it was! Now I remember,' Grisha said pensively. 'Once, Shintemir and I had had too much to drink. I don't remember; it must have been some occasion or other, or perhaps it was for no reason whatsoever. But he told me this story... Of course, you wouldn't know—you were only knee-high to a grasshopper, or perhaps you hadn't even been born—but Shintemir was the chairman of our collective farm. That was after he returned from the front without a leg. There were only women around; even the foremen were forewomen. They say that one of them was very attractive. Her husband had been killed at the front; she had mourned and grieved but life took over. Well, they started seeing each other. You can see that Shintemir is not much of a looker, but they really did get a thing going. They were genuinely in love. So, there you have it, young lad. However, Shintemir held on to what he had; he had his house, his family and he was the farm chairman and that, you know, has its responsibilities. Anyway, one day the two of them were riding in their cart; probably to do with the hay-mowing, I guess. She stopped the horse, got down from the cart and said she wanted to sit down and have a chat. Then she said, *Well, are you a man or what?* And she burst into tears. He couldn't stand his ground.

'Then his wife found out; they had six children and he could hardly have left them behind; he had to feed them all. And so, it all kicked off. Can you imagine, the dressing-down he got at the district committee? They

29

told him to take his amoral conduct elsewhere. It's like in the song: *That's where the love came to an end.* You see, Bibi was that forewoman.'

Grisha may have only just guessed, but I knew for sure that Bibi had once been a forewoman. I had been told that on numerous occasions.

'Now Shintemir tends to cattle in the neighbouring collective farm. "Grisha," he says to be me, "I want to return to my native aul, only my wife and children are against it,"' Grisha concluded and let out a sigh.

We loaded the sacks in no time. Then, we said our farewells to Grisha and our little string of carts crept slowly up the hill.

Kanatay and I travelled in our own cart, while Bibi climbed up next to Shintemir in another. They sat side by side, their legs dangling.

'What are they up to?' Kanatay muttered nervously.

'Let them talk. You don't begrudge them that, do you?'

'Yes, I do!' Kanatay cut in sulkily.

Our roan cantered along; Shintemir's mare also picked up speed and all we could hear was the clicking of its hooves. Then the road shot out of the hollow and climbed steeply into the hills and we had to dismount to make it easier going for the horse.

Shintemir also got down from his cart; Bibi had wanted to join him, but he had stopped her. I could hear them exchanging words at length. In the end, Bibi remained in her seat, while Shintemir walked on

30

ahead, holding onto the cart. Soon we could hear their chatter and laughter once more.

'I don't much like that lame one,' Kanatay growled enviously.

'What don't you like about him? I don't think he's done anything bad.'

'He hasn't. I really don't know why I don't,' Bibi's son confessed. 'Probably because he does nothing but gabble.'

The ascent was steep and the horses continually stopped for breath, puffing out their darkened flanks. We were afraid that the force of gravity would drag the carts back and throw them and their horses into the stream below. However, the creatures made the final push, not without our encouragement, and the journey continued.

Either our roan was stronger, or its load was lighter, but on one of the turns we broke away from Shintemir and he and his cart with Bibi up top soon disappeared from view.

When we reached flat country, Kanatay brought the horse to a stop and we waited there for the others.

'Have they got stuck back there or something? Like they're being pulled by a tortoise, not a horse,' Kanatay said, becoming agitated again.

'Calm down. They'll be here in a minute. What's the hurry, anyway?' I said a little more softly.

But Kanatay had already jumped from the cart and ran back down the hill. Soon, I heard his authoritative voice:

'Faster! Faster! Come on!'

His head appeared from down the slope and then the rest of him came into view. He was pulling Shintemir's grey mare by the reins, crying out,

'Come on! Come on!'

Shintemir was now sitting in the cart, while Bibi was walking to the side; Shintemir was holding his maimed leg and I saw that his trouser leg was covered in clay. His little nostrils were narrow and his lips were pressed tight together. In pain, he looked the spitting image of Kanatay.

'I tripped over,' he muttered guiltily as he met my stare.

'I told you to sit in the cart and that I would walk. But no, you wouldn't listen,' Bibi said reproachfully.

The road now stretched out along the highland plain. We returned to our carts and the horses, having now regained their breath, sped forward to where they guessed our aul stood beyond the horizon.

This time, Kanatay slyly let Shintemir's cart travel in front. We lay back on the sacks and gave the roan free rein.

'Just look at that: that cripple just keeps on gabbling,' Kanatay said again, unable to restrain himself. 'He smashed his leg and still he can't shut up. Ah, the hell with him! He must be nuts or something. But I really don't know what's got into mama. She just sits there, staring at him.'

The creaking of the wheels lulled us; the weather, too, with the dusty haze that covered half the sky and the monotonous steppes brought on a certain drowsiness. My eyelids began to droop. The last thing

I saw before dropping off was the sleeping Kanatay, his cheek resting on the sackcloth.

However, sleep is always light when you're out on the road. I sensed that the cart had come to a stop and that someone had approached.

'Just look at them. Fast asleep like puppies' It was Bibi's voice.

I guessed that Shintemir, too, had approached our cart, from the creaking sound of his false leg.

'What am I to do, Bibi?' he whispered, standing somewhere near my feet.

'What are you to do? Nothing, that's what,' Bibi said, laughing quietly, almost directly into my ear. 'Leave everything just as it is! Warm yourself by your Batima. She's your wife, destined by God.'

'Don't laugh at me, Bibi,' Shintemir implored her. 'Wasn't it you who said back then: *Return to your Batima, have patience and wait for the little children to grow up?*' That's what you said, Bibi. And I have been waiting patiently until now. And now, let me tell you this: my children are now standing on their own two feet and each of them has their own family; Batima has nothing to reproach me for, so there you have it!'

Bibi was silent and then spoke pensively: 'Yes, back then I took pity on your children. They were all so tiny and so, so innocent. And I thought, why should I make them orphans while their father was still alive? Our youth has left us. What would people say if in our old age we came together like some Kozy and Bayan.[3]

---

[3] *Central characters from the ancient Kazakh legend of tragic love Kozy-Korpesh and Bayan-Sulu*]

33

Surely we would burn from the shame of it. What do you say, Shintemir?'

Shintemir was silent. The only sounds were the rattling of the bits in the horses' mouths and the peaceful sniffling of Kanatay in his sleep.

'Well, all the best to you!' Bibi said and beat the roan's flanks with the reins.

Our cart began moving, the wheels squeaked a couple of times and then came to a halt once more.

'Hey, Shintemir!' Bibi called out softly. The squeak of the false leg could be heard once more right beside us.

'You could at least stroke his hair. He is your child, after all,' Bibi said reproachfully.

'He looks awfully cross,' Shintemir said awkwardly.

'Kanatay, hey, Kanatay,' Bibi called out, and I realised she was giving her son a push. 'Come on, son. Wake up. Come on, wake up.'

'Ow, that hurts!' Kanatay moaned.

'What is the matter, sweetheart? Your arm gone numb?'

'No, it really hurts. Can't you see?' And Kanatay showed her Grisha's handiwork.

'Oh, sweetheart, who wrote that on you?' Bibi said in fear. 'Why did you let them do that?'

'I liked the idea, so I let them,' Kanatay blurted out.

'Look, son. You're all grown-up now and you should know everything,' Bibi said firmly. 'There's no point hiding things from you. The thing is that Zhan

Sultan is not your father, like I told you. I concealed the truth from you because you were still so little. Shintemir is your father! There he is; there is your father!'

The cart shook and I sensed that Kanatay had jumped up.

'My father died in the war. In the war,' Kanatay objected.

'Son...' Bibi began, but Kanatay was already shaking me furiously, trying to wake me before his mother had managed to say anything else. I could no longer pretend I was asleep and raised my head.

'Eh? What?'

Bibi looked embarrassed as she motioned to Shintemir that he should be on his way. Shintemir dejectedly sloped off to his cart.

'Safe trip, Shintemir,' Bibi said affectionately.

The carts went their separate ways.

Bibi continually looked back until Shintemir's cart had disappeared beyond the next hill. Her face displayed a hint of sadness and her figure, which had only just now had a striking lofty bearing about it, now seemed suddenly deflated.

Kanatay looked ahead, his teeth clenched, exactly like Shintemir. However, when we had approached the aul, he suddenly buried his face in the sacks and burst into tears.

'My papa died in the war, Mama!'

A WINTER'S EVENING

The new stockyard had been built up on the hill during the autumn. From up there, Zholbai, the new watchman, could see the entire central farm estate stretching out below.

It was now winter. Zholbai was a lad of about twenty-five. Wrapped up warm in his large overcoat, he stood up to his waist in the hay that had been gathered by the gates and looked out over his village. The frost had become much fiercer after lunch as if it had grown thorns. It bit so painfully, that Zholbai's face, with its big, flat nose, had turned a deep red colour. His wide nostrils flared, capturing the smell of the dry hay. At times, the frosty infusion of sagebrush would become overpowering and, wrinkling his nose, the young watchman would sneeze with relish.

He knew that on a frosty day like this one, the people's attention would be involuntarily drawn towards the dark-green hay, piled up on the roof of the barn, reminding them of the hot summer that had recently passed and of the thick, fragrant grass that had filled the meadows. When the piercing frost would set in from the east, the smell of the hay would drift down the hill and through the village, intoxicating every living thing in its path. The animals would lift their noses and, flaring their nostrils, gaze at length over to where Zholbai was sitting.

The day was drawing to a close. The sun was already turning red and disappearing beyond the horizon, flooding the snow-covered expanses in a deep burgundy hue. The frost clasped the steppe even tighter in its icy paws. The smoke that burst from the chimneys would become heavier in the twilight and hang over the roofs for some time before dissipating.

A warm gatehouse had been built next to the cowshed but Zholbai preferred this little hayrick because it afforded him a better view of the house on the edge of the village. It was a house like any other but the column of smoke that rose above it was thin and feeble, most unusual given the frost. Zholbai found this most puzzling.

The house has sufficient coal and firewood. Dzhunus has enough to last two winters, so, why is the stove so miserly with its smoke? the watchman mused.

Asilya lived in this house and, from his elevated vantage point, Zholbai could see her walking around the yard, bringing the cattle in for the night. It would soon grow dark; the light would come on in the house and Asilya's mother would pull the curtains over the windows. Zholbai had no doubt that it would be the mother and not Asilya who would do this, for, during his watchman's shifts, he had learnt the habits of all the people who lived in this house. He knew for sure that light would then break through their curtains throughout the course of the night.

Buried up to his waist in the hay and having quite forgotten about the frost, he kept his eyes fixed on the lit windows, following the shadows that would occasionally fall on the curtains. He had become so engrossed in this past-time, that he had quite forgotten about his solitude. Zholbai believed that it was as if he was sitting in that house and conversing quietly with Asilya. He imagined Asilya changing her son's nappy or breastfeeding him from time to time.

No sooner had he formed an image of Asilya in his mind than a dark figure emerged from her house and headed straight to the stockyard, walking over the rough terrain to shorten the distance. At first, Zholbai couldn't believe his eyes: could it really be Asilya who was coming, floundering through the snow? Had this not been what he had been dreaming of every night as he sat here in the hay?

His dream had come true, for it really was Asilya, making her way towards him. His heart began to beat faster. Excited and nervous, he jumped down from the rick and ran about the yard, trying to busy himself with anything he could find. He felt he was in full view of everyone and as if the entire village was closely monitoring his every move. He involuntarily looked around him, but the dusk had already concealed the first lights of the farm club, from where voices could be heard. Some girls were singing a familiar tune that drifted over to him, the icy air transparently conveying every word of the song:

For no special reason we meet each day,
But, my friend, we cannot find the words to say...
'Hello, Zholbai!'

Asilya was recovering her breath; she had obviously been in a hurry and was panting from her battle with the deep snow.

Zholbai had always recalled her dark complexion, her slender profile and her noble poise, which would disarm even the most petulant young men. *She has lost weight; her face is thinner and she has grown pale. There is so much sadness in those brown eyes of hers. And yet, if anything, she is even prettier than before,* Zholbai said to himself.

Asilya was wearing the same velour coat she had worn back in tenth grade. Now it had become quite shabby and Asilya only wore it for working around the farm. However, Zholbai remembered only too well how she had first appeared at school in that coat. That day, he had been unable to sit still at his desk, and he had spent the whole time staring at Asilya. The teacher had grown tired of telling him off and ended up sending Zholbai out of the classroom.

Oh, how lovely Asilya had been back then! The cunning minx had known this all too well and would cock her nose haughtily at him. There were times when she had been only too happy to make fun of a simple oaf like Zholbai. Once, Zholbai had been unable to take his eyes off her, as usual, and the wily beauty had pretended she hadn't noticed. Later, however, she raised her wonderful eyes to him and winked unexpectedly, making poor Zholbai blush crimson. That was the kind of girl Asilya had been back then.

'Give me a little hay, would you?' the present Asilya asked timidly, and Zholbai noticed she was holding some string.

At first, he was surprised. Why did she need hay, when she had her own rick by her house, albeit not a very large one? She seemed to have read Zholbai's thoughts from the expression on his face and shook her head.

'That's Dzhunus's hay. I don't want it... He scythed and gathered it, so he can have it,' Asilya said with a bitter sneer.

That's Asilya for you. The frost is biting and she still doesn't want to take advantage of Dzhunus's kindness. So, her nature hasn't changed! Zholbai thought to himself, while he said out loud, 'Alright, I'll give you some hay. But what's with that single bit of string? That'll hardly be enough, will it?'

'I'll think of something later. Just an armful will do for now,' Asilya said and quietly added, 'I'm not going to go the chairman, now, am I? I'm too ashamed! You know too well how awkward it is having to ask for something when you've done nothing for the collective farm. I haven't lifted a finger for almost an entire year!'

'Asilya, what are you talking about?!' Zholbai interjected heatedly. 'You talk like it's your last day at the farm. So, you didn't work at the farm for a year. But what about before that? You slaved away with the rest of us, right? Summer will come, and you'll get back to work! No, you go to see the chairman and he'll sign off a whole cartful of hay for you, you'll see. He's a decent bloke.'

'But I still feel awkward,' Asilya said.

'You're worried about evil tongues wagging, is that it? Even now, you're afraid to leave the house,'

Zholbai said with a sigh. 'What's done is done, Asilya, you can't change that. These things happen.'

He felt embarrassed and, in order to hide it, he took to tying up the hay with double the zeal. He spat copiously into his hands, despite the hellish cold, and he stretched out the string, which was as rigid as wire from the frost. However, he couldn't restrain himself and asked, his eyes lowered,

'Asilya, so why did you get divorced? You really loved him. Everyone could see that.'

'Yes, Zholbai, I did love him,' Asilya said simply.

'Perhaps, he offended you somehow?'

'Dzhunus? No way! He never even said a bad word against me. He would always say, *I'd sooner a splinter pierce my head than your heel.* That's the kind of thing he would say, Zholbai.' With that, Asilya let out a sigh.

'So, what *did* happen?' Zholbai asked, alarmed at his own persistence.

'Something I least expected happened... Anyway, you said yourself, these things happen.'

'I see,' Zholbai nodded, although he hadn't understood a thing she had said.

'Zholbai, you're just as funny as you always were. You haven't changed a bit,' Asilya said, smiling involuntarily. Then she added, 'You should put on your mittens. Look, your hands will freeze for no reason at all.'

Zholbai's hands were indeed frozen stiff and he could hardly move his wooden fingers; but the concern he felt in Asilya's voice gave him added energy.

Zholbai spat on his hands once more with a swagger and said as if throwing a challenge to the cold,

'You call that a frost? Ha, that's nothing!'

He pulled briskly at the ends of the string in an attempt to tighten the knot, but the string wouldn't take it and snapped.

'You rotten so-and-so!' Zholbai cursed, but he was still pleased that this had given him the opportunity to show Asilya how strong he was.

He tied the string together again and, as if returning to tying the bundle by the by, he said,

'They say that Dzhunus was a decent lad.'

He didn't want anyone to think, Asilya included, that he was weaving a net behind Dzhunus's back.

'A smart *dzhigit*, that Dzhunus,' Zholbai added.

Asilya, however, pretended not to hear and turned her back...

They had both gone to work at the farm after school. Asilya had been sent to the cornfields and Zholbai, to work as a shepherd. Since that time, he had seldom seen Asilya and had relied on hearsay to learn how she was getting on. That had been how, two years previously, he had learnt of Asilya's marriage.

Zholbai had met with Dzhunus on occasions. He was a stocky *dzhigit* but Zholbai had heard more about him from hearsay.

People said there was no one in the village more capable of hunting down money than Dzhunus. In any case, he had always had pockets of money and, after moving in at his wife's house, he had told her she

43

couldn't go out to work. Just two years after that, Zholbai had chanced on a brief report in the district newspaper that Asilya had filed for a divorce, and this had surprised him. And not just Zholbai, for people older and wiser were also quite at a loss.

Meanwhile, the string had managed to break another three times. It was a rotten piece of string and no mistake. When it broke a fourth time, Asilya laughed and said,

'Throw it away, Zholbai. I'll go and bring a stronger bit of rope. Something that will withstand your strength.'

Zholbai's trained ear caught a familiar intonation in Asilya's voice. She was making fun of him, just like when they had been at school together. Zholbai felt abashed and, by the time he had pulled himself together, Asilya was no longer there. He could see her silhouette hovering on the white snow. Asilya was returning home, floundering in the snowdrifts once again.

'Asilya! Asilya-a!' Zholbai called out, but the young woman didn't even look back. Who knew: either she was deep in thought and hadn't heard him, or his call had not been loud or strong enough in the dense, cold air. Zholbai felt a sense of despair and kicked the hay he had gathered, scattering it all about.

The last of the crimson hue was melting in the West, leaving nothing but a thin line. The winter's evening had dispatched its first stars as it crept up on Zholbai.

The snow was still crunching from a way off. Two people were walking the road towards the stockyard, one of them leading a horse. The horse walked at a measured pace, its head bowed down and letting out the occasional snort. Zholbai recognised the other man from his black fur coat as the chairman of the collective farm. Later he caught sight of his thick black moustaches, white from the frost.

'It's not too warm out, is it, eh, Zholbai?' the chairman joked, as they exchanged a handshake. 'Let me introduce you: this is the chairman of our Birlik Farm that neighbours onto ours. I've had to guide him through this way. Now, you, Zholbai, are a man of principle and you're not one to take in a stranger's horse, but I'm giving you special permission for this one. Take him in until morning, would you, and pick one of the better spots for him, alright? Our pacers wouldn't think twice about kicking out at a stranger and we wouldn't want that, right? What would we say to our guest, here, eh?' he concluded with a laugh.

While Zholbai busied himself with the horse, the chairman and his guest looked over the stockyard, conversing about business.

'Now, why not invite us into your palace,' suggested the chairman. 'We've quite frozen today and I bet it's warmer in there than out here, right?'

Zholbai threw open the door to the gatehouse and the aroma of glowing iron, hot brick and the resin from spruce timber came bursting out.

45

'Wow! It's the height of summer in here, Zholbai! Please come in,' the chairman said, ushering his guest ahead of him.

Barely had they settled down by the stove when voices and the crunching of sled runners could be heard from outside.

'No way, could our lads already be back from Karoi?! Well, it can't be helped. Come on, Zholbai, let's go and meet them,' the chairman said good-naturedly.

That winter's evening, the string of carts looked thoroughly outlandish and fantastical. Steam rose from the horses, their coats shimmering from the frost. The frost had engulfed the haymakers' cumbersome figures and, hovering between the sleds, they appeared like fairy-tale spirits.

'*Aqsaqal*, I wanted to ask you for a cart of hay,' Zholbai said once the haymakers had got themselves busy and had left them alone. 'I'm not asking for myself. It's for this woman, you see,' Zholbai added, looking down at his feet and sensing the flame-red blush of embarrassment creeping over his face and neck in the dark.

'So, who is this woman, then? And why does she not come and ask herself? Or has she lost her tongue?' the chairman marvelled.

'No, no, she hasn't lost her tongue, only she cannot come herself. She feels ashamed,' Zholbai whispered, still looking down at his felt boots.

'Well, who is she then?' the chairman said angrily. He was accustomed to speaking plainly and Zholbai's lack of directness had put him out.

46

I'll have to tell him her name, Zholbai thought. *Whatever way you look at it, he'll never sign out hay to just anyone, let alone a whole cartful.*

'Asilya. She needs it,' Zholbai said, forcing out the words barely audibly.

'Ah, the one who got divorced? And rightly so! That Dzhunus is a right money-grabber, and no mistake,' the chairman said sternly. 'Hey, Manar! Manar! Take your cart to Asilya. And make sure you unload it properly and place it all on the roof of the barn there. And you, Zholbai, you can go and help him. Make sure he doesn't scatter the hay every which way, for there are only women at that house.'

The chairman called his now warmed guest from the gatehouse and left for the village with him. The two short figures slithered down the hill into the darkness, but the crunching of the snow under their boots could still be heard long after they had both crossed the threshold of the chairman's house. Or at least, that's how it seemed to Zholbai.

Asilya was fussing about the yard when they approached her home.

'Hey, missus, where do you want us to put this hay?!' Zholbai called out rakishly.

Asilya had been taken quite unawares by their appearance with the cart. Unable to make head nor tail of what was going on, she became suspicious.

'I only asked for a bundle,' she said, looking askance at Zholbai.

'And there is a bundle here. Well, and another, and another... The extra won't do you any harm,' Zholbai replied, doing his best to look like a jolly decent fellow.

'So, you think of me as lonely and helpless? If that's the case, you're wasting your time, Zholbai. I'm not one of those people who accepts pity,' Asilya said with a determined expression.

Zholbai was taken aback and lost for words. He realised that Asilya was being serious.

What's the matter with her? He thought. *Either she really is that proud, or she simply finds my help distasteful.*

At that moment, however, it was Manar who piped in. He had long been wanting to get off home with thoughts of hot tea, and Asilya's obstinacy had really put him out of humour.

'What's pity got to do with anything?! Well, aren't you the poor wretch! And you think Zholbai is rolling in money? This hay is yours! The chairman sent it to you because you're a member of the farm team. So, get to it! Can't you see the horse is tired?' the ill-tempered Manar added.

Only then did Asilya notice his white eyebrows and frozen-stiff mittens, and she gave in.

'You can put it there,' she said curtly and pointed to the far barn.

The young men shed their sheepskin coats, took up their hay forks in unison and began loading the hay up onto the barn roof. The hay had a particular aroma that day and it reminded Zholbai of the smell of dried melon. Zholbai worked with frantic energy. The one thought that he was making an effort for Asilya's sake gave him indescribable satisfaction. The weaker Manar could not keep up with his mad pace and quickly broke out in a sweat and put down his fork.

'Just look at how proud she is. *I don't need your hay,* she says,' said Manar, wiping the sweat from his brow. He was pleased to be returning home soon.

The young lads suddenly heard a crunching in the snow. Manar's mother, old Kanipa, had approached from behind them, leaning on a wizened walking stick. 'Manar, hey, Manar!' she screeched. 'What are you doing, you good-for-nothing? Why are you carrying hay to this house? Everyone else refused, I suppose?'

'Mama, what are you on about? Shame on you! How can you say that?!' blurted the startled Manar, afraid even to look in Zholbai and Asilya's direction.

'But I can!' croaked old Kanipa. 'Because tomorrow you'll have hell to pay with all the gossip.'

'Don't worry, Manar will be back soon,' Zholbai interjected, trying to calm things over.

The old woman departed, tapping her stick angrily and muttering under her breath.

The frost had become savage, yet this only served to spur the lads on. Asilya had heard the old woman's hurtful words, but she had said nothing, nor even batted an eyelid; she had just stood there, staring straight at Manar and at him, Zholbai. As for Zholbai, he would have been happy to toss hay about all his life, if it meant he could feel Asilya's eyes on him!

The work, however, had come to an end; the hay had all been placed on the roof. Deeply disappointed,

Zholbai placed his fork in the sled and he took out a bundle of firewood before Manar rode away. In an attempt to slow the course of time, Zholbai plucked pieces of straw from his clothes, one by one. Asilya watched him in silence. Her face remained impenetrable.

'I had no wish to offend you. I just wanted to help you as... as a friend. That can't be a bad thing, can it – when someone helps another as a friend, right? Anyway, you know best,' he said tentatively.

Asilya, though, remained silent. Then he found more courage and continued with greater assurance:

'You don't have any firewood either. Dzhunus brought in some coal, but what's the use of that? You heat the stove with any old rotten wood. You think I don't know? I see everything from over there,' and he nodded in the direction of the hill. 'Asilya, you have a small child. He might fall ill in an unheated room. Borrow this wood. You can pay me back later, say, in autumn.'

He extended the wood to Asilya.

'And what if you freeze? It's obvious you don't have the firewood to spare,' Asilya said with unexpected humility.

'Oh, come on, Asilya!' Zholbai shouted delighted. 'I am always outside as it is. And when I'm cold... When I'm cold, the sight of your window warms me up. I look in and feel warmer.'

He tried to sound at ease when he said this, applying unthinkable effort. However, when his eyes met the gaze of the young woman, he stopped short;

50

Asilya's face had dropped and there were tears in her eyes.

'Hurry up and put your coat on. You've run up a sweat and you'll catch a cold,' she said, pulling herself together. She picked up his sheepskin coat, gave it a shake and put it over his shoulders. Zholbai stood there, motionless.

'I don't how else to thank you,' she said tenderly.

'I do,' Zholbai replied bravely. 'Let me kiss you!'

'Well, aren't you a sly one!'

They both laughed. Zholbai had never felt so at ease with Asilya. Now he believed he could even tell her everything that he was thinking about when he looked at her windows every night.

'Asilya, please allow me to come and visit you from time to time,' he said shyly.

'There's no point, Zholbai,' Asilya replied, turning instantly serious. 'The village is full of girls who are pretty and available. I, though, am divorced and with a child in tow. Can't you hear how they're singing over there?'

Zholbai heard the girls singing. They were evidently returning from the club and they were singing the same song as always:

For no special reason we meet each day,
But, my friend, we cannot find the words to say...

He sensed something insurmountable between Asilya and him.

'Asilya, I love you. And I don't need anyone,' he said hurriedly and heatedly, trying to break down the wall before it became even stronger and more terrible.

51

'Love me, what can I do?' Asilya responded wearily.

'Asilya, I make a lot of money! More than Dzhunus! I'll get anything you desire. I'll build you a new house and...'

'You're so funny, Zholbai, like I said,' Asilya interrupted, looking at him sympathetically. 'That is why I broke up with Dzhunus. He never had enough and brought home everything he could get his hands on. You don't get it, poor Zholbai! Goodbye!'

She was about to head for the door, but Zholbai happily followed her and said,

'Is that true, Asilya? Is that really true?'

'Oh, Zholbai, leave me be,' Asilya said at the doorway.

But Zholbai held the door with his hand and stood there with a big grin, saying the same thing,

'Is that really true, Asilya?'

'My dear, let me go, please. Mama will be really cross,' Asilya pleaded. 'Please, just let go of the door.'

'Alright, then... So be it.'

She raised herself on her toes and touched her lips quickly to his cheek.

'There!' and the door slammed shut.

Zholbai turned and slowly walked back. Asilya's kiss burned on his cheek. He could even touch it.

Zholbai returned to his hayrick and lay there, up to his waist in the hay. He immediately strained his eyes to the windows of the house at the edge of the village.

Oh, what a wonderful evening, Zholbai thought.

THE GUEST

The train stopped at every halt and stood motionless at the stations; this tormented Beken. During the last day of his long journey, he never left his compartment. Beken sat looking out of the window with a dull expression. On his head was a hat, made heavens knows when out of blue velvet, but which had faded in the steppe sun to a tobacco colour; his lower lip bulged with a pinch of tobacco. Beyond the window, the snow-covered, sleepy steppe slid by and vanished in an endless ribbon, but, unlike the first day of the journey, none of this interested the old man any longer. He was thinking about why he had set out on this long journey and, if the train stood longer than usual at a halt, he would begin to worry.

'When will it ever end? We spend more time standing still than travelling,' he blurted to the woman who shared his compartment.

'There's no need to rush, pops. You'll have plenty of time to see your children,' she said, to raise the grumpy old man's spirits. 'You said you hadn't seen your son for four years, didn't you? You probably miss him after all this time.'

'It turns out I even have a grandson. He's three years old,' Beken announced as if trying to nettle the woman with the news.

'Well, isn't that something?!' the woman chirped in surprise with a shake of her head. She looked attentively at the old man and, after a silence, spoke in a disapproving tone:

'Well, you can take this how you like, but let me tell you straight: you have a heart of stone, you do! You haven't been to see your son for four years; he's got himself married and become a father in that time, while you... You mean to say you've never set eyes on your own grandson?!'

Beken heard the woman out in silence and offered no reply. Why should he make excuses to a stranger; if he did, he would have to explain how things had worked out as they had. He had no wish to accuse his son of anything. As things had turned out, after graduating, his son Bagan had kept secrets and things had become difficult between them; this could hardly be explained to a stranger in a single breath when Beken himself didn't understand the half of it.

The train slowed as it approached a large station and the carriage became a hive of activity and noise. Still, the old man, who had previously been more agitated than anyone else, remained in his seat, retaining a seemly sense of calm. Breathing onto the window that had become frosty from the evening cold, Beken formed a circle and looked through, but all he could see was a multitude of lights. Incredibly tall buildings surrounded the approaching station, all with countless lights burning in their windows. Beken tried to take it all in with a single look, but his eyes teared up from the effort.

Finally, the train came to a stop. It was a vast station, cast in an even, greenish light and this made everything on the platform appear as clear as day. Beken emerged from his compartment, the last of the

54

passengers pressed into the space by the door. His head spun from the noise and the instantaneous hustle and bustle. He became confused, not knowing where to go and what he had to do.

'Well, pops, where are you off to?' his fellow traveller asked him as she squeezed past the old man on her way to the exit.

'Me? Nowhere, someone's meeting me,' Beken mumbled.

Negotiating the steep steps down from the carriage, he lowered himself onto the platform and began to look for his son. The old man hadn't forgotten the winter clothes he had sent the money to buy, and so he sought a *dzhigit* in the crowd, dressed in a short, black, woollen coat and a grey cap. However, it was quite impossible in that crowd to catch sight of what he needed. Beken was equally unable to get through the crowd by pushing with elbows and suitcases like everyone else. No, there was no way he would find his son here. It was a miracle that anything could be found!

At that moment, a familiar voice called out to him: 'Hey, pops!'

Beken turned his head. The woman from his compartment was standing some distance away.

'Hey, pops, your son's not here? Come with me; you'll get lost otherwise.'

Beken obediently shuffled after the woman, through the main station building and out onto an enormous square. There were even more people assembled here in front of the station and Beken stopped involuntarily, quite flustered. That said, the loud snapping of the rolling stock could hardly be heard from where he now stood.

All manner of motley cars stood a little further on to his right. Beken was about to head over to them for some reason, but a *Volga* car crossed the road right in front of him, almost deafening Beken completely with the screech of its brakes. The old man had never found himself amidst such pandemonium and he lost his bearings.

'Damn it, he nearly ran me over,' he said angrily.

A handsome young man in attractive city clothes jumped out of the *Volga*. A snow-white woollen scarf tumbled casually from under the fur collar of his long leather coat; his shiny, brown leather hat with a narrow brim barely covered his mop of lush black hair. The *dzhigit* turned towards Beken and the street light illuminated him. His face was a little plump and he had thick, curved eyebrows and a straight, narrow nose with a slight crook. Indeed, this was a lad you couldn't fail to notice.

'Bagan, hey, Bagan...' Beken called out tentatively. The *dzhigit* frowned and furtively looked around at the people within earshot.

'Bagan, my son,' Beken cried out once more and, his legs shaking, he went over to the young man.

'Ah, father... You're already here?' the young man said. He took another quick look around for some reason and extended his hand to Beken, but the old man, not satisfied with this gesture, drew his son towards him and kissed him on the forehead. Then, he brought a handkerchief to his eyes and whispered in an aggrieved tone:

'There's no one else, I'm here all on my own.'

To make amends, Bagan slapped Beken on the back and ushered him towards the car.

'You can tell me later, father, but now we're going home.' Bagan spoke quickly as he hurriedly ushered his father into the car. Forgetting about everything else in the world and failing even to give his fellow traveller a backwards glance, Beken sat in the car with his son.

Bagan drove very fast. After their initial greeting at the railway station, they continued in silence. Until that moment, Beken had prepared answers to his son's questions about the village and how his kin and countrymen were doing back home. Bagan's attention, however, seemed to be riveted on the road in front of him, his hands glued to the wheel.

Perhaps, the well-educated don't ask after the health of their countrymen just anywhere, Beken presumed. However, he didn't know what to ask his son about. It seemed to Beken that his questions would have been unworthy of this handsome young man.

They got out of the car by a five-storey white house. Bagan nodded the way to go and entered the building ahead of him. He rang the bell to the apartment and a moody voice instantly called out: 'One moment, one moment,' and the door swung open. Beken saw a young, pleasant-looking woman on the threshold who looked him up and down, her eyebrows cast upwards in surprise. Her cold, black eyes ran over Beken once more and her eyebrows again crept upwards.

'Sania, let me introduce you: this is my father,' Bagan uttered quickly and with some discomfort.

'Eh? So, you have a father, then?!' she asked, looking askance at Bagan, who just stood there as if he wasn't sure if he was going to be allowed into his own house with his father. *Hmm, good for you*, Beken thought gratefully, deciding that his daughter-in-law had wanted to make his son feel ashamed. Then, however, the resentment that had been gathering in his heart against his son somehow dissipated of its own accord.

'Well, you can't stand in the doorway all day long. Come in,' the daughter-in-law said, making way for Beken.

The large room, with pink flowers on the walls, was lit by a blue-glass lamp. Entering the room, Beken froze at the door, astounded at the beauty of it all. All manner of expensive items stood along the walls, things he only knew about from hearsay. Only then did Beken realise that his son must have a decent job. Feeling awkward, he sat down on the edge of the couch and sniffed his tobacco.

Several minutes later, having spoken in halftones in the hallway, the son and daughter-in-law came into the room. It was evident from their frowns that they had disagreed about something. The son walked over to the couch and sat awkwardly next to his father. The daughter-in-law, curved like a swan, glided over the room, looked at herself in a tall mirror and stood there, her elbow resting on the piano. Beken took a secret look at his daughter-in-law's attractive face and her well-groomed hair that lay lightly on her slender, gently-sloping shoulders. *Her parents are obviously bigwigs of some kind*, Beken thought. *She's evidently spoilt and not very well brought up, just standing there without so much as a scarf over her head.* Deciding that he would bring up his daughter-in-law's misdemeanour later, he turned to his son. Bagan smoked one cigarette after the other. The smoke clouded his face, rose to the ceiling and then spread across the room.

'Everyone back in the village is doing fine,' Beken began, for he had had his fill of this awkward silence.

'Ri-ght,' Bagan replied pensively. Beken seethed at this indifferent *ri-ght*. He wanted to reproach his son but, sensing the daughter-in-law's cold stare, he stopped short.

'You've forgotten everything, haven't you?' he said quietly, all his bitterness crammed into this one phrase. His son agreed in silence.

'Sania, my father must be tired after his journey. Perhaps some tea...' Bagan said indecisively after a while, the end of his sentence tailing off.

The daughter-in-law languidly left the room. Beken had waited for them to be alone and decided to voice his grievances. He looked at Bagan. His son was greedily smoking up his latest cigarette, looking ahead with unseeing eyes. Only now did Beken notice that his son's face now had deep wrinkles. His chin now hung down. For reasons he could not fathom, Beken felt pity for him. *He probably works day and night and gets really tired*, the old man thought.

'Rather than staying cooped up in the city all the time, you could have come to the village for a breath of real air,' Beken said cautiously. His son sneered bitterly and reached for another cigarette.

'Oh, father, you think I don't miss home?' Bagan said with a disaffected wave of the hand. 'It's just that I never have the time...'

The three of them drank tea in silence. At the table, Beken asked where his grandson was. Bagan told him that he was boarding at a kindergarten and that they would collect him that Friday.

They finished their tea and the daughter-in-law fussed noisily about the room, making up a bed for Beken on the couch. She disappeared into the adjoining room and Bagan shuffled after her, also in silence.

Beken quickly fell asleep; he was probably tired. He awoke for the first time at dawn, as was his habit. The tobacco he had left inside his lip had become bitter and acrid, and made his heart tighten. He took a newspaper from the table, spat the tobacco into it, cleared his throat, placed the newspaper on the floor, and went back to sleep.

When Beken opened his eyes for the second time, the blue light of morning was already streaming into the room. The daughter-in-law, her dishevelled hair a sign she had only just got out of bed, was snorting squeamishly as she took something out of the room. Beken heard the rustling of the newspaper and remembered coughing and spitting out his tobacco at dawn: *Oh, that wasn't very nice, spitting out my tobacco like that*, he thought sheepishly.

Bagan and his wife ate their breakfast quickly and left, paying Beken no attention. Beken was left in the house all on his own.

Wandering around the kitchen, he found an empty tin can and made himself a spittoon of it. He could find no ash, to sprinkle into the can, as he usually did back home in the village, so he filled the can with pieces of newspaper instead.

Beken decided against leaving the house. He parted the net curtains, placed a chair by the window and sat down. The weather had taken a turn for the worse. The old man could see from the clothes on the passers-by that it was cold and damp outside. Beken was bored and began counting the cars that sped by before him. However, this past-time was continually being interrupted by telephone calls. The first time, it was a female voice that distracted his car-counting, followed by a nasal-sounding man. Both of them asked for the daughter-in-law. Beken told both of them that he had been left at home all on his own.

'What do you mean, *all on your own*?! And who exactly are you?' the woman asked rudely.

'Me? I am Beken, Bagan's father...'

The woman's response was to laugh spitefully and put the phone down. After hearing Beken's words, the nasal-sounding man seemed lost for words and, only after a while, he spoke in a confused tone:

'That's strange. So, Bagan has a father, then? Hm, a *father*... We thought Bagan was an orphan, after all the groom's parents never came to our place...'

This time it was Beken who lost his cool and hurled down the receiver. 'Bagan's my son, damn it,' he muttered, looking in disgust at the telephone. Having calmed down a little, Beken fell into thought:

'So, he'd never seen the groom's parents... What does he mean by that?' he pondered aloud, recalling the man on the telephone's words. 'Yes, and my daughter-in-law also said something strange to Bagan about me yesterday.' Beken stood in the middle of the room, having quite forgotten about the cars outside. He could not understand what all this meant. Could it be that Bagan had told everyone that he didn't have a father? And why on earth had it even occurred to him to say such a thing? He didn't dare dwell on it any further, so he went to the window and sat down, leaning his forehead against the cold glass.

He spent the next day all alone, too, only this time his son and daughter-in-law came back earlier, ushering an adorable looking little boy into the room.

'Look there's a grandpa here!' the little boy cried out with joy when he caught sight of Beken. The old man raised himself a little from his chair and, looking at the boy's face, he shuddered, for he saw a carbon copy of his Bagan when he had been his age. The only difference was the eyes, which were large and black and looked straight ahead and coldly, like the daughter-in-law's eyes. Having removed his outer clothes reluctantly and left them where they fell, the child leapt up and clung onto Beken. First, he removed his skull-cap, put it on and jumped up and down on the couch. Then, he climbed up onto Beken's lap and thrust his little hands into his beard.

'What's your name?' Beken asked.

'Kanat.' The child toyed with and pulled at the old man's moustaches. 'Whose grandpa are you? Mine?'

'Yes, yours.'

Beken drew the boy towards him and kissed him. At that moment, the daughter-in-law emerged from the bedroom, putting on a dressing gown as she went, and took Kanat up in her arms.

'You can't do that, father,' she said in an irritated voice. 'You always have tobacco in your mouth and you don't brush your teeth. The child might catch something!'

Beken had the breath knocked out of him. He helplessly shrunk into his shoulders and couldn't find the right words to reply to his daughter-in-law. Bagan, however, began to speak quickly and agitatedly.

'And you can keep quiet!' Sania blurted at him and instantly Bagan fell silent.

Another three days went by. During this time, Beken found a minute to ask his son who her parents were, hoping to have a frank conversation.

'Well, you know...,' his son replied vaguely. 'Her father holds a senior position...'

Bagan gave no further response and Beken, feeling uncomfortable, decided to pursue it no further.

On the morning of the fourth day, Bagan left for work, but the daughter-in-law remained at home.

'Father,' she said after a while, 'so are you really Bagan's father?'

Beken became very angry at this woman with her cold eyes, but he nevertheless retained his dignity. He didn't answer the question, rather he just remained sitting in his place, his sparse white brows frowning. After a short silence, the daughter-in-law softened her tone and said with some caution:

'Bagan said you had only come to stay for a few days and that you'd be going back soon. Is that right?'

'Yes, that's right,' the old man replied sadly.

His daughter-in-law immediately brightened up, as if the most important matter had been cleared up and went on to speak about her family with evident relief in her voice. Beken sat with his head bowed, his heart aching with bitter, troubled pain. The daughter-in-law's father was, it turned out, a prominent scholar and he had secured Bagan a postgraduate place after university so that he could gain an academic title. Suddenly, the daughter-in-law spoke, as if incidentally:

'You understand, father, that life is hard for us. I understand you are on your own but, in our situation, looking after an elderly person... Well, you understand...'

So that's where this is going! Beken thought. They didn't speak after that. Beken waited for his son to return and gave him some money to buy a return ticket.

'You're already leaving?' Bagan asked, looking rather fearfully at his father and then at his wife. Sania was busy fixing her hair in front of the mirror.

'Yes, I'll be going, I think. I'm afraid the chairman will be cross, for he never did find anyone to sit in for me and someone has to be on watch.' Beken reached for his ivory tobacco box. 'And I am running out of tobacco...'

The train on which Beken had come to visit his son departed late in the evening. His son and daughter-in-law came to see him off. The daughter-in-law was in excellent spirits.

'Father, I'll also be receiving an academic title in a couple of days, like Bagan,' she informed him, explaining why she was in such a good mood. The only thing that Beken requested was that they pop into the kindergarten on the way to the station, to take Kanat with them. The daughter-in-law agreed.

As before, there were crowds of people at the railway station. They approached Beken's carriage and waited for the train to depart. Kanat sat in his father's arms, fidgeting and reaching out to touch Beken's face. Finally, the train's departure was announced and the locomotive whistled.

Entering his compartment, Beken was delighted to discover his place was by the window again. To ensure his gown would not be crumpled, he tucked in the flaps and sat down in his place. The train slowly began to move off. The faces of the crowd seeing the other passengers off receded past him. Beken's children among them.

MY LITTLE SISTER

My little sister, the only sibling I had, used to make a real impression on me when I used to come home to my village for the winter holidays. As I approached my local district, I had thought of her, half listening to the muffled, sleepy clickety-clack of the train's wheels. Alima was a short girl, who would passionately argue with me and try to wind me up, teasing me as all siblings do. It seemed that her little, upturned nose would always be waiting for its owner to laugh out loud at any moment. Her long, thick hair would rest on her back and a thick fringe would curl messily on her forehead. Looking at that messy fringe would regularly drive me bereft and my little sister really suffered for it back then! On the whole, I spent most of my time lecturing her on her moral improvement; as her elder brother, I had unlimited rights as far as that was concerned. Any little thing would give me cause to pass comment, but my attention was particularly drawn to Alima's behaviour and what she wore; I would always find something unseemly or boyish in both these things.

My sister would hear out all my fault finding and posturing with a thoroughly serious expression on her face. However, the moment my strict demeanour softened, her lips would curl with a smile. Continuing to smile slyly, in an attempt to distract me, she would slink towards the door. If she made it to the threshold before me, my efforts would have proved fruitless. Having only just heard out my comments, Alima would transform in the blink of an eye and, standing in the doorway, she would poke her tongue out at me, saying,

'Show off! Smug pants! Brr!'

Then, she would run away, slamming the door in my face. In those moments, I would almost boil over with rage. I would shake my fist at her and cry out a threat:

'Just you wait till you get home...'

Sometimes, I would arrange various kinds of tests on the subjects she was studying at school andmy questions would have no bearing whatsoever on the curriculum. They would come to me from heaven knows where and I would amaze myself at how contrived they were. That said, should my little sister only fail to answer one question, then battle royal would commence once more. In other words, there was an attack but no worthy defence. The *defensive side* of the divide would bare her white teeth at the entire delight of the whole thing. All the same, my sister would invariably emerge victorious. She would unexpectedly deploy the one weapon that was guaranteed to strike me down: a timely poke of the tongue. I was always defenceless in the face of this weapon. Many times, I rebuked her for her lack of respect for her elder brother, but to no avail.

Now, though, sitting on the train, I make no secret of the fact that I was really rather looking forward to seeing Alima. I had really missed her sweet, childlike mischief.

And there she stood before me, my brave, impudent little girl. I stood bracing myself, assuming she would come rushing out to embrace me as she had always done. However, this didn't happen. Despite that, I kissed her on the cheek and still said,

'Right, I'll check and see how well you've been studying without me around.'

She blushed and said,

'Please do, *aga*!⁴'

This surprised me and I looked closely at Alima. She was carrying herself differently and the way she spoke and smiled had changed. She had stretched upwards and grown slender, while her tender face had taken on a certain clarity; she had grown up a little. She was wearing a new red velour coat...

So, my little sister has turned into a real beauty, it finally dawned on me, and I recalled what my mother had once said about girls growing up fast. However, I had expected to see the same sly, teasing troublemaker and I felt a little sad. Not for long, though. Deciding that, at the age of seventeen, my sister had every right to make such a transformation, I reconciled myself to it completely and thought once more with pride that she was indeed beautiful.

For now, we had not managed to find the right words to say to one another. Several times, I had tried to start a conversation but found myself unable. Something was holding me back. My sister, too, remained silent, although in the past, she would have

---

⁴ *Means 'older brother' or 'uncle'. Kazakhs address all older men as aga. However, if a man reaches his 70s, then he becomes ata to everybody.*

showered me with questions about the city and student life, and listen to me with her mouth almost permanently gaping, forever showing surprise and repeating her questions over and over.

Finally, I asked Alima which institute she was aiming for and she replied,

'I don't know. I haven't decided yet,' with a forced smile. Thinking some more, she added, 'Perhaps I'll remain here in the village.'

After dinner, Alima went to her room to do her homework and my mother and I sat down for some tea. My mother took her time, asking me about my college news, where I was thinking of going after graduation and what my future plans were in general. She had long since known my plans and she was obviously asking simply to break the silence. I answered for the umpteenth time that I would possibly return to our village in two years to work as an agronomist. After that, she gave me the village news. It turned out that the collective farm was sending several year-ten pupils to study at a school for machine operators and several other courses as well.

'You probably know Duken's son Nurlan, don't you?'

'Not really. I know of him...'

It was true that I barely knew any of the kids who had finished school after me; I would return for the holidays and they would be off visiting or working somewhere else. I recalled that someone had told me about this Nurlan having finished school the year before and getting a job at a power plant, where he had worked as a fitter.

'So, where does Nurlan work now?' I enquired of my mother, more out of politeness than from curiosity. 'At the plant. He's an engineer's assistant, I think. He has really grown up and could have supported his family, but the farm contrived to send him away to study for three years. Why people need to study for so long is beyond me!' she remarked disapprovingly.

I understood what she meant. She was aggrieved that I seldom came to visit and had even sat a practical training internship the summer before at another village. She had probably moaned to the neighbours with a sigh: *It's not for nothing that they say a mother thinks of her son, but her son thinks only of the steppe!*

Now, she was sighing once again and this sigh, of course, was addressed to me.

'It's a good thing he'll be studying,' I said, wishing Nurlan every success with all my heart.

My mother didn't like what I had said. For some time, she concentrated on drinking her tea, wiping her face with her washed cambric scarf and, drawing back the net curtain, looked outside.

'Don't be too short with Alima; you don't want to offend her,' she requested as if she was summarising her preceding words and thoughts.

I simply shrugged my shoulders. What were these precautions all about, I wondered? I thought my mother had never taken an interest in the way I had spoken with my sister. Her invariable response to

Alima's protestations would be, *He is your elder brother. Do what he says.*

Now, though, things were different.

The next day, Alima returned from school, looking upset. I assumed this was because of her schoolwork; year ten was no easy matter. I decided not to quiz her and picked up her homework diary. Alima, following my every move closely, suddenly burst out,

'*Aga*, did you ask my permission to take that?'

For the first time, I felt awkward before my sister, but I didn't let on.

'I think I can say I'm no stranger here and that I don't need permission.' With that, I started flicking through the homework diary, paying no heed to her protests.

Soon, however, I mellowed and even smiled in satisfaction; every page contained top marks, today's 3 out of 5 the only blemish on the overall picture.

'It looks like you're up for a gold medal!' I said happily.

Alima remained silent. She sat before me, tense, pale and with a yearning look in her eyes.

'Alima, what's wrong? Has someone hurt your feelings?'

My little sister's round chin shook and big tears ran down her cheeks, leaving narrow, wet trails. I carefully closed the journal and wanted to put it down on the table, but something slipped from the pages. It was a photograph. I bent down to pick it up, but my little sister beat me to it:

'I'll get it myself. Give it to me!'

72

I didn't even manage to catch a glimpse of the lad in the photo.

From that day on, my little sister became a total mystery to me. I only had to start talking to her and she would be at a loss for a reply and would get up and leave, thinking up some reason or other. In short, she clammed up completely.

I was sitting reading in the far room in the corner of the house. The sun was still high in the sky, though it was long past midday. A lad in a tracksuit top and a girl walked past my window. A minute later, there was a knock at the door. I sensed rather than realised that I would now discover Alima's secret. I was at the door in an instant. The guests clearly hadn't expected to see me and were embarrassed. I was just about to invite them inside when Alima appeared. Catching sight of me, she flared up a little and turned to the lad in the tracksuit top, who was standing with an embarrassed look on his face. The girl anticipated Alima's question.

'Nurlan has come for the book,' she said, although a secret flashed in her cunning little eyes, as if she was saying to Alima, *Don't believe it for a minute; that's not what he's here for.* Alima first blushed, then turned pale. I even thought my sister was shaking.

'What book?' she asked in a whisper, almost in tears.

The lad became even more embarrassed. I saved the situation by hurriedly saying,

'Alima, why don't you invite your guests inside? Come in, come in,'

They entered the room, but Nurlan wouldn't sit in the place he had been offered.

'I am really in a hurry. I have to be going.'

He has to be going?! It finally dawned on me that I was really not needed, so I went into the next room. However, an almost unconscious anxiety overcame me. I could not sit still and began walking up and down, occasionally casting glances in the direction of the open window. I caught sight of part of the main road, leading to the station. Poplar trees that had been planted along its sides had stretched to form a green corridor of sorts.

Seeing the road and these poplars, I suddenly recalled the day I had first left the village to go to college. Over by a small hill, I had hailed down a passing car. Saule had also been there to see me off along with my other school friends. I can still remember how she stood there a long time, waving after the departing car. She remained there even after my friends had returned back down the hill. Other cars sped past Saule, but she didn't notice them. She stood waving and it struck me that her hand wasn't saying goodbye, rather it was beckoning: *Come back, come back...* In fact, Saule had been whispering, *Farewell, farewell...*

Time and distance, however, see things differently and they often make our decisions for us. Those they don't split apart are the lucky ones.

Saule and I wrote to each other for quite some time. She would impart the village news in vivid detail, while I would simply reply that nothing had changed in the big city, which she had never seen. After seven months of correspondence, she stopped replying to my letters. I responded in kind, and stopped writing them. It was only when I returned for the holidays and learned that Saule had got married that I realised how dear she was to me.

This road edged in green foliage was now the only thing left to remind me of Saule. I can still see her, standing alone on the road; I see her hand, either waving me goodbye or calling me back...

And now my sister was standing on this same stretch of road. She was waving after a cart, which was carrying Nurlan away from the village.

Her hand was also beckoning, or perhaps Alima was doing the same as Saule had done, and was whispering, *Farewell, farewell...*?

I slumped face down onto the settee, my mind awash with contradictory thoughts and feelings. Mama entered the room. She stood in the doorway and evidently didn't know if I was asleep or simply lying there. She then quietly went to the table and began to flick aimlessly through a book. I got up and looked over at her. It seemed she had more wrinkles now than before.

'Nurlan has gone off to college,' she said sadly.

'Good for him. It's the right thing to do.'

Once again, my mother took umbrage at what I had said. She fell silent. Suddenly, Alima burst into the room. Her sweet face was a picture of boundless joy. She ran over to our mother, took her by the shoulders and spun her around the room. Our mother tried to say something, but Alima whispered something loudly in her ear:

'Mama, mama, don't say a word. I believe him, I really do... Aga,' she said as she turned to me, 'I am ready for your difficult questions! Set me as many as you like!'

I couldn't take my eyes off her. I imagined that my little sister of old was once more standing in front of me and it was only in her eyes that I noticed a barely perceptible secret: the secret of that first, strong passion...

FIRST SNOW

The tractor left the farm late, roaring and rasping. The road rolled downhill. It was stuffy in the cab and the reek of diesel rose in Kulipa's throat.

She lowered the window and stuck her head out. That was better.

The wind struck her in the face and ripped at her hair, but it still felt good. The sun's rays broke through the clouds and stretched like ropes to the ground. The storm clouds were growing darker and ever larger. The golden sword of sunlight had already been tightly sheathed and darkness was descending. The road, flattened by the tractor's tread, had become grey and unwelcoming. Muddy puddles dotted the faded and dirt-splattered grass.

Kulipa caught sight of two dots on the now colourless sky. Ducks. *They are probably the last*, she thought to herself as she watched them go. *They are in a hurry, it seems.*

She began to feel cold.

The day had been a hard one. She had risen before the cocks had crowed, but still, she had hurried out, brushing her hair as she went. The stars had still been bright in the sky and she had already called on all the milkmaids. She was cross from having had to knock more than once on their windows.

Then she had headed off to the farm. Once everything had been put in its place, Kulipa had saddled up her obedient little chestnut horse and set off to see the chairman at the office. Finding the office deserted, she had gone to his house. She hadn't even allowed him to finish his ablutions.

'What's all this? You got a fire raging at the farm or something?'

'There's no fire; it's just that the hay needs taking to the farm. Winter's just around the corner. We won't manage it today and tomorrow will be too late.'

The chairman knew all too well that he had to give her a tractor. However, it wasn't as if he had a hundred of them. All the tractors he had were out at work. That said, Kulipa wouldn't leave the chairman alone until she'd got a tractor from him. Then, having got all the milkmaids together, she had spent the entire day ferrying hay from the remote fields. By the evening, only the very last rick remained. The milkmaids couldn't be pulled off the milking and so she had gone on her own.

On the soft, springy seat up in the cab, Kulipa sensed how tired she really was. Her head buzzed, her shoulders ached, her eyes drooped and her head dipped lower and lower.

The tractor driver Sultan was silent, as ever. Sultan had a strange nature about him. Whatever Kulipa might have said, he would just sit there in silence and grin. This riled the girl.

When they were leaving the farm, Sultan spent an age, pottering about the tractor.

'Let's go, shall we, you bonehead!' she cried angrily and then felt ashamed for her rude outburst. However, Sultan merely blushed and smiled as if she had been singing his praises.

Kulipa had taken to observing him. She liked people-watching. The levers looked like toys in the tractor driver's enormous hands, but he controlled the machine nimbly and with ease. *You would have thought he'd have found a more suitable job. He'd be perfect at felling trees with those bear-like mitts and fat, twisted fingers. I can't imagine anyone else with a shape like his.*

Kulipa's gaze slid over his face. *A head just like a melon with a chubby nose protruding awkwardly from his face. Concertina boots with the tops turned over, of course, and a boilersuit shining from the oil. What a picture!*

She had grown fed up with his silence.

'My head's splitting from that fuel of yours,' she shouted over to him.

Sultan frowned at her, said nothing in response and, for some reason, he touched his ugly nose with a fat finger. Kulipa found this most annoying.

'My head hurts from your fu-uel! What are you, deaf and dumb?'

A smile spread across the tractor driver's face. He remained silent for a little while longer and then spoke quietly:

'I am not deaf and dumb. You're just not used to it. It's the same for everyone the first time around.'

This time it was Kulipa who said nothing.

His voice and the very words he used got on her nerves. *What a freak!*

And they call him an eligible bachelor! She screwed up her snub little nose disdainfully and turned away. Before, Kulipa had only heard about Sultan through hearsay. He was the laughing stock of all the village girls. People would say of hapless girls: *Who apart from Sultan would ever take her for a bride?* In recent years, Sultan's parents had done the rounds of the district to find a match for their son. The year before, even Kulipa had not escaped their attention when she had returned home for the academic break. She had welcomed the elderly parents with respect, of course, and had promised them politely to think about it. When she finally saw him in the flesh, however, she realised he had sent his parents for fear of showing himself. Now, though, here she was sitting next to this laughing stock. The poor thing could do with taking a good hard look at himself. A fine specimen, for sure!

Heavy, black storm clouds were closing in from all sides; there was not a patch of blue sky to be seen. The wind was turning ever fiercer. In the west, the sky was like a black abyss. But what was this? One white dot; a small, fluffy cloud, was flouncing amidst the grey giants, transforming first into a duck, then a lamb, then a juniper bush. It threaded its way through as if feeling its way through rocks. Sultan's eyes were fixed on her.

Nice! Such beauty! Even here, nature is incredibly fine, and yet she doesn't notice it. She just groans or purses her lips.

Sultan had heard a lot about Kulipa. Everyone wanted to outdo one another with their praise. She was attractive and modest, and industrious too.

But what was good about her, really? Short and tanned and that was about it. The only beauty in her was, perhaps, the rosiness in her cheeks. She frowns from morning to night and is never happy with anything. Alright, so she worked hard; she seemed to carry the entire farm on her shoulders. Yes, she was pretty, but what a character she had.

The tractor driver coughed, probably from the diesel.

Just think: I wrote her a note this morning, too. I wanted to give it to her when we were to go... A note... Now I just want to bring the hay in as quickly as possible and forget about it all.

'What are you always laughing about?'

'What, am I supposed to cry, is that it?'

'People don't just laugh without a reason.'

'Why not, if it's funny?'

'Hey, just shut it, alright? And step on it.'

So rude! She'll make someone so-o happy. I don't envy her future husband, that's for sure.

He applied the brakes, took a bucket, jumped down from the cab and poured some water into the radiator. Then he lay on his stomach by the ditch and drank the icy water.

Ugh, he drinks like some farm animal.

'What's with you? Eaten too much salty food or something?'

Sultan wiped his mouth on his sleeve and unhurriedly returned to the cab.

The road crept uphill and became rockier. The wheels scraped plaintively over the granite. The feather grass lay flat to the ground from the strong wind.

Not my idea of a nice stroll. I wish we'd hurry up and get there, Kulipa thought. *There are only about two kilometres to that hill. We'll secure that rick with some metal wire and get back.*

Kulipa recoiled from surprise: dense, fine rain had begun to fall.

'Hey! Get a move on!' Kulipa cried.

It seemed that Sultan had been waiting for her order and yanked the levers. The engine roared so loudly; it made their ears pop. Sultan raised the window and this made it unbearably stuffy in the cab.

The girls are probably already having fun... There's a dance at the farm and the lads will be coming from town.

The rain became heavier and Sultan turned on the headlights. They found it hard to make out the road in the thick band of fog. The slanting jets of rain shone brightly in the light like shards of glass. The hammering of the rain and the roar of the engine unified into a single drone.

Perhaps we should turn back?

The girl glanced over at the tractor driver. He was sitting calmly, seemingly unaffected by the sudden change in the weather.

'We won't get lost, will we, Sultan?'

'I don't know,' he replied with a smile. It was as if he even liked all of this. 'If we get lost, we'll stop the tractor and go to sleep. If you sleep next to me, nothing will happen, don't worry. I don't bite.'

This completely enraged Kulipa. She found it hard to restrain herself and scream at him.

'You talk too much! Let's step on it!'

82

Kulipa decided to say nothing more until they had reached their destination. She sat looking out into the dense darkness. Bedraggled sparrows leapt out from right under the tractor, seemingly bathing in the light, and then disappeared from view. As they cut through the thick fog, the tractor's headlights revealed a hayrick up ahead.

They had made it!

Kulipa pushed open the cab door and impatiently jumped out while the tractor was still moving. Sultan merely shook his head and, applying the brakes, he reached for the rope.

'You take one end; I'll take the other. Now, pull! No, no, not like that! This way.'

At last, the hay had been loaded and Kulipa clambered up on top of it. 'Brr... it's wet through.' She tried to rake some out to make things more comfortable, but she didn't have the strength. She huddled up in a ball. *It's alright, no big deal. We'll get back soon.*

She lay down on her back and fixed her matted hair. She opened her mouth, just like when she had been a child, and caught the raindrops. The tractor drove into a furrow and Kulipa was thrown gently upwards. She cursed the driver angrily, even though she knew there was no reason. A biting wind stung her face. Then it died down and the girl sensed something soft and wet on her forehead and cheeks. Snow! She looked up anxiously. Large, soft flakes were falling slowly to the ground. It became brighter, the ground quickly turned white and the hay seemed to have become smeared in a lime-like substance. Kulipa tried once again to rake out a hole for herself but her fingers, now hard as wood, refused to do her bidding.

'What have you stopped for?'

The tractor had come to a halt. Sultan had jumped down and was looking at the rick.

'You are completely frozen through.'

'No, I'm not. Get going!'

'You'll catch a cold up there. Get in the cab.'

'That's not your concern. Let's go!'

Sultan stood there a while and wanted to say something else, but thought better of it. Instead, he took off his padded jacket and threw it up to her. The engine roared into life.

The jacket was large enough for three Kulipas and it smelt of engine oil. She looked at it and screwed herself up even tighter. Then she put it on all the same.

'Ew, it smells awful,' she said and screwed up her nose.

The driver simply looked at her and said nothing.

They came to a stop once more.

'What's happened?'

'I think we're lost,' Sultan said quietly. 'Come down here, if you don't believe me. Take a look.'

Kulipa started making her way down but lost her grip. Her hands slipped on the snow-covered hay and she fell.

Sultan came running up, wanting to help her, but she pushed him away and limped round the tractor, swallowing tears of pain and affront. She looked out at the quivering ripples of whiteness. There was no road;

everything had been covered. The snow continued falling. It went down her back and tickled, it melted on her stockings and crept into her rubber boots.

Kulipa had only read or heard tales of people getting stuck in a blizzard and losing their way in familiar places. It had seemed to her to be nothing but what people made up for a laugh. But now? It was just like in the movies.

'Which way shall we go?' Sultan asked.

'Whichever way you want! Call yourself a driver?'

'Kulipa, I just...'

He didn't finish his sentence. He came back around the tractor, bending over and looking for the road.

'I reckon we need to go forward a little.'

Kulipa silently began clambering back onto the hay.

'Get in the cab.'

Her rubber boots slipped on the wet snow; there was nothing for her hands to grab hold of. The sodden padded jacket got in her way and bashed against her knees.

'Kulipa, why are you so stubborn? Get in the cab. It's warmer in there.'

He picked her up under his arm and lowered her onto the seat as if she were as light as a small child. He closed the door tightly.

Kulipa began shaking. It took her a long time to warm up, and it seemed that she could hear the sound of her teeth chattering even over the roar of the tractor's engine.

'You're behaving as if I'm some fiendish enemy. What have I done that's so bad?'

Instead of replying, Kulipa huddled up and became even smaller; next to her, Sultan's figure seemed even more immense. She occasionally glanced over at him, but he failed to notice her look; instead, he looked intently out into the white gloom beyond the cab's windscreen. It was clear that he was very tired.

The snow continued to fall and fall. The tractor trundled onward through the impenetrable haze.

'Where are we?'

'I don't know.'

The jerking and bumpiness continued. As did the snow. Kulipa sensed they had reached a fateful place.

'Let's travel back and turn right,' she suggested.

They did just that, but there was no road to be found. Kulipa stopped looking ahead. Instead, she looked at the driver. He even seemed to have grown thinner.

Kulipa felt afraid and shuddered from deep inside. The tractor jolted and crept sideways and downward as if devoid of life.

Kulipa let out a shriek.

'Jump! Quick, jump!' Sultan cried out.

He pulled with all his might on the brake lever and the tractor came to a halt. Sultan closed his eyes and wiped a hand over his forehead.

'Don't be afraid,' Sultan said and attempted a smile. He climbed out and soon returned, looking genuinely concerned. 'Do you know how to drive a tractor?'

'No,' the girl replied, not understanding a thing.

'This is what you'll do: first, you squeeze down firmly on this pedal. Then pull to the left and sharply forward... Only be calm and don't worry. Otherwise, we'll go clattering down the ravine!'

'Listen, Sultan. I won't. I'm afraid. Let's walk it. We'll leave the tractor here until the morning.'

'What? You want everyone to laugh at me?'

He explained once more what she needed to do and jumped down from the cab.

Kulipa was overcome with terror. She was all alone. She had to do what Sultan had told her or else they'd be in trouble. She repeated Sultan's words out loud to ensure she wouldn't get the instructions wrong. She pressed down on the pedal and shifted the gear lever. The tractor quietly crept downward and came to a halt. *What next? And where's Sultan?*

'Sulta-a-an! Where are you?'

'I'm right here,' his voice came from below. Kulipa made it out of the cab and stumbled forward. What had happened? The hay had slid halfway off the tractor; any more and it would have fallen off completely. Sultan, his legs spread apart, was holding it up with his head and arms.

'Sultan, what shall we do?' the girl asked with tears in her eyes.

'Get some rocks... and quick... Place them underneath. Then, don't be afraid; just drive forward.'

Clean forgetting about the pain in her leg, Kulipa ran to gather rocks, brought them back to the tractor and placed them underneath.

87

Then she climbed back into the cab. Which way with the lever? Which pedal to press? Aha, that was it. Forwards! The rocks crunched and clattered. How far had she travelled? Was it enough? She applied the brake, killed the engine and there was a sudden silence. All she could hear was the wining of the wind.

'Sulta-a-an!'

Kulipa ran down to the ravine's edge.

'Sultan, are you okay?'

'Just about,' came his faint voice.

He got up, devoid of all strength, and headed for the tractor, barely able to place one foot in front of the other. They climbed up into the cab and sat down. They caught their breath. For the first time in their journey, they looked directly at one another. Attentively and as friends. Then they burst out laughing.

The hay had scratched Sultan's face. Kulipa pulled out her neckerchief and carefully wiped the congealed blood from his face.

What if I held and kissed her? She's so lovely, and her hands are as light as feathers. He carefully took her by the wrist.

'Hey, Sultan, you'll break my arm!'

She said this with a smile and without a trace of anger.

What pretty eyes she has

'Sultan, don't, please.'

He carefully let go of the girl's arm, turned away and grasped the levers.

Surely, he's not offended, is he?

88

The tractor sputtered and stopped. The engine died.

'We're out of fuel,' Sultan said. 'What on earth are we to do now?'

Kulipa began shaking.

'Look for the aul[5]... You got us lost; you look for it.'

Sultan slowly began to remove his jacket.

'You can leave it on; I won't put it on anyway.'

'You know what, Kulipa, I'll pop out, and you take off your wet top and put the jacket on.

'Come on, take the jacket. We're surely not going to sit in this cold and argue about it!'

'But you'll freeze.'

'No, I won't. I have a dry vest on underneath.'

Kulipa changed and began to get warmer. Sultan returned to the cab and pulled the door tightly shut.

'And now, sleep. Don't be shy, just lie down. There's a long time till morning.'

Kulipa laid her head back onto the seatback. *So, here's the night, and so quiet it is, too. The dancing has probably all come to an end by now. All the girls have gone home to bed. And me?*

'Tell me something, Sultan.'

'What can I talk about? I don't know how.'

'Well, tell me how you fell in love with girls.'

'I've never fallen in love before...'

Kulipa didn't see; rather she felt him blush and she wanted to tease him some more.

---

[5] *Generally means 'village'. In Kazakhstan, the aul represents the very heart of the traditional Kazakh community and its values and culture.*

'Yeah, as if... Who would believe you? Tell me the truth, go on.' She made herself more comfortable and grinned. 'If you don't love anyone, why do you send your parents to matchmake for you?'

'I asked them not to, but they won't listen. I don't want to offend my folks, so I don't stop them. I do know why no one wants to marry me.'

That's the truth, Kulipa thought with a smile. *I should never have opened my mouth.*

They both fell silent. The wind, though, both cold and wicked, continued chattering. It found the smallest cracks in the cab and expelled the last warmth that remained there.

Kulipa's feet had become stone-cold in her rubber boots. She wanted to wiggle her toes, but they wouldn't move.

I must have frostbite!

'Your feet must be frozen,' she heard Sultan say thoughtfully.

'No-o... Not really... A little, perhaps.'

Sultan bent over and tapped the rubber boot with a finger.

'Take them off. Sit on your feet and you'll feel warmer.'

'Alright,' the girl agreed without hesitation and began pulling off her boots. They seemed to have become stuck fast; Sultan tugged at them with considerable effort.

Of course... Her feet are like ice. Her stockings are wet through.

Kulipa wanted to pull her feet underneath her, but Sultan began to rub them. Both her feet fitted easily in the driver's enormous hand. A warm sensation spread through her body, and she began to feel drowsy. Then she dropped off. When she awoke, it took her some time to realise where she was and who she was with.

Outside, the wind howled in the black of night. Sultan wasn't there.

But where's Sultan? He couldn't have walked off and left me here, could he? In just his vest. No, he couldn't have.

'Kulipa! Kulipa! You'll freeze to death up there. Come over here.'

Where was that voice coming from? Where is he?

She began to pull on her icy boots and shuddered from the cold. The cab doors flew open.

'No, don't put them on.'

Sultan's strong arms picked up the girl, lifted and then gently lowered her into a hollow he had made in the hay.

Oh, it's wonderful here! And it's out of the wind... The hay is completely dry. When on earth did he manage to warm it up?

The dust got into Kulipa's nostrils and she sneezed. The dry stems of hay tingled, but it was far better here than in the cab.

He carefully sat down next to her, doing his best not to alarm her.

He's so kind. And strong. I wouldn't stop him if he wanted to kiss me now, Kulipa thought and closed her eyes.

However, Sultan had been thinking of nothing of the sort. He was exhausted and frozen. Added to which he knew that no girl would want to kiss him.

No, he is in no way worse than all the rest. He's even better, I'd say. He's brave, attentive and calm. That is how a real man should behave. She recalled his face as if she had not seen it before. *So, why does everyone think he's ugly? He's not ugly at all.*

Kulipa fell asleep. She dreamed she was walking hand-in-hand with Sultan. Everything was bathed in white snow. They walked for a long time and then they became quite lost. Sultan was now walking ahead of her, stamping out a path as he went. His footsteps were enormous. Kulipa couldn't keep up, her feet getting stuck in the snow. For some reason, she was only wearing stockings. She cried out. Sultan stopped and laughed. He waited patiently for her, took her up in his arms and kissed her. It was a long kiss. Kulipa giggled and Sultan laughed. His unshaven cheeks tickled and tingled. A-ah! The bright sun was beating down into her eyes. The dry hay was tickling her face. It was morning. Kulipa looked at Sultan. He was still sleeping. He had Kulipa's feet pressed against his chest, wrapped up in something. Kulipa slowly began to release her limbs. Sultan woke up and looked embarrassed. He reached for her boots, stuffed with dry hay.

'Here. They must have dried a little by now.'

'Thank you, Sultan.'

The sky was now quite clear. The white snow sparkled – the first snow.

92

Kulipa recalled her dream and blushed crimson.

'Can you believe it? Kulipa, look where we got lost.'

The girl looked around. She could see the farm just a kilometre and a half away. They both laughed heartily.

'Come on, Kulipa, let's go. The torment is over. I'll bring some fuel and you can stay at the farm.'

How clean and white that first snow was! Kulipa bent down, picked up a large handful of snow and shoved it in her mouth.

'You're like a little kid, Kulipa!' Sultan said. He overtook her and also filled his mouth with a heap of snow.

His strides were enormous. Kulipa had to jump to keep to his footprints. She missed and slipped.

'Careful, now.'

Sultan slowed his pace. Kulipa crept up on him from behind like a cat and shoved snow down the back of his neck.

'That's cold,' the driver said quietly and continued walking.

The girl jumped up and showered him in more and more snow.

'I'll roll you in it in a minute,' Sultan threatened good-naturedly.

Kulipa ran and laughed. She got caught up in the oversized wadded jacket and fell over.

'Are you alright? You're not hurt, are you?'

He helped her get back to her feet. He looked into her eyes.

'It really hurts!'

She screwed up her face and then burst into peals of laughter. She threw snow into Sultan's face and rushed off ahead.

There was the farm. They could shake themselves down and get their breath back.

'Kulipa,' the young man said suddenly, looking awkwardly down at the snow, 'Would you mind if I gave you a letter?'

'What letter are you on about? Now, there's a turn-up. There's no need for that!'

Sultan's hand with the note lowered slowly and returned to his jacket pocket. He walked on ahead, continuing to brush off the snow from his collar and without looking back.

I'm such an idiot. What have I done?

'Sultan! Sultan!'

He's not stopping. Maybe, he can't hear me? No, he's stopped.

Kulipa ran over to him, plunged her hand into his jacket pocket and retrieved the note.

'Now you can go.'

Kulipa followed him with her eyes, the note in her hand. A sheet of squared paper from an exercise book that reeked of diesel.

GRANDMOTHER

They say that mothers are the happiest people on earth. If that is so, then the happiest of all of them must surely have been my grandmother. Judge for yourselves: she had three sons and a daughter and, from them, she acquired enough descendants to fill a small village. And every one of them was well fed, well clothed and well shod.

The first of her children to appear in the world was my father, Kosembai. He worked as chief accountant at the collective farm and that gave him honourable status, both at work and as the senior member of the family. Her middle son Asembai became a leading shepherd, so often travelled to Moscow or Almaty, to exhibitions or meetings. Things turned out well for her third son Yeselbai, too. He completed a postgraduate course and then wrote his dissertation while working in a highly responsible position at the district centre. In a word, my grandmother brought her sons into the world. And what about her daughter, I hear you ask. Marzhapiya was born last and, like all youngest children in the family, she was the darling of her mother and her brothers. She grew up like the *Princess and the Pea* and turned out mollycoddled and capricious. She continued to believe she could do whatever she liked and that the world revolved around her. Grandmother continued her habit of spoiling her, too.She had only recently married

Marzhapiya off and not just to anyone but the most handsome *dzhigit*[6] in the entire village. After Grandmother had had her children, she began dreaming about having her first grandson. She was given her first grandson, then other grandsons and granddaughters. Now, Grandmother was impatiently awaiting her first great-grandson, which the first grandson was to produce, of course.

And that first grandson was me. That year I turned seventeen, not exactly the age for marriage, you understand. Although, I have to admit there wasn't a girl in the village who genuinely took my fancy, either. Grandmother, though, had her own designs.

'I need to find my Zhenisbek a beautiful bride and then wait for their first child; after that, I will want for nothing,' she said to her neighbour while I was standing next to her.

Naturally, the neighbour stared at me with open eyes as if to say, *is this one able to live up to his grandmother's expectations?* I found it both embarrassing and amusing at the same time, and I made out as if I had understood nothing. The only thing I thought was *My dear, sweet grandmother! There'll come a time when you'll see me with a bride and you'll see your youngest grandson with a bride, too. And you'll have great-grandchildren. The only problem would be that then you'd say you need a great-great-grandchild!*

---

[6] *A word of Turkic origin which is used in the Caucasus and Central Asia to describe a skilful and brave equestrian, or a brave person in general. In certain other contexts it is used to describe menfolk in general.*

I believed she had many more years in her; she was only sixty-three and she moved about easily and nimbly. Grandmother seemed to have heard my thoughts and said to her neighbour, 'There's something not right with my stomach; it's forever giving me grief. It's all in Allah's power! Who knows how long he'll let us live? He'll get fed up with us, remove us from this wicked earth and be done with us.'

In recent months, she had made thorough preparations for the coming of the Grim Reaper and she wanted to meet him well-dressed as is fitting. Her black, wooden chest contained velvet camisoles she had never worn, all waiting for their moment. My father had given her a green one, Asembai, a brown one and her third son Yeselbai had brought her a blue one from town. Marzhapiya had proved herself her brothers' equal, for she had made Grandmother a black velvet camisole. From time to time, Grandmother would sprinkle cloves over her gifts and then hide them at the bottom of the chest once more. She had also accumulated countless dresses for her funeral, made of silk and satin. There were probably enough to clothe all the old women in the village.

However, while she was granted the right to live, she would go everywhere in a cheap-fabric dress and my father's old, threadbare jacket.

Grandmother was forever busy around the household. She would go visiting and make a note of where help was needed or where something needed to be done. As we all know, in such instances, the right attire would never get in the way. Yet, she had no time to put on a pretty dress, what with her never-ending worries.

My father, they say, was a decent employee at the collective farm, but at home, you'd be hard-put to find a worse master. He would bring in firewood by the cartload, but a month later, there would be nothing to throw on the fire. As we Kazakhs say, you might as well throw your legs on the fire. It was then that my grandmother would spring into action.

'Zhenisbek,' she would say, 'go and get the horse ready.'

I would happily carry out her instructions and we would harness our old gelding to the cart and set out to collect fuel by collecting dung out in the pasture and cut saltwort with a sickle or meadowsweet with a grub hoe.

Then, she would head off to Asembai's place and sit late into the night over her ancient sewing machine, her watery eyes screwed up as she sewed and mended old clothes for the little ones. The middle son had an entire mob of the little perishers, running all over the place and poking their noses in everywhere they weren't wanted, so it was no wonder their clothes didn't last long.

At Yeselbai's house, she would take on other tasks. She would cross the threshold and then immediately step outside again with a large bag in her hands, with which she would trawl the shops in the district centre, standing conscientiously in all the queues.

As always, Marzhapiya would do her best not to be outdone by her brothers. Recently, she would hang around at ours for hours, insistently explaining that she was expecting and needed her mother's attention more than anyone else, meaning her mother should move into her place.

If I had been Grandmother, I would never have put up with it for long and would have run as far away as possible from such a life. It would be *Mama this, Mama that* and she would have had no time to put her feet up. Clearly, though, there was nothing more she required from her lot and would have fussed around her children and grandchildren forever and a day. I guess all mothers are like this. We Kazakhs say, *enter the house with firewood, come out with ash*. In any case, I once heard Grandmother say, 'Oh, Allah, if you want to hear my most cherished dream, listen up: I want to die as a slave to my children.'

You see, those were her own words. And Allah was happy to accommodate: say what you will, but she always had plenty to keep her busy, with all her children and grandchildren. And Grandmother was always content with this. She would run from one home to another with a happy smile; I don't know where she got the strength?!

However, at times, her face would darken. She wanted her multitude of descendants to live in peace and harmony, but her descendants had complicated relations and were constantly picking bones with each other, and it pained her to witness this.

Grandsons would get into a fight and she would instantly leap up, pulling the scrappers apart, consoling the weaker one and remonstrating with the stronger. Whenever her patience reached its limit, she would raise her eyes to the heavens and say ruefully, 'Oh, Allah. Why have you made me live in the midst this squabbling mob?! When will you rid me of them?!' At such times, the furrows on her face would darken and deepen. She would become small from her grief; so small it seemed as if you could pick her up in your hand. At times like these, I wanted to fall on my knees before her and plead forgiveness for all those bitter minutes that I was personally responsible for. At this moment, doubt would creep into my heart: is my grandmother really happy?

From an early age, I had always enjoyed special treatment from my grandmother. Perhaps, this was down to me being her first grandson. She had waited and waited and then her beloved Zhenisbek had finally been born. I don't know how to explain it, but she would entrust me with her secrets like no other. When we would be alone together, she would tell me about how hard life was for a widow with a host of children. I found her courage and faith in people truly inspiring. I would look at her work-worn hands and be overcome with tenderness. *Dear Grandmother,* I would exclaim to myself, *had I the wherewithal, I would dress you in silk and place you on the seat of honour. And I'd fold the blanket in four to ensure you were sitting comfortably! And I'd do everything to make sure you never knew sadness or worry.*

Her perceptive heart would read my thoughts; she would run her dry, slender but tender hand through my rough hair and say, 'I should visit Asembai. I wonder if everyone is well at his place. Perhaps he could do with some help. My daughter-in-law is weak and sickly and simply can't manage on her own.'

That summer, she spent a whole month at Asembai's and only then did she return to us. In that time, Grandmother had grown noticeably thinner and her eyes more sunken. At times, it seemed she was listening in to the beating of her heart and she would sigh heavily. However, she would never let on to us that something was awry and continue to busy herself around the house.

One evening, I was sitting alone with my grandmother and my younger sister when Marzhapiya burst in as if the place was on fire. Her sleeves were rolled up, her arms covered in dough and her apron covered in flour. We were alarmed, thinking that something terrible must have happened at Marzhapiya's.

'Mama, you know how long I've wanted to make that new dress with a flowered pattern, don't you?! It would really suit me,' she said, catching her breath.

We sat, dumbfounded, not knowing what to say in response. But Marzhapiya went on: 'So, there I was, mixing the dough and, can you imagine, a thought struck me: Granny, auntie — for that is what she called my mother — has just what I need. Can you believe it?'

101

Before we had come to our senses, Marzhapiya had dived into my parents' cupboard, shoved a roll of something under her arm and promptly disappeared. She had just barged in and taken it away. What a reprobate she was! She really believed that everything good in the world belonged to her and her alone. 'I have spoilt her rotten, I have,' muttered Grandmother with a shake of her head.

My mother soon returned home from work and, over dinner, she said to Grandmother,

'I bought myself a length of fabric for a dress yesterday. Only I can't make up my mind what style to make it in. Let me show you.'

She went to the cupboard and then began rummaging in suitcases and turned over all the linen.

'I don't remember where I put it,' she said, confused. 'Have you seen it, Mama?'

'No, love, I haven't set eyes on it,' Grandmother replied, hiding her eyes. It was pitiful to look at her: all bent over and with drooping cheeks. I realised in an instant where the fabric had gone, but I decided to hold my tongue. My little sister spoilt everything, however. She had been devouring an apple with relish and appeared not to have noticed what was going on. As luck would have it, she finished her apple at precisely the wrong moment. The silly girl wiped her lips with her hand and blurted out,

'Auntie Mazhaya stole it. She tucked it under her arm and took it off home. There!'

Well, it all kicked off then! My mother was so furious she went quite white and her eyes wide and round, her arms akimbo, she laid into Marzhapiya with all guns blazing. I'd never heard the like of it from my mother.

Grandmother managed to gather her wits a little and did her best to calm her daughter-in-law, making out as if there was really nothing to be making such a fuss about.

'Calm down, my dear. It's not worth making yourself ill over it, is it now? It's only four metres of old cloth!' she said as amicably as she could.

This only resulted in my mother turning her guns on Grandmother. She launched into her, reproaching her for the failings of all her children and grandchildren. It all came down to this: whatever pain they caused my mother, Grandmother was at fault for all of it.

'Your brood will take the food from my plate and the clothes off my back!' my mother screamed.

'I'll give you my velvet dress if you like,' Grandmother said.

'I'm not a pauper! I want to wear my own dress,' my mother replied, tossing her head in high dudgeon.

Grandmother didn't utter another word and just cowered under the hail of verbal blows. She went to bed, still cowering. I couldn't get to sleep for a long time and lay there, listening to my grandmother's sighs.

It was difficult for her to keep everyone happy. She pitied everyone and that is why she couldn't stop herself from bursting into tears, with her pity and love for all of us. She wept silently; I don't know how I guessed she was crying. I simply looked across the darkness and understood.

The next morning, she behaved as if nothing had happened. She began by going round to the back of the shed to fetch some dried dung cakes. Then, she stood at the stove until noon, making flatbreads in the frying pan. Once lunch had been made, she said what she always said: 'Right then, Zhenisbek, go and harness the gelding. We need to go and gather some meadowsweet.'

I loved going on these trips with Grandmother, so I didn't hang about and ran to harness our old gelding, threw a couple of grub hoes into the cart, helped Grandmother up into her seat and off we went on our modest expedition.

The horse's pace was even, its head rocking from side to side and its tail swishing, as it took us to the Glubokiy Ravine for the meadowsweet. We whiled away the time, chatting about this and that. These times were especially dear to me because this was when Grandmother would talk with me as if I was an equal. She would share her innermost thoughts, give advice or ask for some herself. It was as if the fifty years that separated us didn't exist.

We had set out when the sun was at its most oppressive. It was so hot that we thought our blood would boil in our veins. There wasn't a single living thing to be seen out on the steppe; everything was in hiding from the hot wind and the scorching rays of the white-hot sun. Only the horseflies endlessly tormented the gelding; it would forever swish its tail and, although we travelled at a slow pace, the horse's perspiring flanks suffered greatly.

We sat in the cart under an umbrella. It gave scant protection from the sun, but I gave it no thought because Grandmother was telling me about how she used to travel to the Glubokiy Ravine to cut meadowsweet when she had been a young girl.

'Back then, over there beyond that rock, we would burn the lime,' she explained, pointing with her whip towards an outcrop a little downhill from the Glubokiy Ravine, 'and we'd cut the meadowsweet for the fire. Back then, my children were knee-high to a grasshopper, each one smaller than the next. Your father, Kosembai, was only eleven at the time. Asembai had turned eight. Yes, eight, that's right. Yeselbai had only just started walking. There was no one to leave them at home with so I would take the kids with me. I would sit them all to one side and then get to work with my grub hoe. Back then, I would cut an entire cartload of meadowsweet in a day. Not every *dzhigit* who could keep up with me, I can tell you. Only the nimblest of them came close. They would say: *Come on, Balzia! There's no way you were born to cut meadowsweet!*'

With all our conversation, we soon arrived at Glubokiy Ravine, unharnessed the horse and walked down into the hollow, each with grub hoe in hand. We climbed up the slope, overgrown with meadowsweet. I went on up ahead and Grandmother walked behind me, leaning heavily on her grub hoe and talking with a barely audible wheeze in her voice.

'Oh, look how they've grown, the beauties. I thought we had cut them all back, the poor things, but just look at them!'

The bushes on the hillside had indeed grown to the height of a man, forming an impenetrable wall. Each branch was as thick as a whip handle. Each bush would provide a sizeable bundle of firewood, but you had to get them chopped first. Seeing the size of the bushes, I had my misgivings at first. Grandmother, though, took a customary, nonchalant look and began dishing out commands: 'Right, then, let's start from here. I remember how we used to do it back then: I would come from over there, Zarkom, rest his soul, would be here and Isabai would chop over there. The same Isabai who now tends the cows. He's grown old, he has. Back then, though... This hoe here feels a bit light. Zhenisbek, let me have yours; it's a bit heavier, I think.'

Grandmother seemed to grow younger before my very eyes: her face was radiant and her lips unable to maintain a broad smile, simply stretched over her yellowed but undamaged full set of teeth.

Grandmother spat on her hands, like a true forester, raised the grub hoe in both hands above her head and swept it down onto the trunk. She struck down, over and over, until the meadowsweet creaked in response to her every strike.

In the blink of an eye, Grandmother had chopped a bundle of firewood, but the effort had taken its toll. She had tired quickly and sat down on the grass.

'Take a break, Zhenisbek. Don't push yourself too hard,' she said, even though I had not made even ten chops.

To be honest, this was just what I had been waiting for and I sat down beside her. She undid the *torsyk* leather bottle with sour milk, drank a little, enjoying every drop, and passed it to me. The sour milk pleasantly refreshed my dry mouth.

Grandmother watched me drinking with tender eyes that were ever-so-slightly mocking, and she wiped her mouth with the corner of her scarf.

'You'd do well to get some sleep, Grandmother,' I suggested, breaking away from the *torsyk*. 'You'll get your strength back after a nap.'

'What are you talking about, my little lamb?! You are my strength. I have so many of you, too. And I'm hardly likely to fall asleep here, now am I?' she said with a laugh.

We got up and took up our grub hoes. Grandmother worked fervently and it was clear that every swipe of the grub hoe brought her great satisfaction. Then, however, she recalled something, her expression became troubled and, there and then, she began to move without the ease of before. Finally, she let go of her hoe and started grumbling.

'Now your father has gone and upset Asembai. He says, "I don't even want to see Kosembai." Why did Kosembai take that sonofabitch's bonus for himself? He signed for it and just took it for himself. And then he comes and says, "What is this all about? We slave away in the freezing cold and boiling heat but he just

107

sits there barely lifting a finger and he's the one who gets the bonus, is that how things should be? Well, I'm going to see the chairman right now..." He's a so-and-so, he is. "So," I said to him, "instead of helping each other and supporting your own brother, you want to go and complain to the chairman about him?" "And what about?" he replied. "He could at least have asked." "So," I said to Kosembai, "did you take money from your brother?" "Yes," he said, "I didn't know he'd get so angry. I thought I'd return it to him later." What am I to do about them?' and Grandmother shook her head sadly.

'I bend over backwards to ensure they get along, but all they do is argue... And yet I fed them all the same milk... And then there was Marzhapiya yesterday... She's no better; she managed to upset your mother. You tell her something and it goes in one ear and out the other. Oh, lord! People say: *Just look at that widow. She's raised so many children and made grown men and women out of them. And now they're all doing very nicely for themselves. The old woman must be very happy.* I am happy, of course, I am. If only they knew what I have to do to ensure they're not at each other's throats the whole time. We lived peacefully. I won't say a bad word to my daughters-in-law, just as long as my sons are alright. After all, I'm not a mother-in-law to their wives, rather a house servant. What will come of you all when I die, eh?!'

Grandmother had probably dwelt too heavily on what would become of us after her death. This terrible image seemed to drain Grandmother of all her strength; she leant on her grub hoe and shook her head in an attempt to dispel these thoughts. Her lips pursed and her chin shook, but the old woman held herself together and stopped herself from bursting into tears. She even tried to wink at me, only her eye refused to follow her bidding.

'Don't you worry, I'm not going to up and die on you. You know what a tough old thing I am,' she said, all the same trying to cheer me up.

But I did worry. Not so much for ourselves; we would be alright; we were a grasping tenacious bunch. I was worried for Grandmother. I worried that she would run herself into the ground with us and end up dropping dead at any minute.

By sunset, we finished up our work, loaded the cart with the chopped meadowsweet, and returned home in the coolness of the evening. Yeselbai's fourteen-year-old boy was waiting for us on the threshold. Of all her grandchildren, he was the shyest and, so, Grandmother went up to him, embraced him tightly and kissed him on the forehead.

'Oh, my little black-eyed, snub-nosed darling,' she said endearingly. 'Zhenisbek, just look how tall your little cousin has grown! He's already a fine *dzhigit*! But where is that good-for-nothing father of yours?' she asked affectionately.

Yeselbai had not been to see us for over a month and Grandmother had come to miss her youngest son.

'Papa doesn't have the time. He's too busy,' the little boy muttered, lowering his eyes.

'Doesn't have the time!' Grandmother mimicked him amicably. 'He never has the time! He could have popped over for an hour in his car. You tell him that your Grandmother said: "He could at least have popped over for an hour."'

The boy nodded obediently and the conversation ended there, but my mother emerged from the house and said, 'They don't really think that much about you, Mama. Especially that youngest daughter-in-law. She could at least have got a present for you, if only a little bag of sweets.'

'The best gift I could have is right here,' Grandmother replied and squeezed the little boy's cheeks. 'Who needs sweets, eh? I am old and my teeth are rotten enough as it is. As long as the children are in good health, that's all that matters. There's nothing more I need.'

'You're just saying that,' my mother said with a smirk. 'You know only too well that that daughter-in-law of yours is nothing but a skinflint. She'd sooner choke that give anything to anyone.'

Grandmother ruefully waved her away, passing judgment neither on my mother nor Yeselbai's wife.

'Mama, how could you? You know how Grandma takes things to heart,' I said indignantly.

'Why you can't even make a joke around here,' my mother said, flushing.

In the meantime, Yeselbai's son had taken note of everything she had said. I had no doubt that he would pass on my mother's insults to his, not to mention the

110

fact that my grandmother had had to hear them as well.

The next day, Grandmother suddenly fell ill. Previously, she could have easily emptied an entire samovar while busying herself with the housework, but on that day, she could barely manage a second cup and went to bed earlier than usual.

'I don't fancy any tea for some reason. My chest hurts,' she complained in response to our enquiries.

Waking up the following morning, Grandmother informed us she had a tickle in her throat as if she'd spent the whole night nibbling sunflower seeds.

Then, she acquired a violent cough and began twisting and turning every which way. Grandmother was choking badly. We gave her water, but this relieved her cough for no more than a minute, only to return with even greater venom.

After that, my father took her to the hospital in his works car. After a series of tests, the doctor informed us in secret, away from Grandmother, that she had cancer of the oesophagus. We also concealed the awful news from the patient and brought her back home. From then on, Grandmother began melting away before our eyes; soon, she was nothing but skin and bone. Any piece of food tormented her greatly and we had to force-feed her with a spoon.

We managed to deceive Grandmother for a few months, assuring her that her illness was inconsequential and would soon pass, despite the fact the doctors had left us little hope of recovery. But her experience of life and her instincts helped her realise the truth eventually. Sensing her end was near, she told us she wanted to gather all her children together. I ran to call my Uncle Yeselbai in the district. A neighbour set off for Asembai up in the mountain pastures.

Marzhapiya was the first to come, bringing her young husband with her. Then, Yeselbai rolled up in his car with all his family. A little later, the middle son Asembai appeared, having caught a lift from a passing truck. Our sizeable family, all weeping and wailing, had flocked to the house and all stood around Grandmother. They kissed her hands and her forehead and each tried to ask how they could help and if they could right any wrongs Grandmother might hold against them. Grandmother lay there under our sympathetic gaze and seemed rather confused by this impassioned outburst of feelings.

Asembai took it worst of all. He pounded his head against the bed by her feet and wailed:

'Ma-a-ma, my mama! We have wronged you! You are leaving us, mama. Tell us what we can do for you. Just name it. If you have a dream, don't take it with you until it has been fulfilled.'

Grandmother clearly felt uncomfortable at being the cause of such grief to those so close to her because of her end. She moved her lips, seemingly saying, *Don't cry!*

Then, she asked for some water. I shot to the kitchen, brought her some water and released droplets into her mouth. It seemed to make her feel better and, when I put my ear to her lips, she said to me, 'Place me in the yard.'

The adults crowded around, getting in each other's way, and took Grandmother out into the yard under the dark-blue twilight sky.

She signalled to us that she wanted to sit by the wall. We picked her up by the arms and carefully set her on a blanket, folded three times. Leaning against the wall, she raised a tired hand to her eyes to protect them from the sun and looked around. She studied every little thing closely as if wanting to etch them in her memory and take these steppe expanses with all their wonderful trifles away with her into oblivion.

'Mama, tell us, what you want. I'll do anything!' Asembai began once more.

'I have one dream, that you should all live in peace,' Grandmother said in a barely audible voice.

At that moment, an ancient song reached us from the street. An adolescent's voice, as yet not fully formed, could be heard from somewhere behind the neighbouring houses. We recognised the voice as that of the village boy Nabiden.

He sang: *The young dzhigit will never rest on a willow stick. The young eagle will never turn down a fox.* Nabiden didn't know that our grandmother was dying. However, she shuddered, raised her hand once again and began looking out ahead, hoping to catch a glimpse of the young singer.

'That is a very old song. It came into this world at the same time as I did,' Grandmother whispered and a tear ran down her cheek.

113

We also felt the onset of tears. Nabiden, though, carried on his way and soon his voice disappeared beyond the edge of the village.

When the sun had rolled from sight beyond the horizon—until just the following morning for us, but forever for Grandmother—the men took the old woman back indoors. Here her condition deteriorated markedly and we realised her last minutes were upon her.

My father nodded to his brothers and they went out into the kitchen. A few minutes later, we heard Asembai breaking into song:

We owe you so much, mother dear.

My mother looked into the kitchen and cried out, 'Quiet, in there, have you no shame?!'

The song broke off and my father and his brothers appeared in the room with red eyes and sat at the head of Grandmother's bed. I could smell vodka on their breath.

Grandmother suddenly breathed, rapidly and heavily, as if a heavy burden had been placed on her chest and she had to apply increasing effort each time she breathed out.

'Oh, Mama!' Asembai's wife wailed.

She grasped Grandmother's hand and drew in close.

Marzhapiya, who was sitting next to her, gasped as if someone had trodden on a blister. She blurted out, 'What's all this? Come on, give me Mama's ring. It's mine! Tradition states that before their death, a person must remove all jewellery and hand it out to their nearest and dearest, to remember them by.'

Perhaps, Grandmother had forgotten this, or perhaps she still kindled a hope that she wouldn't die, only the ring remained on her finger.

Now all Grandmother's strength had deserted her and her daughter-in-law and daughter were doing all they could to remove the ring.

'Hey, love, it won't work,' Asembai's wife objected with an unexpected calmness in her voice.

She bent once more over Grandmother's hand where the gold band shimmered dimly on her middle finger, but Marzhapiya pushed her aside, grasped Grandmother's wrist and began licking the ring, hoping that this would somehow help it move. Grandmother began hiccuping her last breaths.

I think I was the first to come to my senses. I pried open Marzhapiya's vice-like fingers, took the ring from Grandmother's finger and threw it out the window into the darkness.

As if finally free of that ill-fated ring, Grandmother's arm dropped there and then from the bed and hung there limply.

'Mama!' Asembai cried and our home let out moans of grief. Distorted faces surrounded me.

An elderly neighbour approached Grandmother and checked her pulse, then closed his eyes and recited a sad prayer from the Qur'an.

I sobbed from deep down and ran outside. It seemed that centuries had passed in those hours. Even the stars appeared to be confused up in the heavens.

Only the North Star remained in its place like a well-hammered nail. It slowly began to turn light. The green star of Venus appeared above the horizon, portending morning. Relatives and neighbours emerged from the house. Asembai's wife and Marzhapiya came running out after each other, and they began rummaging about under the window.

'Zhenisbek, love! Where did you throw the ring, eh?' they asked me and then turned to berate one another:

'It's my ring!'

'Oh, you're a piece of work! Whoever finds the ring should get to keep it!'

Grandmother's sons were the last to emerge from the house. They stopped in the middle of the yard and embraced one another round the shoulders, creating the impression that their mother's passing had revealed to them at last that they were brothers. I looked at them, unable to believe my eyes. They held one another as if they were afraid of separation. It was a shame that Grandmother had been unable to see that.

'Hey, what have you lost there?' my father asked sternly and the brothers stared menacingly at Marzhapiya and her opponent.

'Well, I want to find the ring... to give it to her,' Marzhapiya said bashfully, nodding at Asembai's wife.

'And I want to give it to her,' muttered Asembai's wife guiltily.

I turned away. The neighbour who had recited the prayer spoke behind me: 'She has gone, having fulfilled her duty. She gave away everything she had.'

I wanted to return to Grandmother and I went inside. The elderly neighbour followed me in.

Grandmother's body had already been moved to the right-hand wall and was screened off by a curtain. The house had become desolate.

I tiptoed over to the curtain and was about to pull it open a little when I suddenly heard a sigh from where Grandmother was lying. I froze on the spot and then shot like an arrow outside. The old man followed me again.

'What's wrong, son? Has something scared you?'

'Grandmother's breathing.'

'Impossible,' the old man said. 'Come with me.'

We returned to the house and the old man read a prayer once more. After that, he threw open the curtains before me.

'See for yourself. Grandmother is sleeping.'

Grandmother lay there, white and haggard, like a person sleeping after a hard day's work. Her cheeks were sunken but an expression I was familiar with remained on her face. *They have all been fed from the same breast. My breast*, Grandmother seemed to be saying.

117

MUKHTAR'S[7] EAGLE

Slowly and inevitably, or so it seemed, the melody made its way into the yurt extending its slender brown fingers towards the fire. A merry magician had settled down with his little *kobyz*[8]. The strings, like a voice, muffled by the distance, calling us to join it from far away. The melody's breathing was suddenly interrupted with a pause as acute as a sharp pain, followed by the dull sound of a heavy premonition rolling in. However, the trouble passed, the strings sighed in deep relief and the *kobyz* sang once more, its melody interjected with the rhythms of an irregular step: someone, mortally wounded, was ascending higher and higher up a steep slope, to where the spring clouds wander and where eagles circle. The music fell silent. The old man sat limply, pressing the *kobyz* to his chest like a shield.

'Zeynep, hang it back in its place,' he said wearily.

A young man with a tea bowl in his hand asked, '*Aqsaqal*[9], is that not the song that we heard back then together with Mukhtar-*aga*?'

The old man nodded: 'The very same. You were here at that very time, exactly two years ago. You were listening...'

---

[7] *Mukhtar Auezov (1897-1961) is considered one of Kazakhstan's greatest writers of the 20th century. His work is revered in Kazakhstan and throughout Central Asia to this day.*

[8] *The kobyz or kyl-kobyz is an ancient Kazakh string instrument with two horsehair strings. The resonating cavity is usually covered with goat leather.*

[9] *A village elder. A position that commands great respect in the aul and in the wider community.*

119

The *aqsaqal* had forgotten about those around him and was now talking to himself. He was thinking. He was thinking aloud about the man who had left books full of goodness and truth for people to remember him by.

'He sat right here, in this place here,' the man's wife said, lowering her eyes.

It had been in the first days of April that old man Urmis had set out bright and early to go hunting. He had visited his favourite spots but by noon he had only managed to tie a single hare to his saddle.

The sun burned overhead. Having sensed the impending heat, the animals had all headed north into the Betpakdaly Steppe. The hunter hadn't encountered a single saiga or gazelle. His horse perspired freely, its sunken flanks heaving heavily. Suddenly, raising- its head, a saiga antelope leapt from a shallow gully right beside them and startled, darted off to one side. With his customary prayer to Allah, Urmis took aim but didn't fire his rifle. The saiga was lame. It was hobbling on its front right leg and by its side, screened by its mother's body, ran a little fawn with ears like mittens.

'Oh my, oh my!' Urmis exclaimed with relief. 'Don't let yourself be blinded by greed and your hand will be delivered from an evil deed.'

He followed the saigas with his eyes, unconsciously heeding that tense feeling that preceded the conception of a new song in his heart. This feeling had remained with Urmis throughout his life. Nearing old age, it had to be said that he

120

experienced it less often than in his distant youth , when he could make the strings sing as keenly as his young heart had once sung.

He and Zhappas knew no equals among all the *kobyz* players. Their get-togethers in the summer evenings when they played their *kyui* melodies, made their countrymen and anyone else listening gasp with astonishment. Zhappas had been a worthy opponent. Then he had departed to the place where grand music is played and the *kobyz* of Zhappas Kalambayev was now only heard in concerts on the radio which were listened to by the entire republic. Good! Zhappas had found his happiness. And Urmis had found his. He hunted and busied himself working the land. However, the wise are right when they say that the soul doesn't recognise the wrinkles of old age. There would be times, most often when on his own at the top of some hill, bathed in the bitter air of his native steppe land, that his heart would sing like it had before.

Urmis lowered his rifle. The saiga was now too far away. However, the popular belief among hunters is that once you've loaded your rifle, you have to shoot.

High above, right next to the sun itself, he caught sight of a black dot.

'Looks like an eagle,' the old man muttered to himself. 'Yes, it's an eagle all right.'

He knew that eagles had long deserted these parts and this unexpected sight genuinely surprised him. The experienced tracker instantly marked the point over which the bird was circling. And it was to this spot that he now led his horse.

121

Eagle country, he thought. *There used to be nesting grounds here. There's a dense almost impenetrable growth of saxaul there. But what if...* The old man perked up and set his horse off at a decent trot.

The heat was becoming unbearable. So much so that looking at the rippling waves of white-hot sand was painful. Having finally worn his horse out, Urmis sought out the right hill. *It must be here*, he thought and dismounted. He started out for the summit. The fine, hot sand shifted under his feet. Each step proved heavy going. The free-flowing sand pulled him down several times. The yellow dust burned his throat and lungs and felt gritty on his teeth. Tormented by hunger, the old man crawled slowly up to the summit. He crawled persistently, refusing to bemoan his old age. And indeed, why would he? Thoughts of old age are not synonymous with fortitude. The shirt on his back was covered in salt from his dried sweat and yet he continued forward, his entire body crouched against the barely perceptible, uneven patches of the steep slope. *Just a little further*, he encouraged himself. *I am not that old after all. Allah may steal the years away, but he cannot steal the iron resolve of this dzhigit.*

He searched for the eagle. He could now see it quite clearly, its broad, blunt-tipped wings spread out as it spiralled downwards through the blue sky, as if following the thread of a screw. 'That's right,' the old man muttered. 'It's seen me and is flustered. That means the nest is here somewhere.'

Urmis finally made it to the summit and sat down to catch his breath. He wiped the dust from his rifle.

'Everything is as it should be.' Urmis screwed up his eyes, satisfied. 'That little saiga will become a big saiga and if I find that nest, fortune will have smiled down on me.'

Making his way through the undergrowth, he looked keenly at his feet. 'There it is!' Beneath the thick, knotted trunk of a saxaul tree lay animal bones , white and weather-worn – the remnants of the predatory bird's feasting. There were even tortoise shells. 'Hm, an experienced hunter.' The old man quite forgot his fatigue. It would be no easy task to take the chicks from the top of a brittle saxaul. However, Urmis knew what he was doing. He crawled up underneath the nest, which was shaped like a wide platform made out of twigs and branches and set about dismantling it from below. Two yellow, big-headed chicks with inordinately large clawed feet and tender, fuzzy skin where the beak had yet to harden, huddled close to one another and stared at the hunter with unblinking, eyes as round as buckshot. The old man clicked his tongue: *Oh, nicely done! Princelings, the pair of them!*

'Right, my princelings, climb into my pocket here.'

Urmis returned home late that evening, tired but happy. Days such as these don't come around that often! He had to tend carefully to his feathered friends in the front room of what had once been the *main office* of the local collective farm. He knew the value of these captured eagles. He sat at the table and warned his wife:

'Zeynep, leave the hare be; save it for our new guests.'

123

Urmis took a particular liking to the smaller of the two chicks. Barely accustomed to its new environment, it immediately chirped for food. It was bold, nimble, mischievous and quite fearless. *With time, you'll become an indispensable hunting companion,* the old man mused with joy.

And what a death grip it had!

Early one morning, some three days later, Zeynep had set the samovar and Urmis had fed and watered his horse. At that moment, two cars appeared from the direction of the collective farm's central estate building. *It's rather early for the management to come calling,* the old man thought in surprise.

The cars stopped by the old man's *office* building. With the exception of two of them, they were all locals and well known to Urmis: district managers and the farm director. *They look rather jolly; they must have good news.* Anyone bringing joyful news was always an honoured guest in the aul and the old man was keen to learn what would ensue. A man with a broad brow stood by one of the cars. He looked around with what Urmis took to be a kind yet wistful, barely perceptible smile; only his bright brown eyes shone from behind slightly slanted, attractive lids. *Who is that?* The old man could see how respectfully the others were waiting for him. It also seemed to him that he had met this pensive man somewhere in the past, although he knew he could never have set eyes on him before. He couldn't have! If he had, his keen steppe memory would surely have remembered who he was.

Urmis stepped forward to meet his approaching guest. He bowed. His guest extended a hand. Having exchanged greetings with everyone, the *aqsaqal* invited the arrivals into his yurt. Once again, it occurred to him that not only had he met this man before, but that he knew him, too. This uncertainty worried the old man. He had not experienced such a feeling before.

'Wonderful,' the guest pronounced as he entered the yurt. 'It's clear that the people here are a jovial lot.' His warm gaze had settled on the *dombra* and the *kobyz*. Zeynep offered the guests tea.

'Some ayran[10], please, if you have any,' the guest requested.

Sipping the thick, creamy goat's ayran from a wooden bowl, he praised the lady of the house. Then he addressed Urmis:

'Please play something on the *kobyz*, if you would.'

The old man took up the instrument, withdrew to one side and sat down.

He closed his eyes. He pictured his guest, with his tanned cheeks, slightly reddened from drinking the ayran. He imagined him walking the ridge of the dune, up to eagle's hill with the undulating infinity of the spring steppe rolling away beyond. Suddenly, he clearly heard the uneven clip of hooves on the hard ground and pictured the joyful darting of a young saiga... The bow wavered, touched the strings and a melody came forth.

---

[10] *A cold yoghurt beverage, mixed with salt.*

125

The guest sat motionless with such quiet concentration that it appeared that he was not with them in the yurt but transported somewhere else, to that place where the melody was taking him. Urmis played. He wanted to convey what he felt like never before in this song. He wanted to transfuse the sonorous force of his feelings into sounds and bestow them upon this man who was his guest.

Urmis shuddered and stopped playing; his guest's gaze had caused him to halt. His gaze betrayed both yearning and pain. *He understands; he knows. I have caused him suffering. I have not played as I should have.* The old man clenched his cold fingers. Not one of the guests uttered a word. The man who was both familiar and unfamiliar was also silent. He said nothing and looked at Urmis, but there was no pain in his eyes any longer: the clear depths of his gaze now reflected wonder and admiration.

Finally, and with some difficulty, he spoke: 'I heard the ancient voice of the strings.' The guest looked directly at Urmis. 'That voice told me that it is in death itself...' For a moment, the guest fell silent, the features of his face displayed tension, his broad brows frozen in arches. 'Yes, it is in death itself that the exultancy of life is confined, its renewal and its ineradicable thirst for creativity.'

The guest spoke quietly, pronouncing each word with a disquieting deliberation. It was as if he was posing the question *Am I right?* both to himself and to his partner in conversation. He was searching for the expression that would convey the right meaning and,

126

when he found it, he would delight in it and this joy would be reflected in his bright brown eyes.

Urmis listened, marvelling at the truth that he had long been carrying inside, without ever suspecting that it was there; that it was everywhere and in everyone. He had guessed as much but had never been able to explain it. His guest, however, had.

Urmis no longer doubted that he knew this extraordinary man. *If only I could recall...*

The guest began saying his farewells. He thanked the lady of the house. He held Urmis's hand at length in his dry, warm hands.

'Thank you. We will certainly meet again,' and, heading for the door, he added, half in jest and half in earnest, 'That is, if neither of us falls from their horse first.'

Urmis had wanted to ask the revered guest his name but couldn't pluck up the courage.

The eagle chicks that had been left unfed, began to chirp. The guest, who by this time had sat in the car, turned to Urmis.

'Are those really eagle chicks?'

He got out of the car, looking considerably brighter and unrecognisably younger in appearance.

'Show me.'

When he saw the chicks, the guest ahh-ed with pleasure, bent over them and laughed fervently, like a little boy:

'How marvellous! Bravo! What a rare treasure! You like birds, *aqsaqal...* So do I; they can fly, after all!

And these too will soar into the sky with time. Would you mind if I fed them?'

Who on earth was this man? Urmis asked himself once again. *He recognises eagles from their chirping and feeds them so skilfully.*

'Which of these two will have an iron grip?'

'The smaller one...'

'How did you find out?'

'From the talons and its gaze.'

'It's gaze?'

Urmis nodded:

'It has a steady, acute gaze. Not so much a gaze as a piercing needle!'

'Oh! What else?'

'When I took them, I saw the shells of giant tortoises near the nest. Not every eagle can take them but the mother of these two certainly could.'

'The gaze, the talons... And wings with powerful joints! Right, *aqsaqal*?'

Urmis smiled:

'Right.'

'And the beak...'

'And the razor-sharp beak?'

The two men laughed and embraced.

'Thank you for the joy you have brought me!' the guest said. 'This considerable joy. I'll see you in Almaty.'

Only at that moment did Urmis remember who he was... He recalled the fact suddenly, like one often does when one cannot recall something essential.

Oh my! How could I? But his guest was leaving. And what a guest. The old man rushed after him, embarrassed and perplexed:

'I must be blind,' he said, catching his breath. 'Please, don't take offence...'

The guest was surprised: 'Take offence for the joy I have been granted? Surely such a thing is not possible in the steppe?!'

For the first time that morning, he smiled with such a warm smile that it took the old man's breath away.

'It is a popular custom that something should be presented to a welcome guest. Please do not offend this old man, my dear Mukhtar. I present you an eagle chick. Take it, please,' was all he uttered.

The guest bowed before him.

'This is a gift beyond price, *aqsaqal*. And I...' He fell silent.

'Please take it. Please do not refuse me!'

'What can I do? We are on the road, after all.'

One of the other guests offered a solution: they would not take the chick just yet, but leave it there until autumn, whereupon they would bring the then strong bird to Mukhtar Auezov.

'Yes, that is indeed a better solution,' he agreed. 'Most important, *aqsaqal*, is that you will be my guest. We will go hunting and test the eagle's skill. And we'll have a good old chat to boot!'

The guests departed. Urmis was in high spirits and simply couldn't calm down. He was never without his copy of Auezov's *Abai*, a book he had already read many times over. Now, though, he would look for a long time at the portrait of his extraordinary guest, a man who knew the language of music and the language of the birds.

The workers arrived from the collective farm. There was much to be getting on with. Urmis had to be in many places at once and yet he managed it all. He had a meeting to look forward to. *That is, if neither of us falls off their horse first,* he recalled. *Not a chance! This old Urmis has many years to gallop yet!*

The days went by and the chicks grew and gained in strength.

One day, however, Zeynep, who had entered the house for something, came running out, screaming,

'Oh, *aqsaqal,* come quickly! I don't know which one, but one of the eagles is dead!'

The old man, who had been relaxing in the yurt, turned cold. *Allah, let it be mine, not his bird.* He ran over without dressing. *No, it's not Mukhtar's.*

The very same day, Urmis wove a strong cage from purple osier.

On the twenty-eighth of June, as always, Zeynep turned on the radio for their morning tea. Someone was singing a merry song. The presenter then spoke in an equally jovial voice but then fell silent mid-sentence. There was a pause, a long pause and then the same presenter, only this time in a voice that was tense and breaking, as if he were shifting heavy rocks, read out the following statement: *Mukhtar Auezov died today in Moscow.*

130

Zeynep looked across at Urmis. Her husband sat slumped, failing even to notice that his tea was pouring from his bowl. The desert could be seen through the open canopy at the entrance. Urmis looked out into the distance. Mukhtar's words emerged into his consciousness, the merciless truth in them slowly gathering momentum: *That is, if neither of us falls from their horse first. He knew that*, thought Urmis. *He knew everything.* His grieving gaze stopped on the hills and the old man thought that they too had slumped, that they too had been affected, like he had, by the sad news that had carried across the steppe. The dial on the forgotten radio had turned dark. A *kobyz* was playing a lament. Urmis, however, no longer heard a thing.

One sunny autumn day, Urmis rode out into the steppe with his nurseling. On the hill where he had seen the wounded saiga, the old man opened the cage.

The eagle stepped out awkwardly, extended its neck and with a single leap, flew to its freedom. Its plumage shining bronze, the eagle ascended higher and higher.

The *aqsaqal* followed it with his gaze until it disappeared in the cold blue autumn sky, up where the sun was at its zenith.

THE CROSSING

The village shopkeeper Turash had just been released from prison after a three-month stretch inside.

The main gate opened before him and Turash stepped outside, his eyes greedily taking in everything he could see. Three months earlier, there had been a savage winter. The last thing he had seen back then, from inside the police car, was the dead-blue ice in the ditches, the deep snow on the roadside and a cloud of snowy dust, blown along the street by the biting wind.

Now, though, it was spring that met him. The rays of the pre-dusk sun struck his face softly. His starved gaze instantly took in the cloudy, yellow water, running merrily in the ditch, and the buds on the fruit trees, so full of life. He became quite heady from his sense of freedom.

The time had come, however, for him to make his first step, and he suddenly came over all timid. He thought that the moment he stepped out onto the street, the passers-by would realise from where he had only just emerged.

He drew his head into his shoulders and, barely able to hold back, he all but sprinted along the pavement towards the bus station.

The bus station was empty. Turash guessed that the bus to his native village must have left only recently and this meant that the next one would be a long while coming, or it might not come at all, seeing that the evening was drawing in.

133

Perhaps it's for the best that I missed the bus, Turash thought. *There'd have been so many people I know that I'd have gone out of my mind. I think I'll walk home. That way, I won't get noticed. It'll be getting dark in the village by the time I get there and, one way or another, I'll be able to sneak home.*

He turned onto a quiet side street, which took him unnoticed to the outskirts of the town, from where a track led away into the hills.

The path looped around the foothills and then rose to a plateau, brown and flat like a dining table. Here and there, Turash encountered verdant needles of fescue grass, breaking through the clumps of last year's grass. Skylarks flew up noisily, startled by his appearance. They hung in the blue sky, chirping like the peal of bells, but then dived back into the grass once they were happy that Turash meant them no harm.

Turash walked and thought about how his trouble-free life had come to an end. He tried to imagine how his existence would now unfold but he felt completely out of sorts from the first image that came into his mind. He would emerge from his house in the morning, to be met with his neighbour's gaze. He didn't dare to think what would happen after that.

Over those three cursed months, it seemed he had forgotten how to walk. His legs quickly tired and sweat poured from his forehead. Turash stopped to rest and looked around. The district centre below had disappeared from view; before him, the mountain tops shone white and the sky hung overhead like an upturned bowl. The sun had turned red as it began to set, its dimming edges forming a distinct outline.

All this beauty is no longer for me. And nor is the people's respect, Turash pondered bitterly. All he had left in this world was his slow-witted wife.

He recalled their first meeting in prison when his she had naïvely asked him, *Can they really leave you in prison over some stupid rag? Don't you fret; you'll see, they'll sort it out and you'll be out in no time. And if it comes to it, we'll find a person, you know, what do they call them... A lawyer,* she had concluded blithely.

Her nonchalance had piqued him. Was your prison term really the most important thing? Although, to be honest, all he had thought about up until then was how he might get free. But now that he had been released to go on his merry little way, did he feel any better? What a stupid woman she was! And it was because of her that he had taken that rotten piece of velvet home in the first place.

Turash wanted to give vent to all the grievances that he had accumulated against his wife. However, he decided not to, when he recalled how he had missed her those three months and how he had dreamed about her those long nights.

He guessed how much further he had to go. Taking this path meant it was barely ten kilometres from the district centre to the village. He would descend into the ravine and reach the Tastana winter pasture and that would mark the half-way point. From there, the road would be a continuous, downward slope. That would mean he should make it home just as it turned dark.

Turash began to walk down into the ravine. There was almost no fescue grass here, just the odd bit of meadowsweet and peashrub, beginning to display their little leaves. Majestic cliffs rose like giant walls on either side of the path.

The path itself threaded in a melancholy fashion around the rocks, the smaller pieces of which broke away under Turash's feet and clattered into the abyss. The rumble gave Turash solace because the silence had made him feel out of sorts. He happily kicked stones off the path, but when the grey-green head of a giant fennel reared up from behind one rock, looking just like a lizard's head, he gave the foul plant a wide berth. One touch and it would emit an awful stench.

The crimson sun set behind the mountains. Only the highest, snow-covered peaks still reflected its glow. It became dark in an instant down in the ravine and the air, the rocks and the grass suddenly turned grey; the enormous cliffs turned completely black. Now he had to be careful where he was putting his feet.

The Tastana winter pasture loomed below and ahead of him. At the same time, a light flashed in that lonely, deserted pasture, formed from uneven boulders; Turash also noticed that thick black smoke was billowing from a chimney.

Who could that be? Turash thought in fright. *Who on earth has ended up in that godforsaken wintering ground?*

136

His legs began to feel weak from the cowardly fear that was creeping into his heart. He crouched down to pull himself together. Then he sensibly decided that there could only be people there and people who knew him, and this second thought was not to his liking.

However, there was no way he could make it past the winter pasture in secret. He would be unmasked by the smallest stone rattling treacherously under his feet. In the end, he fell into a trap of his own making.

While he was dithering in uncertainty, a slender girl in a multicoloured dress and white headscarf emerged from the winter pasture. She walked with the agility of a gazelle, the ends of her long, pitch-black plaits fluttering around her legs.

The girl, bent over under the weight of a bundle of meadowsweet, was humming a song under her breath but then she inadvertently turned her head. The song came to an abrupt halt, the girl straightened up, looked for a moment at Turash and, with a shriek, rushed away home. Of course, she had been frightened by him lurking and observing her in silence.

Excited voices were heard from the winter pasture, and a tall lad with broad shoulders came out into the open. The same young girl was peering out from behind him. The lad crossed strong arms across his chest and stared at Turash in expectation.

Turash, too, looked at this strange pair in silence; they were not known to him. Convinced that he had never met them before, he breathed a sigh of relief. However, this inner peace did not last long because Turash heard the girl whisper,

'Yes, that's Uncle Turash!'

'Who? Who did you say?' the young man replied, his voice also whispering.

'Uncle Turash. Don't tell me you don't know him. He worked in the shop over in Tastyube.'

'Ah-h,' the lad drawled, 'but he's in prison!'

'Sh-h!' the girl hissed.

Here we go! Turash thought, his spirits sinking.

'Hello, Turash-*aga*,' the girl said, emerging from behind her young man.

'Hello,' the lad repeated and, as if he'd changed his mind, he extended a broad hand in greeting.

Turash shook his hand, trying somehow to explain his unexpected appearance, muttering incoherently,

'You see, I was too late... The bus had left... So, I decided to walk... You know, so as not to wait.'

The lad nodded, readily agreeing, while the girl began to chatter:

'We're from over there, *aga*,' she said, pointed over to the neighbouring village. 'We have an allotment not far from here, up on the plateau. But it turned cold up there.'

Both the lad and the girl looked at Turash with wide-open eyes, but Turash was still expecting a catch and didn't know how to behave with them. Therefore, he hastily said goodbye and headed off.

What does this mean? Are they pretending or don't they understand the shame that has been brought on me? he mused as he hurried away from the pasture.

Despite his wishes, however, things did not end there. The lad and the girl both called after him:

'*Aga! Aga!* Wait a minute!'

He was forced to turn around; the young couple were running after him along the path.

'Stop, *aga*. The Kaskaldak has broken its banks. You'll have to wait until morning; it'll be too dangerous to cross in the dark. You must understand, *aga!*' the girl blurted in a single breath.

'We didn't realise straight away, well, that you didn't know,' explained the young lad in a guilty tone.

Only then did Turash remember the mischief that the River Kaskaldak can get up to. In the summer, it might be no more than a stream but, in springtime, it would carry the meltwater from practically the entire district and the overspill would make crossing no easy matter. He caught the sound of the distant roaring of the elements, as if affirming his thoughts, and he took this is as a legitimately ordained piece of bad luck. What other misfortune might he now expect?

He stood on the spot, unable to decide what to do next.

'Come and stay with us, *aga*! You'll be our guest! We have only recently got married,' the young lad explained and, seeing that he was embarrassed, Turash realised that the young couple had not yet grown accustomed to their new status.

'That's right, you weren't at our wedding, so now you can be our guests tonight instead,' interjected his young wife.

'Yes, please do, sir,' the young man said.

Turash looked at their clear, happy eyes and believed the couple were inviting him to stay from nothing but the kindness of their hearts.

Twilight had set in at the winter pasture, on which the occasional crimson flicker would appear from the bright flames in the stone stove. The young couple accompanied Turash to the seat of honour next to the stove and sat him on a canvas raincoat, under which supple branches of meadowsweet had been placed.

'Perhaps you'd like to have a rest,' the young man suggested and placed a folded sweater under Turash's elbow.

The young woman fussed about the stove, throwing in brushwood, and then put the kettle on, all blackened with soot. Soon it became warm and cosy inside. The kettle whistled, the twigs crackled in the stove, bitter smoke filled the nostrils and glimmers of red adorned their faces and arms.

The mistress of the house laid a white tablecloth, took half a loaf of poppy bread from a bundle and cut it into delicious mouthfuls. The kettle finally came to the boil, the hot water hissing as it fell onto the hot coals. Turash caught himself thinking that each of these little things brought him joy.

The girl poured the tea into glasses and she brought one to her guest.

'*Aga*, please help yourself. We'll be sharing.'

'Yes, indeed! We like it better that way!' the young man echoed.

Burning his lips, Turash sipped the hot, fragrant tea. After every sip, a blessed warmth spread through his veins. It had been so long since he had tasted tea so wonderful. He had now delighted body and soul as if he had not only been making up for lost time but had also been laying stock for the future. The only thing that darkened these festive moments for him was his expectation that the young couple would nevertheless bombard him with questions.

However, his hosts had decided to observe the strict laws of hospitality, or they attached no significance to his past. They exchanged trifling phrases, continuing to show him every possible kind of respect. They also gave one another long looks, the meaning of which concerned them and them alone.

Turash drank tea until the hot water came to an end. The young woman arranged an almost luxurious bed for him while she lay down with her husband under the canvas raincoat. The newly-weds whispered to themselves about something and then fell silent; Turash guessed from their even breathing that they were sleeping. He was unable to get to sleep, however. In any case, now was not a time when he could sleep easily. He lay for a long time with his eyes open, thinking over and over until fatigue set in and he fell asleep.

He slept lightly and warily, which was why a light noise instantly woke him up. Turash raised his head and saw a late moon had risen, shedding a white square of its light where the newly-weds were sleeping. He saw, in fact, that they were not sleeping at all. The young wife was sitting as if behind dull glass, moaning pitifully with a finger in her mouth. Her husband was hovering around her.

'Well, give it to me, come on,' the young lad said and took her finger. 'Don't worry; it'll heal in no time. There, look!'

He took her finger to his lips and kissed it. His wife fell silent for a moment and then whimpered even more.

'It's all right for you; you're not the one who's suffering,' she snivelled, snatching her hand away. 'You catch my finger in a rock and tell me *it's fine*. Can't you sleep still? You roll about like some grizzly bear.'

'Let me at least bandage it,' the lad whispered guiltily.

He ripped a rag with a cracking sound and dressed his wife's finger with it. She lay down and continued snivelling. Then he bent over her and began kissing her tenderly, muttering,

'Come on, don't cry. It'll pass in no time and everything will be fine. Come on, stop it. You don't want to wake our guest, now, do you?'

'Let him wake up, for all I care. It hurts. Oh, my finger! Oh, I am so unhappy!'

With that, the lad leapt up as if he'd been stabbed with a knife, and he began screaming,

'What are you saying? Say that again!'

His face glowed a dull white colour but Turash thought he saw the desperation that distorted his features.

The frightened wife fell silent; she had been caught unawares by this turn of events. They were silent for a while and a tense quiet hung over them. Then, the lad spoke in a tragic voice, as if there was no alternative:

'Perhaps you regret ever marrying me? And, perhaps, your finger is just an excuse to cause a scene, right? I was honest when I warned you: I have nothing, but you said, *Oh, I don't need anything as long as you are here with me.* But only three days have gone by – three! And you are already in tears. Today, you cried as if you'd injured your knee. No, this has got to stop!'

'I won't do it again. Lie down. Go to sleep. You said yourself: you said yourself, we shouldn't wake our guest,' his wife said peaceably.

Her husband, however, kept an aggrieved silence. She then rose and began caressing him like a child, kissing and whispering to calm him down. The lad lay obediently on his back, his mighty chest heaving up and down like a pair of bellows. His wife continued whispering:

'Don't be angry, my knight in shining armour,' and she ran her hand over his face. 'My bold knight...'

'And don't you go telling me about how unhappy you are,' the lad finally requested in a shaking voice.

'I won't. I'm sorry. I am happy. Really happy. Hold me.'

'Alright, goodnight.'

'Goodnight. We have to be up early.'

Turash listened, bewitched by the happiness of these strangers. They quickly fell asleep. The lad slept like a strapping hero, his arms spread across the floor, bathed in the moonlight. His chest now heaved up and down in a measured fashion like some living mountain. His wife was snuggled up by his side as if she had been seeking protection under his mighty wing; finding it, she now slept peacefully. Once, she whispered something briefly in her sleep; she chuckled heartily and snuggled up even closer to her husband.

They were indeed happy and carefree, as only people of their age could be. Perhaps, that was why they had been so welcoming towards Turash.

Oh, how carefree one is in one's youth, he thought to himself and sighed because he recalled his own earlier years.

Yes, it would seem, he had been young and happy himself only recently. And he was as handsome as the young lad, for that matter. When he was in his prime, not a soul would dare ignore him. In a word, he was a true *dzhigit.* He had married the most beautiful girl in the village. Many lads in the district had held a candle for her, but he left them all high and dry. It had all kicked off back then and it was both fun and terrible to recall. His hapless challengers hadn't dared to have a go in the open, but during the night, when the happy Turash had brought his young wife home, the village lads had got the halfwit Khusan drunk and given him a loaded rifle.

In the deep of night, the wedding guests had left for home, merry and replete. The newly-weds had only just retired beyond the screen and laid down in their marriage bed, when a deafening shot had gone off, smashing the window to smithereens. The bullet had flown over his head but what was surprising was that he had not been in the least frightened at having escaped death, but instead had stood right up and laughed arrogantly, throwing down the gauntlet to the next bullet. Quite out of his wits from fear, Khusan had thrown down the rifle and ran away to the farm stables. Turash, brave and proud, had embraced his terrified young wife, caressed her and calmed her down.

In the early part of their married life, they too had had minor quarrels over nothing, which had frightened them and at times even brought them to tears. However, the making up had been stormy and passionate. Oh, how they had loved one another! These had probably been the best days of his life when he could have wept for joy. Recalling this later, they had laughed at one another: *Oh, how foolish we were back then!* If he had ever burst into tears after that, his wife would make fun of him for it. They had changed and this meant their notion of happiness had changed.

A lot of water had flowed down the Kaskaldak since then. Some ten years had passed, that was all, and yet it seemed a whole eternity was behind him. Everything had become so distant and implausible as if these were tales from the lives of others. Back home, it was as if another woman were waiting for him, a stupid and cantankerous soul and only her beauty was left to remind him of what he had had before.

Then there had been the incident with the velvet and the three months in prison. *What are three months compared with eternity?* his wife would probably say, in

145

an attempt to calm him down. *We are together again and it's as if nothing has happened*, would probably be how she would continue. However, he had lost three months of his life. To be more precise, he had never had them. He had missed so many happy days and nights.

Turash lay with his eyes open, his arms folded behind his head. It was dark and quiet on the winter pasture. The newly-weds were sleeping sweetly. Fantastical shadows danced over the uneven stone walls and the cliffs, still covered in night shadow, could be seen through the shabby window. In that hour, it was as if there was no distance; the shapeless mass of rock had almost come right up to the little house, threatening to crush it. An echo added to this surreal picture, carrying the roar of the raging mountain River Kaskaldak.

Beyond the wall, unseen, life carried on as before in all its mystery. Suddenly, it seemed that someone had stamped loudly past and rocks crashed noisily down. Then, a cry was heard as if from the depths of the earth:

'Oo-oof! Oo-oof!'

Content with the effect it had caused, the echo picked up the ominous sounds, doubled or trebled their intensity and carried them over the mountains. Turash felt goosebumps all over, a mixture of fear and curiosity. He had a sense that someone would come in at any moment. When the invisible being emitted its noise a second time and then flapped heavy wings past the winter pasture, Turash was dismayed to realise this

146

was the last time before dawn that an eagle owl would fly past.

When shades of blue appeared in the overcast sky, Turash got up. The newly-weds were still fast asleep, leaving the restless world behind them and not regretting a bit of it. Turash went outside, trying not to make a sound.

The sharp, morning air burst into his nostrils that had still retained the smell of smoke. The world opened up before him in all its magnificence. Everything around was clean and sprinkled with dew: the rocks, the grass and the newly glazed buds of meadowsweet and peashrub had seemed to have dressed themselves long and carefully in readiness for his appearance. So, the world didn't see him as an outcast. It welcomed him with open arms. Still unable to believe what he was thinking, Turash slowed down and walked along the path, still dark with dew. He felt human again, a human returning home after a long journey. He still found it hard to believe that he was walking his native soil. He strained his eyes and was relieved to see that he recognised faces and things that were dear to him and close to his heart.

A splash of sunshine burst out from behind the mountains. It caught fire over the peaks and then slid down, enveloping the ravine and Turash himself. It was probably nothing but a coincidence but it was at this moment that Turash realised that everything depended on him. He had a life, a wonderful, faithful wife, a heart and hands, all capable of returning him the respect of the people he had lost. He had to go to them openly and honestly, in the bright sunshine and not skulk in the shadows.

Turash quickened his step and had gone so far from the wintering pasture that he guessed someone was calling to him only from intuition.

A man and a woman were standing on the edge of the plateau, waving to him. They were bathed in sunlight, which gave the impression that they had been cast from bronze. The sun's rays captured their joy and this joy spilt out across the world. The echo of their voices reached him:

Aa-ah!

Turash almost wept with joy, as if he were being seen on his way by people that were very dear to him. He imagined that they were shouting, *Every happiness to you!*

The echo carried their voices along the ravine.

The warm, morning dew streamed down the wrinkled faces of the cliffs like tears of quiet joy.

'And every happiness to you, too' Turash muttered quietly, feeling a lump in his throat.

However, the echo still captured his words and rolled them back across the ravine. Or, perhaps, he just imagined it.

This echo contained an enormous, unbridled joy, a joy that makes you want to cry out for all the world to hear. He turned back once more.

The echo was still conversing with itself in jubilant voices.

NOVELLAS

ABOUT A MAN

The man was about to raise his rifle, but the *chukar* partridges had anticipated his intention, it seemed, loudly flew up and crossed to the other side of the ravine. Heavy with fat, they flapped clumsily and almost sideways against the headwind, through the mesh of falling snow. Reaching the opposite side of the ravine, they flopped down into the snow and ran off between the rocks, their heads bobbing now and then between the patches of grey.

The man ran there too, his arms awkwardly flapping as he waded knee-high in the snow. The prickly specks of snow lashed against his face, but he ran on, with no feeling in his legs and not even noticing the snow or the sharp claws of the dog rose that caught the tails of his coat. He was thinking about one thing only, and his eyes remained fixed on the opposite side of the ravine, where the partridges bobbed between the rocks. The most important stage of the hunt had arrived. *At least two*, he said to himself. *I must get two partridges – no less than that. I'm in luck this time and no mistake!* Indeed, luck was finally on his side: he had been wandering since morning, in search of these cursed birds and there they were, right in front of him. Now he would put his plan into practice and force Alibek Dastenovich to utter his favourite *that's something* and cluck in wonder. *Two at the very least...*

Suddenly, a deafening shot rang out somewhere close to his left ear. Someone pushed him sharply in the shoulder, he lost balance and fell onto his backside in the snow. A second shot thundered from somewhere right by his side. His head was spinning. Unable to comprehend what had happened, he had wanted to spring straight back up, but he collapsed once more into the deep, loose snow. Who had pushed him? Who had let off a shot so close, right under his ear? His left shoulder felt an intolerable heat and his left hip ached as if in response to this pain. So that was what it was! Someone had been shooting the partridges but had hit him instead! But who was that idiot? He gingerly rolled over onto his right side, raised himself a little on his good arm and looked around. There was no one. There was only light but persistent wind and a grey gloom hanging low, from which grains of snow came falling. So engrossed had he been in the excitement of the hunt, that he had noticed this only now. But what about the partridges? He glanced involuntarily over at the rocks, where the partridges had only just been darting and bobbing. Now there were none.

They've flown away! They heard the shots and took off. Every last one of them! What cursed luck! And they were good and fat, too. If only I could get a couple. Then Alibek Dastenovich would be sure to cluck, he thought with annoyance. But now he had to sort himself out. Obviously, there was no one else around.

It had been his rifle that had gone off. The branch of dog rose that had caught on the trigger was still swaying, and the smell of burnt powder still lingered from the barrels. The thought that he had almost killed himself made him feel sick. *But look, fate has looked kindly on me; it didn't want me to die,* he muttered happily in surprise. And there he was, and he had almost felt blessed with luck. He was alive! He was alive!

He rose to his feet carefully, overcoming the aching pain in his left shoulder and hip. An unpleasant shudder ran in waves through his body. His head was spinning. He caught his breath, undid the top buttons on his fur coat and carefully felt his wounded shoulder with his right hand. His fingers felt something warm and moist. Removing his hand, he saw it was covered in blood. He didn't need to inspect his left leg to realise all too clearly what had happened: blood had seeped through the hole left by the bullet on his trouser leg and patches of crimson now marked the white snow. All the same, he was satisfied with his inspection. His internal organs were intact, his bones were not broken, and that meant his injuries were nothing to be worried about. Now he didn't know whether to laugh or cry. Call himself a hunter?! There didn't appear any point in crying. That said, there wasn't much cause for laughter either. He was wounded, that was for sure.

He thought he should dress the wounds but then realised that nothing would come of it. In that frost, by the time he had removed his thick fur coat and wadded trousers and put them back on again, he would most probably have frozen to death. Assuming he did undress and tear strips from his undershirt, how would he bandage his shoulder and hip if his fingers couldn't function? Any dressing he applied would slip off in a matter of minutes. No, he should leave things

153

as they were. The wounds themselves were generally tolerable, and he could even continue his hunt for the partridges. They had flown off to the precipice. There had been nowhere else for them to go.

It was the thought of returning to the town empty-handed that he found intolerable. His very first steps down the slope, however, brought his thoughts back down to earth: with every step, the snow was becoming deeper and more treacherous. Would he have the strength to climb back up again? On the other side, he would have to jump from rock to rock as well. In short, while it was not too late, he would do better to return to the aul and head straight for the clinic. Even with a slight wound, it would be dangerous to joke around. Just the year before, one fine young man scratched off a spot on his face and died; he caught a blood infection, and you'll save no one with that.

He hobbled back over his footsteps, leaning on his rifle as a crutch. A nervous shiver ran over his body once again. He had not got over the shock, which still lingered deep inside. He stopped and waited to give himself the chance to calm down. The pain in his shoulder continued to sting, but his leg hurt him less, and this gave him heart. He continued on his way.

Up top in the open, the snow had also drifted to knee height. White flakes continued to fall, covering the man's tracks as he went; they became less and less visible, their outline less and less clear until they completely disappeared under a layer of fresh snow.

154

It's nothing, he said to himself. *I'll get over two hills and then come out onto the sled road, they use to carry hay to the farms.*

Just in case, he looked around to get his bearings. There was the Kurkuldek hollow where he had run many times in childhood; under the snow, beneath his feet, was a field of clover. It was six, at most seven, kilometres to the aul and he could make it home from there even with his eyes closed. If only his strength would hold out and he wouldn't lose too much blood. However, it continued to ooze, and the inside of his left boot had already become wet. His shirt and jacket, too, were sodden at the shoulder. He came over in a chill, and that meant his temperature had risen. *Just don't panic; nothing bad has happened,* he said to himself. *You'll soon be among people and in the warm. You'll be bandaged, and the only thing you'll regret is that you returned without any partridges.* Indeed, it was a shame he had not managed to catch any of the birds. That was the sole reason he had come to his native aul. He had wanted to see Alibek Dastenovich and hear him cluck and say, *That's something!* Never mind, he knew where the partridges nested and the next day, weather permitting, he would return here. He would still surprise Alibek Dastenovich and make him cluck.

The thick snow seemed to grasp him around the legs, slowing his pace. His wounded shoulder became heavier, and he had to carry it as if it were a heavy load. Never before had he realised how heavy his rifle was; it felt as if it had been cast from a solid chunk of iron. He undid the strap and dragged the rifle along the

155

snow behind him. He reckoned that if he continued at this pace, he would make it to the village in two hours. However, someone might pick him up on the sled road. At least one person would be travelling for hay, damn it! Most important was that he mustn't think about his injuries. Think about anything, but not that.

He started thinking about his cousin Batish and her sons. That morning, when he had been getting ready to go hunting and was finally checking his cartridges, Batish had asked to borrow some money. They had brought in some children's clothes at the shop, and she was fifteen roubles short for a coat for her eldest. His preparations complete and his rifle over his shoulder, he had gone outside to meet his sister and nephews, who were already back from the shop. Batish's youngest son had put on the coat destined for his older brother, its tails and long sleeves dragging along the snow as he went. The coat's rightful owner plodded along behind, almost in tears, trying every so often to get his new coat back. However, every time he drew near, his little brother would let out a blood-curdling scream. 'Leave him be,' Batish had said to her eldest son. 'He'll soon grow tired of it and return it to you himself.' The little one had finally got himself caught up in the coattails and fell; deciding he had been pushed, he had begun wailing indescribably. *Aitash and I were just the same when we were children*, he had recalled back then. Aitash, his older brother, had always put up with his whims and naughtiness. There had been times when he wouldn't even let on that he

156

was cross. However, his older brother Aitash was no longer among the living. Tears welled up in the man's eyes, and he wanted to lie down and cry, over his brother and everything in general. It was probably because he was tired and because he had allowed himself to drop his guard. That was something he should never have done. *Hold yourself together; don't come undone. Clench your fists and stay focused. This snow just keeps falling; it's a real blizzard now. Hurry up! You have to make it before it gets dark or things will only get more difficult.* For now, though, he had to make it out onto the sled road. But where had it gone? And was he going the right way? On which side was the hollow? He looked around once more. All he could see was open steppe and nothing but snow. There was nothing to fix his gaze on. But there was also the wind. The wind had been blowing into his right cheek when he had been making his way out of Kurkuldek. So, he had to turn this way. Now everything was alright. The aul had to be on the other side.

What had happened next? That's right: he had waved to Batish and strode out into the steppe. Some distance away from the aul, he had stumbled upon a black dog. It had been a wonder how it had caught itself in a trap set deep in the steppe. However, there had been no time to wonder. The poor animal had probably laid there suffering for two days or so. It has wasted away and grown exhausted, trying to free itself. It had been no easy matter to release the animal. The dog had launched into a frenzy, evidently taking

157

the man as the party guilty for setting the trap. He had circled the hound for a good half hour, trying to approach from one side and then the other. He had tried to calm the dog with kind words, but the creature had growled, bared its fangs and refused to let him anywhere near him. He had decided to give this whole idea up and leave, even saying angrily, 'Go on then, you're on your own; drop dead for all I care.' He had then thought about how tormented the poor dog must have been and decided to shoot it. However, his hands had refused to lift his rifle. A dog is not game; it lives among people. Shooting it would be almost the same as shooting a person. In the end, it had dawned on him to take off his thick, heavy fur coat; he had covered the dog with it and, with considerable effort, had opened the trap. The dog had decided not to tempt fate and had run flat out, its snapping bark echoing long in the snow-covered hills.

I wonder what idiot could have set a trap? What were they expecting to catch at this time? Not a dog, I'd wager. Well, it looks like I'm no smarter. The wind is blowing from the right, as it should. But why are there bushes here? And a slope down into the hollow? There is no hollow on the way to the aul. The man's shoulder hurt intolerably, his left arm had become heavier than his rifle, and blood had soaked through his clothing, his boot and into the inside of his coat. His weakness was dragging by the coattails to the ground; he wanted to lie down on the soft snow and rest. The fact that he had come over in a chill made him realise that his temperature had risen even higher.

Don't stop! Keep going! The problem now was that he didn't know which way to go. There was nothing but snow all around as if someone had been sprinkling from above through a giant sieve. Unfamiliar dog-rose bushes, with branches rising from beneath powdery caps, peered out from who knew where through the thick snowy mesh. *My God, am I lost? It simply can't be true.* Just in case, he cried out; the wind took his cry and carried it off no one knew where. What is more, shouting at the top of his voice caused him yet more pain in his injured shoulder. Then, he loaded his rifle and, lifting it awkwardly with his right hand, he fired upwards. However, this sound, too, was lost in the mushy snow. *What a pickle. You couldn't make this up.* However, he had to move; he had to walk somewhere. The evening was already drawing in. He thought wistfully, like a child, that it would be great if, even for two or three seconds, the blizzard would disappear and help him get his bearings; then, let heaven and earth blend into one, for he would then still make it to the aul.

He realised that he had come to a stop again, so he forced himself onward. He had to keep moving... It was no matter that his head was spinning and that he had probably lost a lot of blood. His body was strong; he was not a weak person. This wasn't the first time he had had to endure hardship. Just the year before, when he had been ferrying a student construction team out to a remote enclosure, his truck had broken down, and they had sat three days out in the sand. The heat had been hellish, there had been only four bottles of water between them, and they had been a hundred and fifty kilometres from the nearest settlement. Everyone had flaked on the second day except him; he had taken a bucket and gone off to look for water. On the third day, he had found an old well, dragged the bucket of water back from there and, it could be said, he had saved the lives of the entire team. No, say what you like, but he was strong as an ox.

Up ahead, through the twilight veil, a stumpy tree appeared. The man recognised it. It was a hawthorn tree, after which a deep ravine began. This ravine was called the *Lone Tree*. So that's where he had ended up! He felt it was time to sit down on the snow and wail, for the *Lone Tree* was on completely the other side. The aul was at least ten kilometres from there. He looked spellbound at the tree as if it were a bad omen. The hawthorn's sparse, twisted branches stirred in the wind like the dishevelled hair of an old woman. The bead-like berries, dangling here and there like meagre decorations, appeared merely to supplement this impression. He pitied both himself and the lonely tree before him. Who likes being all alone? He too now seemed alone and abandoned. Would he now make it to the aul? The aul and his cousin Batish's house suddenly appeared unattainable to him, shifted somehow to the end of the world. And yet this small part of the steppe was as familiar to him as his current city apartment; was that not an irony of fate? Back in his childhood, he would run here, carrying water to his mother, out in the fields, haymaking. He would clamber up the hawthorn and tear off its berries. There had been times when he would tighten his shirt in a knot at the waist and fill it with berries.

He would gather a great many berries, making his stomach bulge through his shirt. It was under this hawthorn that he had wept with his mother when they buried his father. He had been only small and foolish then and hadn't realised the meaning of the word *died*; he had wept and filled his face with berries simultaneously. His mother had only to turn away her eyes or cover them with her hands in her grief, and the boy would stuff berries in his mouth, munching hurriedly, spitting out the stones in an equally secretive way. His elder brother Aitash, who would walk behind the horse and harrow, would notice these tricks and give him a clip round the ear. There were many events associated with this tree and the ravine beyond, to which it had given its name. There had been too many games to list.

However, all of this had taken place during the summer. The hawthorn had not appeared so sad and lonely in the summer. From spring, it would spread splendid leaves and stand like a *bogatyr* warrior who has imbibed the strength and power from all around. Birds would flock here to build their nests on its broad branches, while the haymakers would seek salvation from the scorching heat in its shade. All of this had taken place during the summer. In winter, however, the tree had indeed been growing desolate. Once the last rick of hay had been taken away, the people would not return until the spring. That meant that the man had no right to count on a chance meeting. People would hardly be out looking for him. A couple of days, or perhaps more, would pass until Batish would notice his absence. He had spent many a night out in the steppe before, and his cousin was accustomed to his delays. When this had happened the first time, she had brought the entire aul to its feet in alarm. He had got carried away with the hunt, travelled far and failed to notice the darkness setting in.

It was the same now: it had already begun to get dark, the day was drawing to a close, and yet the blizzard showed no signs of abating. Thank God, Batish had persuaded him to dress in warmer clothes. Otherwise, things would have been far worse than they were.

He turned to face the aul and walked forward. The wind now pressed into his painful left shoulder. The pain had migrated to his head, and he began to feel sick. His rifle had become such a burden that he even thought about discarding it and carrying on without it. But this was something he shouldn't do. What if he were to encounter wild animals?

The wind howled and hurled handfuls of blinding snow into his face. The man had to close his eyes over and over. That said, they were not much use to him as it was. A gloom had set in over the steppe, and it had become as black as soot. He could see no further than the hand in front of his face. He felt completely helpless like back in those distant childhood years. Back then, however, he had had his elder brother Aitash to rely on. Were he here, Aitash would have done something to save him. But his elder brother wasn't there. *What did I do wrong? What have I done to deserve this? If I don't die, I'll destroy everyone! Everyone! Everyone!*

Hurt and anger had built up inside him; he was in a bad way while everyone else had it good. He walked, cursing and weeping and blaming the entire world for his trouble when he suddenly struck something and fell onto his back. Gasping for air and swooning from the pain, he managed to get up from the deep snow. Something like a small house engulfed in a snowdrift stood black before him. He walked along its side and, reaching the leeward side, where there was less snow, he realised that this was no house, but a hayrick. The rick wasn't much of a gift, but it was something he could thank fate for all the same. It was certainly better than nothing.

Hiding from the wind behind the hayrick, the man regained his composure a little. *Oh, if only I had a box of matches; I would light a fire and get warm. Like an idiot, I never thought to take one with me.* He reproached himself. Aitash would have placed a box in his pocket. Who knows what might happen out in the steppe in winter?

He sat on his haunches and began pulling out the hay with his good hand, to make himself a den of sorts. The tightly packed hay wouldn't budge, and every effort made his shoulder explode in pain. Frequently stopping to catch his breath, he finally managed to make himself a tiny cave inside the rick. He crawled in backwards and, placing an armful of hay into the entrance, he lay down. The rough, sour smell of the

163

hay tickled his nostrils. He held himself together for as long as he could but eventually sneezed and groaned with pain. Kicking the bucket from his own sneezing was all he needed. He decided to bury his nose in his collar until he grew accustomed to the smell of the hay. The warmth and the quiet made him drowsy, his body became as limp as cotton wool, and he drifted into a blissful state as if isolated from the world around him. The steppe was whirling in the storm by itself outside, while he was on his own inside. Each party was now isolated in their little part of an enormous universe. His consciousness seemed to be living apart from his body, too.

He mused indolently: *They take the hay from here by early winter, so why did this rick remain here in the snow? Perhaps someone cut it for themselves? If that were the case, then there would have been all the more reason to take it away earlier and look after oneself. But they didn't and all the better for me.* He hovered between wakefulness and sleep as he drowsed, and it was hard to say how long this lasted. It was fear that woke him up. Someone was ferreting in the hay he had placed by the entrance. He listened out, and he imagined he heard someone breathing. It seemed that a hand had entered his shelter and was pulling at his coat.

'Hey! Who's there?!' he cried in a heart-rending voice.

That invisible someone indeed retreated.

'I asked: who are you? Hey, answer me!' he demanded, half in fear, half in hope. Perhaps someone had remembered the hay and had returned for it.

However, no one answered. His drowsiness left him in an instant. He felt for his rifle that lay under him and loaded it in the darkness. *If they come in again, I'll give them both barrels,* he thought and then questioned his own decision. *What if it is a person, but they're just afraid? Or perhaps someone's animal has got lost?*

'Hey, don't be afraid! Come over here!' he cried out just in case.

His voice had completely failed him. It was a squeak and not a man's voice. The sharp pain still pierced his shoulder like an awl. But who was it out there? No one responded. It was quiet out in the steppe. *Maybe, I just imagined it?* However, the wind now blew into his den, bringing flakes of snow with it, and that meant that someone had definitely pulled at the hay that covered the entrance.

He waited, watching cautiously into the darkness and listening out for a sound. Then he replaced the hay at the entrance in a denser layer. *It was probably the wind swirling it up.* This assumption calmed him a little, and yet he had to remain vigilant every minute and not sleep.

Blood continued to seep from his wounds, albeit not heavily. It had soaked through his underclothes on his left side and his felt boot now squelched. How much more blood would he lose by the morning? And would this loss prove fatal? Whatever the answer, there was nothing he could do to help himself. All that remained was to wait patiently for dawn. *Don't think about that; think about something else,* he reminded

165

himself again and directed his thoughts to the town and Alibek Dastenovich.

That's something! Alibek Dastenovich would say, pronouncing the words in his stentorian manner, flashing a gold tooth as he did so. He was an interesting man and a complex one to boot. A fine fellow, for sure, although, to be honest, there was something unpleasant about him as well. He enjoyed the power he had over others...

Stop! You have no right to judge Alibek Dastenovich, your teacher. Who else if not Alibek Dastenovich set me on my feet? I will still shoot a brace of partridge and send him an invitation; I'll make him cluck his tongue, yet, I will. So, how did all this happen? Yes, it was that time when we were visiting Kapar, and my teacher fancifully said that there is no better meat than partridge and that it has healing qualities. Well, and you waded in with your promise, too. And how could I not wade in when that beggar Kapar had rolled out the caviar and the sturgeon? Said it was sent from his native aul. And he probably spent all his measly salary on it. Outscored me, the son of a bitch. And that was when the position of head of department sat vacant. He knows how Alibek Dastenovich likes to eat. And eat he did, as if he had never seen anything better in his life. He raised a toast to Kapar, too. A certain someone took this as meaning Kapar, not me, was now the leading candidate for head of department. Oh, if only Aitash were still alive, he would surely have thought of a way to get the better of that cunning fox Kapar... Oh, Aitash, my dear brother!

He became overcome with nerves, and a bitter lump rose in his throat.

166

He hadn't noticed the rustling of the hay straight away. Someone was once again audaciously trying to enter his shelter and was digging away at the entrance.

He shuddered in fright and cried out,

'Hey, I'll shoot!'

His finger, however, squeezed the trigger of its own accord; the unwelcome guest recoiled with the thunder-clap of the shot. This time, the man saw the black silhouette through the hole in the hay.

He hastily took aim and fired from the second barrel, but he missed, and the wolf disappeared somewhere into the gloom.

The man retrieved two cartridges from his belt and reloaded his gun, his hands shaking and chattering excitedly out loud in an attempt to encourage himself:

'Ah, so you think you can just come here and find me easy prey, do you? Well, you've got another thing coming!'

He took courage from his own words. And right on time, too, for the melancholy howling of a wolf carried over the nocturnal, snow-covered steppe. The creature howled like it was keening over the dead; it fell silent and then picked up again, floating in from the left and then the right. With a wailing sound, it was calling all the wolves in the world to join it. This awful howl was so terrifying, it froze the man's soul.

He shifted the cartridge belt on his stomach and counted the remaining cartridges in the dark. He had six left. Not that many for such a situation. *I must have been mad. And this is called going hunting! Anyway, it's too late to lament. Now, think about how best you're going to use your ammunition. You'll probably want to shoot when the wolf comes right up to the entrance.*

The creature didn't have to wait long for reinforcements, for other wolves soon responded to the call. First, one howled in the same melancholy manner, followed by a second and then a third.

The man thought he could even hear the wolves' fangs clicking between their howls. He heard this first from the left, then from the right. The third wolf seemed as if to have climbed right up onto the hayrick.

The man's own teeth chattered, only from fear. *My God, where have they come from?* he said to himself with a shudder.

Having congregated, the wolves began to act. One of them leapt like a dark blur up to the entrance of the shelter. The rifle fired and the wolf, with a quite pup-like yawp, recoiled to one side. The howling subsided for a while. Then the man heard growling and some scurrying. When he had been a child, people had told him that wolves devour their wounded brothers; they only had to smell the warm aroma of blood. Perhaps that was true. In any event, the wolves left him alone for a while and seemed almost to have forgotten about him.

Snowflakes flew into his den. He opened his mouth, parched from the heat, and caught the flakes on his tongue. Then, he thought better of it and replaced the used cartridge with a new one. If there were only three of them, then this ammunition would probably suffice, and he would handle the situation. One cartridge per wolf and he would even have something left over. He just didn't want them to delay their attack until he had become completely weak or, worse, until he had lost consciousness. *But where had these wolves come from? I was told that they had rid these parts of the wolves or that there were only very few left here.*

He had heard many times about campaigns to protect the wolf: people would say that, without nature's clinician, all other life would die out from disease. These wolves had probably bred as a result of a shooting ban. Interesting creatures, these humans! They had forgotten that during the war, the wolves would send shivers through the steppe auls; they would walk about in huge packs of ten to fifteen and these same people were frightened of venturing out alone beyond the last house. He had been only little back then, but he did remember Aitash one day climbing up onto the shed roof to get hay for the cow and crying out, 'Wolves! There's so many of them!' He had clambered up onto the roof there and then and seen a procession of wolves. A uniform, grey colour, they were running calmly in between the houses on the outer margins. He had counted nineteen of them. The people had screamed and kicked up an almighty fuss, the dogs barked as if possessed, yet the wolves had paid them no attention; they had simply ambled unhurriedly over the hill and down into the hollow. Back then, if a person or animal disappeared and didn't return from the steppe, they would say they had been torn apart by the wolves. The terrors people related about these cruel creatures! It would take nothing for them to devour a man down to the last bone, except for the palms and soles, which people say are poisonous to wolves. Once it's brought a man to the ground, the first thing a wolf does is to tear at his side and go for the liver. When the man had heard these tales, the hair on his head had stood on end from the fear. Then the men had returned from the war and set about clearing the steppe of the wolves. They would pay money for each predator caught and for some hunting became a profession. Now, though, the people had forgotten what they once suffered from these creatures, and they cried, 'Don't touch the wolf, for it brings good!' They had cried themselves hoarse, and now no man can venture out into the steppe!

His body felt heavier as if it had swollen and now occupied the entire den. He licked his dry, hot lips, but his tongue would barely move; it was now more like a lifeless slab. However, what was going on in his head was far worse. It spun and drooped to the floor, quite unable to hold itself on his limp neck. *If only I could sleep, even for just one minute.* However, he knew that he had no right to drop off, even for an instant.

As if in confirmation of this, the howling began again. How many of them were out there now? Two... Three... Four... No, new ones had come running too. The howling was coming nearer and nearer. They now surrounded the hayrick.

He was quite breathless. Restraining the trembling in his hands, he moved the cartridge belt to ensure it was close at hand, and he grasped his rifle tighter. *Easy does it: shoot only when they appear at the entrance.* However, the wolves appeared to have cottoned on to his simple tactic and kept out of range. Instead, they approached from the opposite side and, gathering together, they began to howl in chorus. Lord, how vile their voices were and yet how different. It appeared, though, that he had no time for these finer details at that moment. That said, he also noticed some of the wolves howled in a more lingering way as if their teeth were hurting and their jaws clenched tight. Others howled more sporadically as if they had a cough. Some howled in a high pitch and some in almost a baritone. If he survived in one piece and returned to the town, he would have something to tell his friends and Alibek Dastenovich in particular. For he would make him lay it on thick, meaning paint his picture without holding back on the fantasy or the colour. That said, it would be hard to imagine anything more terrifying than what he was going through at that moment. *This is what happened to me when I went hunting for* chukar *partridges,* he would tell Alibek Dastenovich, to conclude his tale. And Alibek Dastenovich would respond: *The poor thing – so, that's what he had to endure in his attempt to do something nice for me.* Yes, all this was for Alibek Dastenovich. And for his sake, he had asked for a whole sheep to be smoked, and he had set off to shoot those cursed partridges. Well, if he were lucky, Alibek Dastenovich would support his candidature once again, help him get the keys to the department and then, what the hell, even help defend his dissertation. Then these torments would be forgotten in a moment. Of course: one so young, still under forty, and here he was heading a department, and with a candidate's

171

degree to boot. Of course, were Aitash still alive, he would not have had to get all this at such a terrible price. A year before, his smart brother would have taken an entire smoked horse, set aside for the winter, and given it to Alibek Dastenovich, thus, as they say, *putting both feet in a single boot,* cutting off all means of retreat and forcing him to grant assistance. *You and I, dear Alibek, are the same age. Stop spinning like a top and listen. If this isn't enough, I'll bring more. I'll bring you everything you want and even what you don't want. But you have to help my brother.* That is what Aitash would have said in his deep voice, and that would have been that. His elder brother had had an iron grasp, and it was no wonder that Alibek Dastenovich had feared him. He would look away when he listened to Aitash and, although he would say, *Well, aren't you a coarse one – quite something of a Kazakh,* he would do anything that Aitash wanted. *Aitash, my dear brother, you are not here, and I am in trouble...* Bitter hurt and anger flooded his consciousness once more. He squeezed the trigger in his rage. The recoiling butt struck him in the shoulder, and the pain brought tears to his eyes. Now, though, his anger had acquired a target. The wolves! 'Come on then, come on! What's keeping you?' he called, replacing a cartridge. 'Ah, so you value your lives too, I see! Oh, how I'd blow Every one of you to kingdom come; Every last one of you!'

Thanks to Aitash, he had never known what it was like to be an orphan or live in poverty, even after his mother's death. He had grown up somewhat of a darling. The elder brother never felt sorry for himself;

172

he didn't go off to study but went to work and let his young brother go instead. After finishing secondary school, he took him to the town, found him a place at the institute and then did everything possible to ensure he stayed on for postgraduate studies. Who knew how he had managed all this, but only in the first days, Aitash had made it to Alibek Dastenovich and used his will to win him over. 'Study well and as much as you need,' his brother had told him. 'Fill your boots. While I am still alive, I've got your back and I'll show you the way. I've got your Alibek in a firm grip. I open my hand and I'll let you run over my palm; I clench it and you won't hear a squeak from him.' Aitash kept his word, helped his brother, cleared the way for him and even laid a carpet down for him. He would have had a degree certificate in his pocket, but he refused at the last and hog-tied himself like a bad racehorse. You see, he didn't want to sit down and write a formal dissertation; he had looked for a unique subject, for he had wanted to make his own contribution to science. What a naive little puppy! When he changed his mind, things weren't so simple for him. And he no longer had his trusty guardian Aitash by his side either. Two years had passed since his elder brother had died suddenly; his heart hadn't held out and had stopped suddenly. Only then did he understand who he had lost and only then did he appreciate how much his brother had cared for him. Before, he had even made fun of Aitash for having not completed his studies. How many school years did he have under his belt? Five? Six? He couldn't even remember that. *What an ungrateful swine!*

He shuddered. A wolf howled directly above his head, from the top of the hayrick. *Damn, it howls like the poor thing's offended! If I didn't know about them, I would have pitied the creature. And there it is, standing right over you.* A second wolf howled in a lower voice and climbed up next to the first.

Don't lose your head. Hold yourself together. What have I done for the world to come crashing down on me like this? The moment Aitash passed away, all manner of misfortunes began plaguing me. One after the other. He sighed and moved his stone-cold legs. It had been as if someone had replaced his wife with another as well. At first, when they had married, she had been slender and agile. She had been quite unable to sit in one place. She had been like a happy child, everyone's favourite. She would sometimes cast up laughing, shining eyes, shoot a glance and then lower her lids once more. In recent years, however, she had suddenly started to put on weight and had transformed into a real woman of the steppe. Now, she would only smile when other people were around; the moment they would remain alone, she would start frowning, giving him the silent treatment or complaining. He would always have done something wrong in her eyes. Most often, she would talk about what she believed he hadn't done or missed out on. She would give him particular grief for not having written his dissertation, and for walking around without a degree. 'So-and-so is long since a candidate of science but you are nothing more than a candidate for a candidature,' she would tell him through her teeth. If anyone, it had been the man's wife

174

who had hit on Alibek Dastenovich when they had been at Kapar's: 'It's been a long time since we've seen Alibek Dastenovich at our house. We haven't offended him, have we?' Naturally, Kapar had begun convincing her of quite the opposite and that he would certainly come visiting the moment he received an invite. When they had returned home, his wife had told him angrily, 'Clearly, unless I do something myself, you'll be dithering about until it's time to draw your pension. Go to see your relatives in the aul and make them smoke a whole sheep. And don't forget that Alibek Dastenovich likes partridge.' So, it had been her idea that had led to him lying huddled in a ball under a rick of hay, surrounded by wolves. Now, the wolves were the hunters and he, the prey.

What will my wife do if I die? he suddenly mused. He was surprised to realise that he couldn't answer this question, not even approximately. It was as if he was thinking about a complete stranger. She would cry, of course. To herself. She was accustomed to living with everything handed to her on a plate. For some reason, however, he didn't really feel sorry for her either. The children he did feel sorry for. His heart sank the moment he thought about them. They were still so young. His son was studying in third grade, while his daughter had only just started first grade. They would find it difficult without their father. He loved them a great deal because, in essence, he had not had a father. His children sensed his love, and they showed him more affection than they did their mother.

175

Hey, so I've started talking about death, I see, he wondered and was surprised that death was no longer something he feared. Way more important now was to get at least a mouthful of water to douse the blazing heat that burned within him. And besides, it was running somewhere nearby; he could even hear its clear, ringing sound.

I must have imagined it, he said to himself. *Where am I going to get water out here in winter? In this cold?!* He extended a numb arm, gathered a handful of snow from the pile that had built up by the entrance, and stuffed it in his mouth. What bliss! He took another handful. Who could have thought that snow could be so delicious?! *If I survive this, I'll become a street cleaner. I'd have plenty of snow in the winter. And it's a fantastic job, too. There'd be no need to pander to anyone or put on airs. You'd get up early in the morning, put on warm clothes and then wave a shovel or broom about in the fresh air all day! You'd be healthy, full and not have a care in the world. Your clothes would be simple and strong. There'd be no one but you out on the street, no one to distract you. You'd be alone with your thoughts; you could think as much as you want and about whatever you want. You'd be alone! But wait, here comes the first passer-by... My God, it's Aitash with a huge grin on his face.*

'What's got into you? What about your studies?' he asks, looking at the broom.

'I'm tired of it all, and I gave it up. Don't be cross with me, Aitash, and don't scold me. I couldn't do it any more.'

'Don't worry. I won't scold you. Let's go and get a cold beer,' Aitash replies, taking his brother affectionately by the arm.

176

'Yes, let's. I am gasping for a drink, now you mention it,' he said, preparing to follow his brother. But what was this? His broom had got caught on something and wouldn't let him go. He tugged at the broom and then woke up from the loud bang of a shot going off.

This time he was lucky. His rifle had been lying barrel up, even pointing slightly outwards. He rubbed snow on his face to wipe away the last of the sleep.

Nothing had changed out in the steppe: the night was still dense and dark and the snow was still falling. *That dream could have ended badly for me. I mustn't drop off under any circumstances. I might never wake up again*, he said to himself and, replacing the cartridge, he peered out into the darkness. But where were the wolves? Why were they silent? Had they really lost hope of getting a decent meal? But no, he caught sight of two twinkles of light, then another pair, then another and then another, They had lined up and were waiting. What if they weren't wolves? He remembered the words of his deceased grandmother: 'Go on, beat it! Get lost, you devils!' he barked as loud as he could, although he couldn't hear the sound of his voice. What had happened to his voice? Or, perhaps, there was something wrong with his ears?

He shook his head; a blade of grass had got into his nose. He sneezed. He felt as if needles had pierced his body, but at least he had cleared his ears. Right then, the drone of the wind and the howling of the wolves burst in. It seemed that everything had joined in one against him: the steppe, the storm and the wolves.

He was growing weaker with every passing minute. *Those who die as a man is meant to die must be happy,* he thought. *Their nearest and dearest carefully commit their body to the ground. But what will become of me if I die? They will leave nothing behind. They'll even drag my bones over the steppe. What a humiliating way to go! I won't hold out for long, that's for sure. Only one thing is important now. If I am to die, then it must only be among people. I must save my body from the wolves' fangs. I must survive until dawn at any cost, and then I'll crawl to where people are if I have to. That is now my cherished dream! Isn't it funny? But why is the night dragging on so long? I can't wait for the dawn to come!*

Snow struck directly in the hole before him. The wind picked it up and blew it into his eyes. He feverishly let off a shot to be on the safe side. A desperate yelp rang out and the snowy whirl died down. Where pairs of lights had just been twinkling, there was now a ball of dark bodies rolling. He heard an ominous growling and the gnashing of fangs that had not sunk into their prey. The ball dispersed, joined up again and then disappeared in the heart of the storm.

He was no longer afraid or desperate. All he felt was the lead-heavy burden that weighed down his body and the stiffness of his joints. Then his consciousness crumbled away altogether and he saw muddled images, where events and time had become jumbled. He saw Aitash as he had been a year before his death, as stern and powerful as a *bogatyr* warrior. He was replaced by the man's mother when she had

178

been very young. She was gathering ears of wheat in the folds of her threadbare dress made of nothing but patches, sewn together. Then he saw his daughter and son running towards him: '*Papa, papa, are you back from work so soon?*' '*Ah, my dear little ones...*'

He hadn't noticed that the storm had died down and the sky had gradually begun to clear. He didn't stir either when the sun cast its first cold beams onto the snow and thousands of sparks shimmered across the steppe. Finally, a ray of sunlight ran over the hayrick and peeped into the man's desolate shelter. Then he opened his eyes and saw the sunlight. However, he no longer had the strength to enjoy the coming of the new day. Barely able to move his disobedient arms and legs, he crawled outside, dragging his rifle behind him and with considerable difficulty, he rose to his feet, clutching onto the rick for support. He looked out over the steppe. Something like a tractor pulling a sledge floated in the distance. Or was it something else? He could barely see anything, and everything was floating before him. With considerable effort he forced himself to raise his rifle and fire a shot off. He stepped forward, still holding onto the rick, but his legs gave way and he began to sink onto his side.

THE JOURNEY THERE AND
THE JOURNEY BACK

It had all been his mother's fault. He had tried to persuade her, but what was the point? The moment she heard that Kokbai was travelling to town, she would hear nothing about the bus. She decided on her own terms: 'I'll sit you in the cab next to Kokbai, you'll get to town in the farm truck, buy what you need – textbooks, exercise books, etc. – and you'll come home by evening the same way. After all, Kokbai is no stranger; he's one of our own and will look after you if anything happens.' If his mother set her mind on something, she would never back down.

Boken himself had had quite a different idea of how his journey. He had wanted to go on the bus that travelled from the *aul* to the town every other day. On even-numbered days there, on odd-numbered days back. Boken had planned to catch the bus the next day. Once in town, he would take his time visiting the bookshops and buy everything he needed: seventh-grade books, ruled exercise books and thick white sketching paper to draw the mountains and steppe. He had wanted to buy paints of various colours, too. If you added the glistening, glossy notebooks Boken also had his eyes on, then you'd be quite right in thinking his plans were nothing short of ambitious. However, he could hardly achieve all this in the few hours he would be allowed by travelling with Kokbai. He would have spent the night in town, visited the shops again the following morning and then returned to the *aul* by the

181

evening. Boken explained all this to his mother but his mother just started screaming at him:

'Just look at him! You're a constant affliction! Do you know what you're even saying? How can I let you go on your own? To town, where there are so many cars and strangers? And where do you plan to spend the night, you mutton head?'

'In a hotel, where else?' he replied, surprised at his mother's ignorance.

'What am I to do with this walking affliction, eh?' she called out in the middle of the deserted street. 'I really don't know what I can possibly say to this simpleton. A hotel, he says!

'Did you hear that? He probably wants to go all the way and become a hoodlum or something! Just look at him! And he still plans to spend the night in a hotel! Where next, I wonder. Prison? You know what? I'd be better off wringing your neck right here and now! I'll give it to you so hard you'll be driven into the ground like a nail into wood! Take that!' And she gave him a firm clip round the head.

Boken had already shot up and was a good head and shoulders taller than his mother; she had to stand on tiptoes for her blow to hit home, but that was not going to put her off one bit. There was really nothing that could ever put her off, such was her nature.

'Alright, stop screaming. I'll go with Kokbai,' Boken said hurriedly, flushing red. He carefully looked around, hoping that no one had seen his disgraceful humiliation.

He was particularly fearful of his classmates; if they found out, he would be the laughing stock of the school. And heaven forbid if Gulya saw him. Her house stood no more than a couple of paces away and if she had found out, he would have had to flee the *aul* to avoid the ridicule. Fortunately, though, as before, there was not a soul on the street. Calming down, Boken recalled that Gulya didn't have a maths book, and he decided he would pop into see her, to ask if she wanted him to buy anything for her while he was in town.

However, he couldn't bring himself to head over to her place; he knew his mother well. Without fail, she would say something like, *You get what you need first and then worry about your friends.*

'Come on, let's go home. It's time to get you ready,' his mother said laughing, having finally got her way 'It's about time but, all the same, it's nice when your child does as he's told. What am I to do with you, my little colt!' She stroked Boken's head with a rough hand.

She led him home by the hand, forced him to get washed, pouring water over him from a bucket, and dressed him in clean clothes: a white shirt with short-sleeves and smart black trousers. Then she moistened Boken's curls and combed them over onto one side. She still couldn't stop herself from berating him, even then:

'You've grown yourself such a mane of hair that you look just like a girl.'

Thankfully, though, that's where it ended. She sat him at the table and, even though Boken had no wish to eat, she forced him to drink down a whole bowl of *ayran*.

'It'll be there in your stomach in case you get hungry,' she explained.

Having fed him and made him presentable, the mother took Boken to Kokbai's house.

Kokbai's truck was already parked out front. The driver himself was immersed to the waist under the bonnet, rattling around the engine with a spanner. His shirt had become untucked from his trousers, revealing his tanned back and sides. Despite this, Boken could see that Kokbai had also smartened himself up for the journey into town; he was wearing a new shirt.

'Hey, Kokbai, we're here,' Boken's mother informed him before waiting for his head to emerge from under the bonnet.

Kokbai straightened up, realised in an instant what was afoot and rolled his eyes in displeasure and spat through his teeth for good measure. His face was red from bending over the engine; the blood rushing to his head. His ginger hair tumbled in grubby tousles from under his beret.

'You'll take this one into town with you,' Boken's mother said, quite unmoved.

'Better if he goes on the bus,' Kokbai blurted out. It soon became clear, however, that he had been over hasty.

'What?' she screamed at him. 'You don't want to put wear on your tyres, is that it? The truck's empty and yet you're worried about getting a puncture? Just try saying another word, you good-for-nothing!' she continued, not giving the driver the chance even to open his mouth.

Kokbai was her nephew, the son of her brother. For some reason, the fact had slipped his mind that day. A fatal error. Boken's mother laid into him good and proper.

'You swine – you only ever look after yourself!' she screamed. 'We are still on this earth and you go around behaving like that?! What will become of you when we've all gone? You rotten scoundrel – I'll rip out your mangy tongue for speaking to me like that!'

She decided that a verbal reprimand was not quite convincing enough, so she reached down for a thick stem of wild grass and charged at Kokbai.

The driver himself had already realised his mistake, for his face was now crimson-red and fear had appeared in his cat-green eyes.

'Auntie, come on, I was only joking! Of course, Boken will travel with me,' Kokbai mumbled, retreating to hide behind his truck. 'Who else would I take if not him, eh? Boken, you hear? Go on, get in the cab. If you don't, your crazy mother will smash my head in. Just like last year.'

'Ah, so you remember!' the mother said. 'And I'll smash it in again if you carry on like that. Here, son, take this,' she said, quickly calming down.

Boken's mother plunged her hand into a deep pocket, specially sewn onto her dress, and retrieved three crumpled three-rouble notes and handed them to her son.

'That will be enough for you, for your books and paper. Plus, a rouble to get a bite to eat. Make sure you don't go hungry now. And you keep an eye on him,' she ordered Kokbai, who had already climbed into the cab.

'Auntie, why don't you add another five roubles? Money is never a heavy load to carry,' Kokbai joked and scratched his chin expressively, hinting that some money for a drink wouldn't go amiss.

'Are you off again?' the mother threatened with a frown. 'Next thing we know, you'll be charging for the ride.'

'Auntie, what are you talking about? You really aren't getting my jokes today, are you?'

Kokbai made himself more comfortable in his seat and winked playfully at Boken as if the two of them were in it together. If only Kokbai knew how Boken didn't want to travel in this truck, he would have understood everything. The thing is, he didn't know, he only ever played the fool. Boken distrusted Kokbai's passion for clowning around. He was already a grown man and it was high time he settled down. He even felt ashamed at Kokbai's antics in front of other people. He was his cousin; one of his own, after all.

Kokbai, as if nothing had happened, turned the mirror, looked at his reflection and let out a whistle:

'I forgot to shave.'

186

He ran his hand over his thin stubble, pulled the grubby beret from his head and, spreading his fat fingers, began tousling his ginger mane and generally preening himself in the mirror.

'D'you have a comb?'

Boken handed him his comb. Kokbai combed his hair and wiped his eyes with his fingers.

'There, now we're ready!' Kokbai said, admiring himself. 'You're a good lad, you are, carrying a comb around with you and everything.' And, with that, he shoved Boken's comb into his own pocket.

At last they got going. Kokbai jerked the truck away so fast, that Boken's mother was a long distance away in no time at all. Kokbai drove the truck at a furious pace, as if he were being pursued by some evil spirit. He paid no attention to the ruts and bumps. Carefree chickens in the road clucked madly and flew out from under the wheels like clumps of clay. Kokbai always drove his truck like this, which was why people, young and old, would step aside and wait for him to pass, whenever they caught sight of him approaching from afar. Even the dumbest of the dogs that roamed the streets barking and getting under the wheels of the passing vehicles would keep their distance, tails between their legs, to avoid Kokbai.

This trip was no exception. Kokbai's truck raced through the *aul* like a bullet, rattling its iron skeleton and jumping with every pothole. Two men carrying sacks ran out of the end house and waved for a lift, but Kokbai didn't give them a glance and rushed onwards.

'You could have picked them up,' Boken said.

187

'They'll manage,' Kokbai replied with an insolent grin. 'At the end of the day, I am not obliged to take them to the bazaar. There's a bus for that.'

The truck turned onto a dirt road and fine gravel rattled against the bottom of the chassis. Kokbai looked first one way and then the next, as if he was looking for something.

Up ahead, dog rose bushes came into view, growing along the roadside. There was someone sitting in their shadow, wearing red and white. Having drawn up close to the bushes, Kokbai suddenly slammed on the brakes. The truck came to a halt with a terrible screech, as if it had struck an unseen obstacle. Caught unawares, Boken was thrown up against the windscreen, almost smashing his nose in the process.

Looking up, he caught sight of a woman, dressed in a red top and white scarf. She rose to her feet and, picking up her shopping bags, emerged onto the road. When she had drawn nearer, Boken recognised her as the young wife of Mashen the shepherd, who lived at a cattle yard some two kilometres from the road.

Kulshara, the young woman, was as pretty as ever. Boken had admired the soft features of her face and her large black eyes before. Her eyes were a little slanted but this was a feature that became her well. Kulshara had caught the sun over the summer and Boken thought she looked even prettier than usual.

A smile played on the woman's lips, as if she was very pleased to see the truck. However, her smile disappeared for some reason, when Kulshara noticed

Boken in the cab. It was as if he was somehow in her way.

'Hello, beautiful, where is it you're off too?' Kokbai asked, looking askance for some reason at Boken.

'I decided to go to the bazaar in town,' Kulshara replied, continuing to stare at Boken, as if she was replying to him.

'Jump in, I'll give you a lift,' Kokbai said, shrugging his shoulders and looking askance at Boken once more. He was playing the fool as always.

'But the three of us won't fit,' Kulshara said plaintively.

'Sure we will. Don't worry, I'll get you there,' Kokbai said in a lively voice.

He winked frequently as he said this and Boken decided that Kokbai must have something in his eye.

Boken shuffled up closer to the driver and Kulshara sat by the door. They set off, Boken in the middle, sandwiched between Kokbai and the woman.

Kulshara quickly grasped the situation. She undid the buttons on her top and removed her headscarf. Boken's keen nostrils caught the pleasant aroma of perfume.

'It is unbearably hot,' Kulshara said languidly and fanned her face with her scarf. 'Kokbai, I see you've brought along a spare wheel,' she said with a slight chuckle.

What's wrong with that? thought Boken in surprise. *You never know what might happen on the road. What wheel*

189

is she talking about, though? He had looked in the back as he was getting into the cab, but it had been empty.

'You know: Kazakhs are Kazakhs. The moment you plan a journey, someone will always give you something to carry or fob someone off on you. It's always been the way and there's nothing you can do about it,' Kokbai responded to Kulshara and Boken could sense a poorly concealed disappointment.

'Yes, well, there's nothing to be done about it,' Kulshara confirmed with a sigh.

Kokbai shot a glance out of the rear window, as if there really was a wheel back there and, winking at Boken, he said,

'No matter, it's not doing anyone any harm.'

Of all people, Kokbai knew for sure that there was no wheel in the back. Boken realised that they were talking about him. It was he who had been *fobbed off* onto Kokbai. He was the spare wheel in the truck. He flushed red in embarrassment and resentment.

The other two, not even suspecting that he had deciphered their signals, continued with their conversation.

'That spare – is it a decent one? I mean, it won't let the air out all of a sudden, will it?' Kulshara asked.

'No, don't you worry. And if it does, we'll stick a patch on it. Isn't that right, Boken?' Kokbai asked, smirking as he glanced at him from the corner of his eye; he still thought that his younger cousin Boken wasn't the sharpest tool in the box.

Boken remained silent and pretended not to hear. Inside, however, he was angry with himself for giving in to his mother and getting into Kokbai's truck. And another thing: he had been hurt to have heard those words from the pretty Kulshara. It was obvious that Kokbai hadn't wanted to take Boken with him. But what had he done to get in Kulshara's way? Of course, it was cramped and hot with the three of them in the cab, but who could have guessed they were going to meet Kulshara on the way? And there was certainly no way she could have known. However, if anyone had told him that this was how things would turn out, he would never have got in Kulshara's way and would have definitely taken the bus into town.

The broad steppe lay all around and a chain of hills stretched out before them. The air over the steppe quivered and ran down from the hills and into the hollows and valleys below. A stiff oncoming wind either chilled their hot faces or burned with intolerable heat. Wormwood, burnt by the sun, stood waist-height on either side of the road. The wind rocked its yellow heads from side to side.

'You get back alright last night?' Kulshara asked. 'You kept the headlights off, right?'

'You want the entire *aul* to know about it?' Kokbai said

'But what if you'd had fallen down a hole or crashed into a post?' Terror and delight filled her voice in equal proportion.

'Don't you worry about me,' Kokbai replied, self-satisfied. I can make it back on your road blindfold and I won't even roll the truck. Just tell me: your old man doesn't suspect anything, does he?'

'Thank God, no. I came back and he'd already gone to bed next to the children and was snoring with both barrels,' Kulshara said wickedly.

'I thought you wouldn't be going, even though you promised.'

'Why's that?'

'I thought your husband wouldn't let you go. He's the jealous kind, he is.'

'Let him be jealous,' Kulshara said with a wave of the hand. 'So, what, I'm supposed to sit there by his side because of that? Women don't stay young for ever. It's gone before you know it. But all he needs is a stiff drink and somewhere to lie down.'

The truck drove through a pothole full of water. Boken and Kulshara were thrown so violently that they even knocked heads. Boken was startled and recoiled, burnt by Kulshara's hot temple. It was as if he had committed sacrilege. Thankfully, however, Kulshara failed to notice and capriciously said,

'Kokbai, can't you slow down? I thought my heart would give out.'

Kokbai reduced speed a little. With a look of surprise, he said,

'So why did you marry him? You could have found yourself a much more worthy *dzhigit*.'

'We all make mistakes and don't know why, don't we? Such is fate, I suppose.' Kulshara sighed and, leaning to shuffle closer to Kokbai, her hot face came close to Boken and said to the driver, 'You were more worthy, but you left for the army.'

'It was my time. And you could have waited, you know. Or was it too hard to wait two years?' Kokbai sneered.

'Yes, it was too hard,' Kulshara said and gave out a ringing laugh. Then, however, she stopped herself, as if she had caught sight of Boken for the first time; she put a hand over her mouth and then said angrily,

'How awful: we are gabbling about anything and everything in front of the boy. You're particularly good at it! You've clean forgotten about the shame,' she launched into Kokbai.

Kokbai, it seemed would have held his tongue, but then he clearly didn't like being shouted at by a woman.

'Give me a break! Nothing bad has happened. Boken's a big lad now. He'll soon be out on the hunt himself. For now, though, let him listen and learn. It'll come in handy later. Isn't that right, Boken?'

Boken came out in a sweat and blood rushed to his head. He had never felt so ashamed. He was afraid to turn his head, to meet Kulshara's gaze, so he kept stock still, looking out ahead. His elder cousin really was a piece of work: he might have been an adult, but the things he could come out with were worse than a small boy.

Kokbai, however, interpreted Boken's silence differently.

'You see, Kulshara? He agrees. Silence is a sign of agreement.' With that, Kokbai gave a satisfied laugh, as if he had thought up the phrase himself.

The scallywag had wanted to add something else, probably derogatory, but he thought better of it and brought the truck to a halt. The clear waters of the Zharbulak spring lay to the right of the road. The clean, cold spring water ran down from a rocky precipice into a gully.

Kokbai got out of the cab and walked around the truck, kicking the wheels with the toe of his boot. Then he lifted the bonnet and began rummaging about with the engine.

'Hey, Boken! Grab that bucket from the cab and run down to the spring for some water,' Kokbai ordered, raising his head.

Boken took the rubber bucket, made from part of a canister, and headed off along the edge of the gully, scrambling through the thick undergrowth of dog rose. The thorns caught and scratched him, while the dusty leaves and spiders' webs soiled his white shirt and face. Having reached the bottom, he realised that no one had come here for some time. The spring had become overgrown with grass and the water had become a feeble trickle. Boken found a sharp rock, unblock the outflow and, placing the bucket under the water, sat and waited for it to fill to the brim.

Returning with the water, Boken caught sight of another farm truck. Its driver, a short, dark *dzhigit* called Abiltai, was pacing animatedly in front of Kokbai and Kulshara, saying something and waving his arms in the air.

194

'Hey, Boken, get a move on, will you!' Abiltai cried out impatiently, as if Boken had fetched the water for him.

All the same, Boken picked up his pace and, panting from the speed with which he had made it up the slope, he handed the bucket to Kokbai. Kokbai walked slowly over to his truck and began pouring water into the radiator. For some reason, however, the radiator was full and the water spilled out onto the grass.

'Well, mate, you're in luck! You don't have to go for water,' Kokbai said to Abiltai. 'There's plenty here for you,' and he passed him the bucket which was still pretty full.'

So, he had sent Boken for water for no reason. Kokbai had just been making of fun of him, then! Boken glowered and when Kulshara stepped to one side, allowing him first into the cab to his previous place, he blurted out angrily,

'No, I'll sit by the side, thank you very much!'

Once inside, Boken slammed the door with all his might as a sign of protest.

'Go easy, Boken! It's not a toy!' Kokbai cried and slammed down the bonnet.

Boken realised that something had happened in his absence that had annoyed Kokbai.

They set off once more. Abiltai followed them to the fork, then hooted his farewell and turned towards the livestock farm. Kokbai sounded his horn in reply. Then he spat angrily and said,

195

'What the devil brought that Abiltai out here? Why couldn't he fill up at the garage, the idiot?'

'And where did he come from so suddenly?' Kulshara asked in support.

'When I was leaving, it didn't look like he was planning to go anywhere. He was just standing around the garage. He must have just turned up at the wrong moment! Where is he now?' Kokbai leaned out of the cab and looked back. 'I can't see him. He's gone.'

After that, he crunched the gears this way and that and the truck jumped and jerked over the ruts in the road.

'I wonder what's wrong with her?' Kokbai said, surprised. 'Let's take a look.'

He turned off the road, continued over untouched earth for a while and came to a halt. He slowly lit a cigarette, as if gathering his thoughts.

'Well?' he asked Kulshara with a meaningful smirk.

'Tahw ot od?' Kulshara asked, glancing over at Boken.

'I tond wonk,' Kokbai replied with a laugh

They were speaking in some strange tongue that Boken didn't understand. He even gaped in wonder. The man and woman exchanged another two or three phrases and Kokbai then uttered clearly and concisely:

'We'll have to stop here for a bit. I'll check the engine.

All three of them got out of the truck. Kokbai started rummaging around with the engine again, while Kulshara took his old jacket and sat down on the

196

grass. Boken took to flattening the long stems of wormwood, for wont of anything better to do.

'Damn it, where's that wrench?' Kokbai suddenly asked himself and felt in his pockets. 'It must have fallen out when we were by the spring. So, what are we going to do? Hey, Boken, go back and take a look, would you? It's not far at all.'

Boken was accustomed to doing the bidding of his elders and was indeed about to set off to the spring, when he remembered how his cousin had sent him for the water as a joke and belittled him in front of Kulshara. He turned back.

'What are you doing?' Kokbai asked, growing wary.

'Go yourself if you want. You never dropped your wrench, that's why!' Boken cut in.

'I said I dropped it, so I did. I am older, so you have to do what I tell you.'

'I'm still not going,' Boken replied stubbornly.

'God, what a disobedient little boy!' Kulshara exclaimed and clucked disapprovingly.

They looked at one another, perplexed.

'Then you'll have to go, Kulshara,' Kokbai said after some thought.

'Me? Well, of course, I'll go and take a look. Otherwise, we'll be sitting here arguing forever,' Kulshara agreed.

'But there's no wrench there!' Boken butted in heatedly.

'Are you arguing again?' Kulshara said with a frown.

197

She got up and spoke to Kokbai again in a strange tongue:

'Uy mingco?'

'Li eb trigh hindbe uy,' Kokbai replied.

Now Boken understood. They wanted to conceal something from him and were simply moving letters and syllables in their words. How could he not have realised that before? He felt considerable resentment, but lay the blame squarely at Kokbai's feet.

Kulshara, seemingly playing by either clicking her fingers or untying and retying her scarf, stepped from mound to mound, rocking her shoulders as she went, as if she was carrying some fragile glass ornament. She strode across the field and soon disappeared over the hill.

Kokbai paced around the truck, as if he was inspecting it in anticipation of receiving the wrench. Soon, though, his patience appeared to have come to an end.

'You can hardly rely on a woman, now, can you?' he complained to Boken. 'I'll go and look for it myself.'

And he decisively set off in the direction of the spring. Boken went after him.

'And where are you going?' Kokbai asked, turning around.

'I'm also going to look for the wrench,' Boken replied, unable to think up another explanation.

'But you only just refused to go. You didn't believe I'd dropped the wrench.'

Boken said nothing but continued to follow Kokbai.

'Please stay here, Boken! Keep watch over the truck and make sure nothing gets lost.'

Kokbai had asked him for something! This was something unexpected for Boken, but he didn't remain behind. Kokbai picked up his pace and Boken followed suit.

'Listen, stay behind! You hear me?'

That was the former Kokbai with all his coarseness.

'No, I won't!' Boken said firmly.

'Go on, clear off! What is so hard to understand? God, you're such an idiot!' Kokbai said, finally losing his cool. Spitting, he walked away, not even looking back at Boken.

Kokbai was wrong. Boken did understand something and therefore wanted to protect Kulshara.

The woman, meanwhile, stood in the gully beyond the hill and was looking in their direction. The Zharbulak spring was in a completely different direction. That meant that Kulshara, too, didn't believe that the wrench had been lost and had made no attempt to look for it. She had come here to meet with Kokbai alone. There was Boken trying to protect her and yet she was waiting for Kokbai!

'Damn that wrench! Let's go. It's time we got going!' Kokbai called to Kulshara and, leaning down to Boken, he hissed angrily: 'I should wring your neck, you mangy pup!'

The green catty eyes of Boken's cousin were red with rage but Boken met his threatening gaze boldly, as if saying, *Just you try!*

Just as Boken had thought, there was nothing wrong with the truck. Kokbai turned the key in the ignition, pressed his boot down and the truck sped off along the road just like that.

No one said a word. Kokbai frowned and bit his lip angrily. Kulshara glanced over at Boken and winced, as if she had toothache. Boken, meanwhile, was suffering from a different hurt, this time caused by Kulshara. *She's pretty, too,* he thought bitterly.

Soon, the rough, dirt road which had shaken and rocked them from side to side became a broad asphalted highway and the truck travelled swiftly and smoothly as if it were moving on glass.

The traffic here raced along in a steady flow: seemingly fragile passenger cars and giant ZIL trucks towing trailers with grain that looked like trains. They drove along like kings of the road, taking up almost the entire width of the highway. They created the impression that if they were not allowed to pass, they would crush everyone in their path or mow them into the ditches. The ZILs, however, rushed past like arrows buffeting the oncoming traffic with a strong gust of turbulence as they went.

'Oh, to spend just a year driving one of them,' Kokbai suddenly mused out loud.

'We have trucks like them,' Kulshara reminded him.

'Yes, indeed, but they're clearly not for us. I went to see the chairman to ask him. But not once! The moment he sees me coming, he gets meaner than a wolf. "That top equipment," he says, "is not for you."

I wanted to get work on a road train, but my mother doesn't want to move to the district centre. She says, "How are we going to live without our kinsmen?" "Well," I said, "others live like that and they're alright." But still, there's no changing her mind!'

'And she's right!' Kulshara said. 'What, and you really want to leave?'

'Don't worry, there's someone I won't forget. No, no, I'll come and visit,' Kokbai said and looked at Kulshara with a twinkle in his eye.

'You still shouldn't go!'

Kokbai laughed loudly, embraced Kulshara with his free arm and drew her closer to him.

'I'm kidding! I'm not going anywhere.'

'Let me go!' Kulshara cried, wriggling away and feeling ashamed. 'You could at least remember your younger cousin is sitting with us!'

'Why doesn't he just take a running jump!' Kokbai said angrily.

Take one yourself, Boken replied, although only to himself. He turned away and stared out of the window.

An uneven band of mountains stretched out in the distance in a bluish haze as if marking out the jagged end of the world. *It's a good thing I studied geography*, Boken thought to himself. *Otherwise, looking at this, I really might have believed that this Earth of ours was flat with jagged edges. The old, uneducated people still believe in all that. After all, it really does look like a sheet of metal with ragged edges, too! You couldn't but help thinking this way if you're illiterate and had never read anything. I wonder if*

201

Kokbai has ever studied geography. He probably has, but most likely still has no idea.

'I can't drive over surfaced roads. I mean, this is hardly driving for a real man. It just sends you to sleep,' Kokbai complained with a yawn.

You just want to ferry chickens down our street and count the ruts and bumps as you go, Boken thought to himself sarcastically. *And you want to work on a road train. Yeah, they really need you, don't they?!*

The scorching wind burned their faces like a flame. All three of them were red from the heat and perspired freely. The sleepy Kokbai rubbed his eyes, fearful of dropping off at the wheel. Kulshara continually fanned herself with her scarf. The smell of her perfume, which only a short while ago pleasantly tickled Boken's nostrils, was now a source of irritation. He screwed up his short nose.

'All Kazakhs are alike,' Kokbai said, in an attempt to perk up and endeavouring to continue the curtailed conversation.

'Quite right,' Kulshara echoed.

And you are the last people to judge others, Boken objected to himself.

The town came into view in the distance. There were green clusters of trees visible on the horizon and, between them, the white walls of multi-storey buildings. Then they saw the sparkling ribbon of water that ran before the town.

Kokbai perked up and suddenly suggested:

'Hey, why don't we go for a dip in the Koktal? We could wash and freshen up! We'll arrive in town as good as new!'

Kulshara and Boken didn't object, so Kokbai turned off the road, brought the truck to the banks of the river and, stopping in front of a dense willow coppice that rose up right by the water, he was the first to jump down to the sand, stretch his arms and legs, limber up and undress.

'Boken, you and I will swim here!' he cried out merrily, as if Boken were his bosom buddy.

Boken followed his call, removing his shirt as he went. Kulshara silently moved away from them and disappeared into the willow undergrowth.

Once undressed, Kokbai and Boken went up to the steep edge of the bank and stood shoulder to shoulder with one another.

'One! Two! Go-o!' Kokbai commanded and together they jumped into the crystal clear, slowly drifting water below.

The water was cold and goosebumps instantly covered their skin. Kokbai and Boken dived under a couple of times and then emerged onto the bank with their teeth chattering and lay down on the hot sand.

'Good, isn't it?' Kokbai said, barely able to move his blue lips.

Boken simply nodded in agreement.

'Lie here; you'll warm up in no time,' Kokbai promised and, scooping up the sand in his hands, proceeded to pour it over Boken's back.

Boken laughed blissfully.

'Better already, isn't it?'

'It tickles! Now, let me warm you up!'

Kokbai rolled over onto his stomach and Boken began pouring handfuls of hot sand onto his back.

'Oh, that's so hot... yikes, it burns!' Kokbai pretended to groan.

They played around, quite forgetting their recent argument.

'Can you swim across the Koktal? You know, to the other side?' Boken asked.

'Nothing doing. You call that a river?' Kokbai said, getting up and shaking off the sand. 'I swam across the Don when I was in the army. Have you heard of it? You know your geography? It must be at least four hundred metres across.'

'You swam four hundred metres? Really?' Boken asked in disbelief.

'Honest to God! I'll show you, if you want. I'll swim this Koktal ten times without stopping!'

'Show me!'

Kokbai recklessly dived into the water and swam across to the other bank in a smooth stroke, raking the water as he went. His dark, moist skin shone like a snake and his head stuck up, also snakelike, above the water. Reaching the opposite bank, Kokbai turned sharply back. He swam confidently and gracefully. Watching him was a feast for the eyes. Boken envied and admired him in equal measure.

Returning back to shore, Kokbai jumped from the water.

'Brrr, that's cold! Real alpine, icy water, that is! Makes your bones ache, it does,' he said, shivering. 'The water in the Don is as warm as fresh milk. And there's not much of a current. But if you insist...'

'I believe you! You're an excellent swimmer, Kokbai,' Boken blurted.

Kokbai slumped down onto his belly and Boken warmed him with handfuls of sand. His elder cousin lounged and groaned with pleasure but then he remembered something, jumped to his feet and rushed off into the undergrowth to where Kulshara had gone. Boken soon heard his cry:

'Ooh-la-la! Aren't you pretty without your clothes! You're completely white, it turns out!'

Kulshara shrieked and Boken heard a splash as she plunged heavily into the water.

'How dare you?!' Kulshara said angrily. 'I hope your eyes burst! Sneaking up on a woman while she's bathing!'

'Oh, come on, Kulshara, you're not going all shy on me, are you?'

'And why shouldn't I be shy? Or do you think I have no shame whatsoever? Go on, clear off! I've turned to ice. Go on, get lost! Leave me to get out of the water!'

Kokbai stumbled like a bear from the willow undergrowth with a crash. He had a slightly disheartened look about him. He slumped down onto the sand next to Boken without a word. Boken also remained silent. They lay there for a while, sunbathing. Kulshara appeared, fully dressed and, without a glance in their direction, headed for the truck. The young men rinsed themselves down to wash off the sand, and put their clothes back on.

They reached the town by midday. Kokbai set his passengers down at the very first bus stop and, agreeing a place to meet, he drove off to the other side of town on his farm business.

Left alone with Boken, Kulshara instantly transformed into a gentle pussycat and purred at Boken: 'Bokentai, my little one, you won't leave me here all on my own, will you?' she pleaded. 'You know every last street, but I'll only go and get lost on my own.'

Oh, listen to her sing! I might be Bokentai to some, but not to you, Boken thought vindictively. Not long ago, he would have been delighted to accompany such a beauty and shield her from trouble. Now, however, Kulshara's treachery was still fresh in the memory. What is more, Boken had his own plans for the day, which most likely were not the same as Kulshara's.

A bus approached the stop and, without a word, Boken stepped towards the opening doors.

'Bokentai!' Kulshara squeaked and rushed after him, almost knocking him over.

They stood together at the back of the bus and Kulshara spoke loudly, as if there was no one else on board:

'Oh, I was so scared! I thought I'd been left behind! Bokentai, first we'll go to the shop with the gold rings. Then...'

The other passengers looked at her, some in surprise, others with smirks on their faces. Two pretty girls who were Boken's age giggled openly, nudged and whispered to each other while looking at Kulshara. It had to be said, the *aul's* top-ranking beauty was dressed somewhat absurdly. Her dress hung from her like a sack and her scarf was lopsided. Only now did Boken see this, comparing Kulshara with the townswomen.

'Then we'll go to the clothes shop,' Kulshara continued loudly, not in the least embarrassed.

Boken didn't know what to do for the shame: shame for Kulshara and shame for himself for having such a travel companion. When the bus approached the next stop, he jumped out without a second thought. *Phew, I'm rid of her at last!* he thought with relief. *Now I can head for the stationer's.* However, his joy was short-lived. The bus travelled only several metres and stopped again. The rear doors creaked open and Kulshara emerged onto the pavement with her shopping bags.

'Bokentai, why didn't you say we were getting off?' she asked in a whining voice.

Boken looked at the bus involuntarily. The young girls had their noses against the rear window and were making faces.

'Bokentai, have we reached the bazaar already?' Kulshara asked, looking around.

'The bazaar's another two stops away. But I'm not going to the bazaar. I need to go to the bookshop,' Boken said, lowering his eyes to the ground.

'Oh, what a pity! So, I shouldn't have got off. We've wasted those tickets for nothing,' Kulshara complained.

Thankfully, however, another bus arrived, the woman got on and set off for the bazaar. Boken let out a sigh of relief and turned onto the main street.

He did indeed know the town well; he had been there many times with his mother and had been around the bazaar and all the shops. This time, too, he easily found the central department store where they sold books and all manner of other things that he needed. After queuing for half an hour or so, he purchased textbooks for himself and a geometry set for Gulya. Then he bought paints and glossy-covered notebooks. The only thing he couldn't find was the thick sketching paper. However, he ate some wonderful ice cream and drank two glasses of fizzy soda water. That is why he liked the town: if you have money, you can buy whatever takes your fancy.

Emerging from the department store, Boken crossed the street and entered the fabrics shop, where the bright colours and wide array sent his eyes spinning. Oh, if only he had enough money, he would by a length of dress fabric for his mother! But never mind, that time would come soon enough. He would be an adult soon and earn for himself; then he would buy twenty different lengths for his mother!

Going from shop to shop, Boken slowly made his way to the bazaar, admiring all the wares in the windows as he went. He had not seen many of the displays before; they had changed since he had last been in town. He particularly liked the hardware store. He joined the crowds by the counter, ran his hands over all manner of devices and felt the weight of new axes, rakes and shovels in his hand. He found one shovel particularly comfortable to hold and it was inexpensive, too, so he decided to purchase it just before leaving.

When Boken emerged from the shop, he was struck by the strong smell of meat broth. He felt incredibly hungry and hurried to the canteen, nestled by the entrance to the bazaar.

There was a long queue, stretching from the serving counter. Boken took his place at the back of the queue and planned to wait patiently in line, but suddenly he heard Kulshara's voice:

'Bokentai! Bokentai!'

She was standing at the front of the queue and had already been served a bowl of attractively steaming soup.

'Bokentai, come up here, quick. I'll get some for you, too,' Kulshara called.

Boken, however, pretended not to see or hear her. Others, though, had heard Kulshara and started chattering around Boken:

'Young man, you're being called! You're Bokentai, right?'

'Don't be shy, young man, head to the front.'

'Comrades, let the boy through to his sister. He's obviously being shy.'

'These village children are all so timid. Not like our town lot.'

'It's a good thing they're timid, too. Our kids are already running circles around us.'

He was pushed forward and soon, against his will, he found himself side by side with Kulshara.

'What do you want for your main, Bokentai? I'm having stew. They say it's beef,' Kulshara informed him.

'Well, then I'll have the stew as well,' Boken grumbled, still endeavouring to preserve his sense of independence.

To add to the stew, Kulshara bought him some soup, two glasses of tea and some sweet doughnuts. They took their trays laden with food and sat down by a vacant table at the window.

Boken took some money from his pocket and offered it to Kulshara for his lunch. Kulshara, however, not only refused to take it but proceeded even to tell him off.

'Put your money away! Let these city dwellers count their every kopeck; here, they're all strangers to one another. You and I, though, thank God, are both from the same *aul*,' Kulshara said angrily.

Boken wolfed down the soup and the stew but refused the tea.

'I'll have a soda when we go outside,' he explained to Kulshara.

His companion, though, poked her fork about in her stew, drank down her tea and took a third glass from Boken's tray. Streams of sweat poured from her; she wiped her face on her neckerchief and continued drinking the hot tea. It was just as if she was sitting at home, back in the *aul*.

'I think I might be ill; it was so disgusting. They made that stew with pork,' Kulshara said as they emerged outside.

Boken approached a glass drinks dispenser and drank down two glasses of soda water. Then they sat in the shade near the canteen, relaxing and watching the passers-by. Kulshara giggled when she saw women in short skirts, pinched her cheek and said,

'What a nightmare! The next thing, they'll be walking around in nothing at all!'

Boken turned away and blushed, ashamed that Kulshara might think he was deliberately staring at all that bare female flesh.

At three o'clock, just as Kokbai had ordered, they approached the main gates to the bazaar. To Boken's surprise, his cousin kept his word and arrived on time. Seeing Boken's books, Kokbai offered his praise: 'Well done!' Kulshara showed off what she had bought and complained that she had not managed to buy herself a new dress.

'They told me to try it on. But how could I do that? I couldn't very well get undressed in front of everyone, now could I?' Kulshara explained.

Kokbai winked merrily at Boken and said,

'They have curtained off changing booths for that. Don't worry, we'll accompany you to the women's clothes shop; we'll get you the best, don't you worry. As for you, Boken, why don't you take a stroll. There's no point in you stewing in a shop. We'll meet right back here at five.'

Boken strolled through the bazaar and bought his mother some raisins and dried apricots. He bought himself two ice creams and sat down on a bench by the bazaar gates. He set one ice cream by his side and began eating the other. He had to eat hurriedly and in large bites, to ensure the second portion wouldn't completely melt before he got to it. This haste made his teeth ache and froze his throat, turning it quite numb. However, he savoured the second portion slowly, licking it and enjoying every last morsel.

Kokbai and Kulshara were a whole hour late. Boken had already begun to fret, thinking that Kokbai must have decided to have a laugh at his expense. However, when a taxi rolled up and the two of them emerged, he quite forgot about his fretting. He didn't recognise Kulshara at first. Standing before him was a wonder to behold: a beautiful young city woman in a splendid dress and a sophisticated hairdo. She was looking directly at Boken and smiled at him as if they had known each other for years.

'Do you like my dress, Bokentai?' the vision of wonder asked him in Kulshara's voice, then blushed in embarrassment.

'Oh, it is marvellous!' was all that the dumbstruck Boken could utter.

'First, though, I had to go to the baths,' Kulshara informed him, 'to put the dress on a clean body. That's why we were so long.'

That day they had evidently decided to address their appearance seriously, for, having settled the taxi fare, Kokbai went off to the hairdresser's himself. Kulshara sat down next to Boken. Still in awe of the beauty before him, Boken ran off and bought Kulshara an ice cream. Naturally, he didn't forget about himself either.

'Tell me, Bokentai, what kind of *dzhigit* is Kokbai?' Kulshara asked, carefully licking her ice cream and holding it at a distance to ensure it wouldn't drip onto her dress.

'What do you mean by *kind*?' Boken replied, confused.

'Well, bad or good?'

I don't think he's very serious. In fact, he's not all there, if you ask me,' Boken blurted out.

'Then you haven't seen what *not all there* actually means,' Kulshara said with a heavy sigh. 'You should see my husband Mashen. He seems like a regular bloke but once he's had a drink...'

'Yes, I saw him just the other day. He was drinking by the shop. Straight from the bottle, too. Then he climbed onto his horse and began racing about the streets. He looked like he might fall off at any moment. It was terrible to see your husband like that.'

'Yes, Mashen really isn't all there,' Kulshara repeated sadly.

Boken then thought he had been wrong to have been angry with Kulshara. There was something he didn't understand: she couldn't have had anything going on with Kokbai if she asked such questions about him.

It was at that moment that Kokbai himself called over to them, waving, as if to say, *come on then, let's get going*. He too had undergone a dramatic change. That morning Kokbai's hair had been so dirty and tousled , a passer-by would never have guessed what it's true colour was. Now though his ginger mop had been neatly combed with a parting and it shone; clean, white skin was visible where the hair had been parted.

While they travelled through the town, Boken sat in the back of the truck, to make sure the traffic police wouldn't stop them. Later, he climbed back into the cab.

The heat had subsided by the evening and a pleasant, refreshing breeze blew through the cab's open windows. The shadow of the truck that followed by their side stretched out into the steppe and onto the hills, reaching right up to their peaks.

Having covered three kilometres or so, Kokbai turned the truck off the highway onto a dusty-grey steppe road that had once connected the town with the *aul* in a straight line. However, after comfortable bypasses had been built, this road had become deserted. Only very occasionally would the odd traveller be encountered on a cart pulled by a melancholy looking bull.

'It's eighty kilometres to our *aul* over the surfaced road, but only sixty over this road,' Kokbai explained to Kulshara. 'Not only that, but it passes right by your house as well. I'll drop you off right to your door!'

'I wouldn't mind if you didn't. I could travel to the end of the world with you,' Kulshara said and laughed loudly at her own joke.

Once again, the truck jumped from bump to bump, sank into potholes and rocked from side to side. The cab shook violently and Kulshara and Boken bumped shoulders with each other and bashed the tops of their heads on the cab roof. Kokbai, however, felt very much in his element amidst all this shaking; he sat back in his seat and steered with a single hand. His eyes shone craftily, as if he had devised yet another mischievous plan.

An old, half-filled-in irrigation ditch appeared in front of them. Kokbai involuntarily dropped his speed and the thick trail of dust following the truck caught up with them and filled the cab. All three of them began to cough and sneeze but they all found it very funny.

Boken poked his head out of the cab and began surveying the steppe. It had appeared quite different from the moving truck. It seemed to be moving just like they were, never standing still. This was particularly evident when he looked at the hills. Those in the distance, round as skull caps, ran up ahead, as if they wanted to overtake the truck and block its path. Those that stood closer to them were like the humps of camels and they appeared to move backwards. Their motley movements made his head whirl; the steppe seemed to spin on its axis like a carousel.

Behind the truck, the red ray of the setting sun pursued them. The truck and the ray appeared to be

215

racing one another with the truck eventually coming out on top. Before long, it could only be seen after the truck had made it to the top of a big hill, caressing the peaks of the neighbouring hills. The truck tumbled forwards on a downward trajectory, much like a falling star and the last ray of sunshine then went out.

Boken drew his head back into the cab and sat up straight, looking out ahead. Kokbai and Kulshara had been talking about something but instantly fell silent. Boken, however, attached no significance to this.

'That's half the journey done,' Kokbai said cheerfully.

'Only half?' Kulshara replied with disappointment. 'I want some water. I need a drink. I'm gasping,' she said in a fading voice.

'Hang on just a little longer. There's a spring just beyond that hill. We'll stop there and you can have a drink,' Kokbai told her.

Dense twilight had set in over the steppe, but the road could still be seen, rising sharply upwards ahead.

'Oh yes, Kokbai, I wanted to ask yesterday, only I forgot. People say that you're planning to get married. Is that right?' Kulshara asked animatedly, quite forgetting about her thirst.

'Who told you that?' Kokbai asked in surprise.

'I just heard, although you've kept that a secret.'

'I have nothing to hide. Those people! They hear something in passing and then gabble God knows what. It's all Chinese whispers. Here's what actually happened. I was sitting having tea with my mother the other day and she said to me, "How about we hitch you up with old man Zhumagul's daughter?" Well, and I said, "Whatever." The people, meantime, have me married off already!'

Kokbai made it over the steep hill and brought the truck to a halt.

'Let's go. I'll show you where the spring is,' he said to Kulshara.

They got out of the truck and went off from the road into the darkness. Once they had disappeared from view, Boken also felt thirsty and headed off in the direction they had gone.

He almost stumbled right into them. They were standing, pressed up close to one another and, at first, Boken didn't realise that two people were locked in an embrace in front of him. He only realised when the couple noticed him and separated to either side.

'What do you want?' Kokbai cried, embarrassed.

'I want some water too,' Boken muttered, no less embarrassed than they were.

'What are you following us for? Did someone ask you to?' said Kokbai resentfully.

'I also want a drink,' Boken repeated obtusely.

'You idiot! There's no water here,' Kokbai said and laughed wickedly. 'Kulshara, would you just look at him! He really believed there was a spring here!' Then he shouted at Boken: 'Go back to the truck right now, or I'll wring your neck!'

'Alright. Let him look if he's not ashamed,' Kulshara interjected. 'Come on, Bokentai, what are you standing there for? Come a little closer!'

'You are bad people, both of you. And you are a deceitful cheat, too, putting on that pretty dress,' Boken blurted out, almost in tears.

'Hey, say that again. What did you say?'

Kokbai took a step towards him and slapped him hard across the cheek. Boken turned and ran to the truck. The key was hanging in the ignition. Some time ago, one of the farm drivers who took the milk from the farm had taught him how to start a truck. Boken turned the key and the display instantly came to life, the arrows shaking into position.

He turned on the lights and pressed the starter. The truck rumbled obediently and moved away. 'They're not people, no way' Boken whispered.

'Hey, Boken! You son of a bitch! Stop right now! I'll kill you!' the incensed Kokbai screamed from behind him.

Boken, however, pressed harder on the gas. The truck, roaring and shaking, wobbled from side to side, striking the steep sides on the road and threatening to flip over. Kokbai's heart-rending shrieks flew after him:

'Bo-ken! Bo-ken! Stop! You'll crash!'

The old ditch appeared in the beams of light only too late. Boken didn't even have time to think and, even if he had, he wouldn't have known what to do. The truck rushed downwards and then rocked up. Boken was thrown painfully onto the roof of the cab and bit his tongue. The truck somehow straightened up but the road for some reason seemed to become ever narrower. Wormwood and wild rye along the roadside grew in the headlights to the size of trees, attacking the truck from both sides.

'Bo-oke-en!'

It appeared as if Kokbai's voice had caught up with the truck. The truck slowly and heavily made it up the hill. Boken furiously applied the accelerator. The engine whined and roared as if it wanted to render the earth in two. At last, on its last legs and shaking fitfully, the truck made it to the top of the hill. Then, it seemed as if someone who had been holding on from behind, released their hands from the truck and it went down the hill as if flying down into an abyss...

WHAT'S BOTHERING OLD BEKEN?

A strange noise had woken Old Man Beken before dawn. At first, he had heard in his sleep what he thought to be someone climbing into the zinc washtub his wife had left on the other side of the wall, stamping around in it, relishing in making as much of a din as possible, then flying up to the roof and rattling about above his head. Light filled the room, then disappeared, the yard rumbled deafeningly and the earth shook beneath Beken's feet.

Startled, the man sat on his bed. Then he got up and went to the door wearing only his underwear. He had barely opened the door an inch, when a lifeless blue light flashed in his face as if someone were sitting with a torch behind his earthen yard wall, waiting for him to open the door. Beken was stupefied and then the rumbling returned with full force. It was only then, once he had shaken off the last of his drowsiness, that he realised it was thunder.

Blessed be, blessed be, the old man muttered and returned to his room.

He sat on his bed in thought and slowly began to wake his old wife:

'Balsary, hey, Balsary!'

However, the old woman was wrapped up tight with her head under the blanket and didn't stir. Beken shook his head.

He thought he knew what was going on outside but the next thunderclap still caught him unawares. This time, there was barely a pause between the flash of lightning and the clap of thunder. The barrage appeared to sound right by his ear as if a decent-sized bag of salt had just been thrown on the fire. The old man's instinct of self-preservation forced him to climb under the blanket. While he was wrapping up his thin legs, his wife woke up, poked her nose out and, fearing that she may fall back to sleep again, Beken said to her quickly,

'Get up, Balsary! Don't tell me you can't hear. It's thundering out there!'

Balsary reluctantly rose from the bed, threw her white *kimeshek*[11] around her head and dabbed her puffy eyes with a corner of the fabric. Only after this did she look out of the window with a yawn.

Beken became annoyed by the unhurried motions of the old woman and blurted out,

'What's with all this pottering about? I'm telling you: it's thundering out there!'

'Alright, I'm up, I'm up! What more do you want? You'd think we'd never seen a thunderstorm!' said Balsary, irritated.

She retrieved a crumpled doublet from under her pillow, put it on and, with a mutter, went out into the yard.

'You're getting old and you're flapping about like a lost little boy,' his wife said once she had returned.

Has she got out of the wrong side of bed? The old witch went to see herself if I was right and there she is still nagging away, Beken grumbled to himself, but averted his eyes,

---

11 *A white, calico, traditional, national headdress, sometimes with an embroidered decoration, which covers both the head and the shoulders.*

to be on the safe side, trying not to catch his wife's fearsome gaze.

He started fussing around the room in an attempt to look busy, but his wife managed to get everything done perfectly well without him. She clattered the crockery in the kitchen as if competing with the noise of the storm and took an aluminium ladle out into the yard. Beken poked his head around the door and saw her processing around the house, intoning to herself,

'More milk, less coal... more milk, less coal,' waving the ladle about as she spoke.

In the meantime, dawn had broken. Black clouds continued to gather above the earth like a pack of ravenous hounds. The lightning continued to flash, the thunder clapped and only then did the torrential rain begin to pour.

'It was dry all night and now it's chucking it down,' Balsary said as she entered the room.

Having covered the earth and thoroughly drenched it, the torrential rain died down. The thunder rolled over the horizon; the last of the clouds galloped away to the east, whipping themselves with their fiery lashes.

That was how the first thunder of that spring had roared over Beken's house and the rumble from which the old man had awoken had been its first call.

'Balsary, that's a good omen,' Beken noted, sitting down to his bowl of tea. 'Just remember, it was today that I decided to take to my horse and today the first thunder has rumbled! That's a happy coincidence, old woman, and so, I'm going to go to Uizhygylgan to

223

recite a prayer over the grave of my ancestors. You've been complaining all winter that you can't wait for spring to come so you can have some wild steppe onion. But what could I do? You know as well as I do that you can't pick wild onion until the first thunder has passed. Well, now you'll have a whole bagful and gorge to your heart's content.'

The earth had dried out over the course of the morning. The heavy rain had washed away the dirt left by the meltwater, the sapless, withered green grass had acquired energy and vibrancy, the stems now thicker and airier, and the steppe had become clean and multicoloured, like a newly woven rug. In short, the storm had forged the way for the new spring.

Travelling out of the village, the old man turned his horse towards Uizhygylgan. The first thing he did when he found himself out in the open was to check the pace of his thick-maned chestnut steed: first, he rode it at a trot and then a gallop. He had been really impatient to try out this horse, which he had finally got his hands on after no small amount of trickery. Beken kept watch over the collective farm's crops and was convinced that only a special horse would do for such an important job, to ensure he would make it in good time to any part of any field where stray livestock may be running riot. After all, what would be the use of a horse that couldn't drag his rider where he wanted at any time of day or night?

The chestnut steed had looked the part. Previously, it had been ridden by a fat foreman and this had kept Beken up at night, for he believed that a horse this fine had been born for worthier things. The old man had accosted the collective farm chairman to convince him to hand over the steed. In the end, he had got his way, almost literally pulling the horse from under his big-shot master.

He had been helped in this venture by a meeting to which all the farm watchmen had been summoned. The farm chairman himself addressed the crowd, making a long speech and singing Beken's praises left, right and centre. He said that, despite his venerable age, the respected Beken would remain in the saddle, be it day or night, so highly did he value his work, and that everyone else should follow the example of this fine fellow.

Beken liked the flattery; he knew it was a weakness of his but was quite unable to do anything about it. On this occasion, when the chairman had voiced the first words of praise, he removed his cocked wadded hat, took a skull-cap from his pocket, straightened it and, as was customary, stretched it onto his shaved head. His wrinkled face became animated, his narrow eyes sparkled with satisfaction and a wide grin appeared on his face. Beken had nodded approvingly at each of the chairman's words as if to say, *Yes, that is indeed the case.*

When he had been given the stage and the audience had vigorously applauded, Beken suddenly lost his nerve and came over in a cold sweat.

'I promise to watch over the fields with care, boss,' he blurted out.

Everyone waited for him to say something more. Beken wiped his brow with his sleeve, surreptitiously ran his eyes over all those present and suddenly became overcome with old grievances.

'But that's not all I want to say,' he added with passion. 'It's a thankless job I do, you see. All you hear is abuse. One thing after the other! And so many accusations. Someone doesn't like this; another doesn't like that! Until they bring in the harvest, you get no sleep and no rest! You're in the saddle the whole summer long. Why, you never even get to take your belt off. All you ever do is argue with everyone. Those who own livestock – they hate you! Ever since I've been a watchman, since the end of the war, I've seen and heard all manner of things. If even the slightest of the curses had ever come to fruition, my poor old bones would have long since dried up and turned to dust. To be honest, there's not an ounce of gratitude for this work. That's what I want to say and that's that!'

'We have heard how hard it is for our greatly respected Beken. But how does he manage to do such a good job in such conditions? That's what we'd like to learn from our *aqsaqal*,' the wily chairman remarked and the people nodded in agreement.

'This is how I do it...' Beken began and unwittingly divulged all his experience.

However, at the end of his speech, he did manage to get one over on the shrewd chairman.

'Well, boss, you've given me high praise and for that I am grateful! Now, though, give me the wherewithal to do my job. Do what you like, but take the foreman's chestnut horse and give it to me,' Beken declared.

And so, there was Beken, now in the saddle on that same chestnut steed, which now quailed beneath him. Despite that, it displayed some skittishness: it would recoil from sparrows flying beneath its hooves with shrill squeals and, even when all was calm, it would still chew on the bit. *Zhuanbai[12] himself used to ride on a chestnut horse like this. That was a famous horse and yet it would behave much the same as mine*, Beken thought proudly, although he had to admit that, not only had he never sat on the renowned Zhuanbai's horse, he had not even led it by the reins. Quite immersed in these pleasant thoughts, he reached Uizhygylgan before he knew it and brought his horse to a stop only when he had found himself at the top of a hill overlooking a valley.

A six-sided yurt had once stood here but a terrible hurricane had blown it to the ground. From that time, the place had become known as Uizhygylgan, which means the *Fallen Home*. According to family legends that had been passed down to Beken, his ancient, nomadic ancestors had been buried here many years before. His family had later moved on to a new place and the burial mounds had become barely visible to the untrained eye beneath the perennial grass.

When the wind would blow into the valley, the feather grass would stir and sway, shimmering in the sun, like the fleece on a fat sheep. These places had not

---

[12] *A character from the Kazakh film 'The Beardless Deceiver'*

been touched by farming. The grass had long since died away and new growth had taken its place, just as in the time of Beken's ancestors.

Casting a customary glance over the valley, Beken started in the saddle and his eyes suddenly darkened. *What is the matter with me? Something is wrong here*, he thought in fear.

Before him, a fallow field stretched uniformly as far as the grey rocks in the distance and Beken scanned the land for his ancestors' graves, before which he had prayed every spring. However, they had been completely swallowed up by a wave of ploughed earth. Beken's face turned grey and the blood drained from his heart.

'Whoever ordered this steppe to be ploughed shall rot in hell,' he whispered, shaking his thinning beard in anger.

The horse foundered in the deep furrows of black earth. Beken made it to the place he reckoned his ancestors' graves had once stood, got down from his horse and, holding it by a long rein, started to look for signs of a previous burial mound among the clumps of soil that dimly glimmered where they had been cut.

Where were the graves that he had knelt before since childhood? The sanctuary to which he had entrusted his troubles and which had supported him in his most difficult moments had disappeared. He looked around, hoping to find even the smallest sign to confirm that this was the resting place of the heroes he had celebrated and the people he had revered, whose kinship to him elevated Beken's estimation of himself in his own eyes.

In desperation, Beken fell to his knees where the earth was a slightly yellowish colour, and his lips began to recite a prayer. Tears clouded his eyes; he caught his breath and his lips failed to do his bidding. He was unable to finish.

He felt like the earth had been pulled from under his feet and he was hanging in space. His thoughts tried to seek something to hold onto; tales of the heroic deeds of his ancestors, passed down through generations rose to the surface of his memory.

There were times when he would shepherd lambs from dawn to dusk and then return home and slump on his blanket from fatigue. His legs would ache frightfully from the thorns and barbs that had perforated him over the day and he would scratch them furiously, but the aching pain would only become worse. He would be hungry and the aroma from the cooking pot where the meat would be bubbling would tempt his nostrils. Finally, he would fall drowsy from the warmth of the hearth, drop off and cough from the smell of the dung cake fuel. He would remain in this strange state, neither dreaming nor awake, until the old, white-bearded man lying on the seat of honour would speak in a voice which time had broken.

'Long, long ago, our ancestor the hero, may he rest in peace...' the old man began and Beken felt his drowsiness and fatigue disappear in an instant. His hunger was a mere trifle compared with the heroic deeds of his forefathers. At times he would see himself as if from a distance and with someone else's eyes. He would see a skinny little nipper, his mouth gaping wide in admiration. Back then he remembered every last legend, not like today, now he had reached old age. Indeed, he even thought his childhood had been a half-forgotten dream.

'Oh, my eyes,' Beken whispered, 'it would have been better to have gone blind than witness this disgrace.'

His knees had begun to hurt on the stiff clumps of earth and this irritated him. He got up, rubbed his numb legs and climbed up onto his horse. He had barely put his foot in the stirrup when the chestnut horse began spinning on the tilled earth. It was the first time he had failed to mount a horse at the first attempt. Beken took this as a bad sign and became utterly despondent. Stumbling over the loose clods, he eventually made it to a dry irrigation ditch at the edge of the tilled earth and stopped his horse. He adjusted the stirrups but, having lost his former confidence, decided to take a rest and sat down at the ravine's edge.

The tilled earth here had dried out and become warm, with currents of heat rising from deep below. Beken thrust the handle of his whip into the ground and rested his forehead on it, his tear-filled eyes closed. His head was devoid of thought; he didn't want to think in any case.

His horse paced evenly nearby, tugging at the green grass on the banks of the ditch and chewing loudly. Suddenly his steed jolted warily. The old man had not managed even to raise his head when he heard a woman's voice:

'Ata[13], what's the matter? Grandfather, grandfather!'

He recognised Sabira. He had heard that she had graduated from an important institute two years before and she had come to the collective farm as its chief agriculturalist.

Sabira was sitting on a shaggy-looking colt with stumpy legs and was wearing a padded jacket, wide trousers and canvas boots. Spring had only just arrived and yet Sabira's face had already managed to take on a dark tan.

Beken had always liked her, perhaps because of her energy or maybe because she had always struck him as a serious person. (Was it a joke that she was dressed as a man?!) However, her appearance had now generated a sense of resentment.

'Go on, off you go, my dear! You've done what you've done so now be off with you!' he said, unable to control himself. He got up.

'What on earth are you talking about?' Sabira said, startled.

Beken, though, believed he had said quite enough.

His anger had given him more strength; he jumped up into the saddle, just like in his youth, and he was even surprised at this.

---

[13] *Literally means 'kind grandfather', but is used as a term of endearment for elderly men.*

The chestnut horse chewed on the bit, scattering flakes of foam. Beken lashed it with his whip, turned on the spot and headed off. His steed had been waiting for this and ambled away. Beken slouched heavily, almost lying on the horse's neck.

He met a tractor pulling a sowing machine up on the hill. The red-haired tractor driver Samat poked his bare head out of his cab and called out in a hoarse, deep voice,

'Hey, old man, any chance you could come a little closer? Come over here, I tell you!'

Samat would show off all year round, his red hair aflame, as if he were issuing someone a defiant challenge. His thick red hair was always sticking out in all directions, perhaps because of his constant exposure to the elements. He would use the *tu* form with everyone, whatever their age. Things would never go beyond words, but everyone in the village secretly feared the man. Beken too found himself involuntarily quailing faced with this gruff *dzhigit*.

'Come on, pops, get your tobacco out! Don't be stingy now. I've been stuck in this tractor for two days now. You could easily forget what cigarettes taste like. At least give me a bit of snuff to sniff. Everything smells of smokes,' Samat said, unceremoniously diving his fingers into Beken's tobacco pouch.

He pulled out half the contents in his grubby hand and winked with a sleep-deprived eye.

'I know no peace,' Samat went on. 'I won't rest until they bestow the title of Hero of Labour upon me. Otherwise, I'll know no satisfaction from my work,' he declared, either seriously or simply to mock old Beken. 'I've decided that from now on, I'm going to cultivate a record harvest. Mark my words, old man, if you cause any damage, you'd better watch out. I'll rip your beard out hair by hair! Mark my words! Ha-ha-ha! Nah, I'm joking with you, father, don't take offence. If I didn't, I'd go mad stuck here at the wheel. So, what's with you? You look dreadful. You're not sick, are you? Don't you go falling ill, now, alright? You've only just got yourself a prancer, and a fine one he is too! Get yourself home and get your old woman to make you some tea. Sweat it out and everything will return to normal, you'll see. Go on then, off you go!'

Without waiting for an answer, Samat shoved a pinch of tobacco in his mouth and placed his grubby hands, black from engine oil, on the wheel.

That day, seeds had been sown on the earth where Beken's famous ancestors had been laid and no one but Beken had even remembered about their graves. They had long since forgotten them and some perhaps never even knew about them at all. The ploughshare had passed over the ridges, overgrown with feathergrass and saltwort, and had levelled them completely. The tractor driver hadn't even given it a thought; so what if there were humps in the ground? If one were to stop and think about how many little hillocks there were in the earth, how could the human race even carry on living? The time had come for Beken's shrines to go and they had been ploughed up into the soil.

Beken didn't leave his house for two whole days. He wallowed in bed, barely ever rising, as he endured his pain.

Barely a slip of a girl and yet she has caused me so much upset by trampling the graves of my ancestors, he said to himself about Sabira. At first, his blood had boiled and he almost went to the district to file a complaint, but he calmed down a little and realised there was nothing to be done. What would be the point in complaining? He decided to be a man and take the offence in his stride. Added to this, his old wife had had a prophetic dream and this gave him a certain sense of relief.

'I saw a man come in with a long white beard,' she said. 'He was tall and dressed all in white. He came in and asked me to make him a bed in the corner on the right. *Aga*[14], I realised it was our forefathers, who sensed our troubles and they had decided to visit us. May they rest in peace!' Balsary concluded, adding, 'Oh, I heard they are giving out wheat bread in advance. Why don't you pop over there and sign out a hundredweight of flour until the new harvest has been reaped?'

'Oh, would you look at that rain!'

'It's just a cloud. But it's a black one, for sure. What do you think it holds?'

'Water, that's what. And lots of it! It's holding the harvest, so let it pour down on the seedlings, I say.'

---

[14] *Means 'older brother' or 'uncle'. Kazakhs address all older men as aga. However, if a man is in his 70s, then he becomes ata.*

The people had scattered from the field, seeking cover in the nearest hut. A violent whirlwind had rushed after them, churning up clouds of dust from the earth. Lightning flashed and thunder clapped, sending warning of an imminent storm. It was already advancing from the nearby highland. True enough, no sooner had Beken reached the hut and taken the cushion from the saddle than the deluge came hurtling to the ground, obscuring the rest of the world from sight. Torrents of dirty black water gushed loudly all around the hut and the earth seemed to shudder with every clap of thunder.

Once inside, Beken picked himself a spot by the entrance and sat down. There were no windows in the building and the light only came in through the door, so, entering the gloom from outside, the old man was unable to see a thing at first. He could discern there were other people inside from their murmuring and he was also struck by the heavy smell of wild onion, which Beken found almost stifling.

As his eyes grew accustomed to the dark, the faces of fellow villagers began to emerge. He caught sight of Sabira. Of course, who else would give off such a smell of wild onion? Everything bad was sure to be coming from her, he mused, with a certain vindictive satisfaction.

Sabira was sitting deep inside the hut and was indeed chewing on a stalk of wild onion. An entire bunch of the wretched stuff lay in her lap too.

Beken recalled how the year before he had offered her half a bag of wild onion, secretly depriving his old

235

woman of her share. He had wanted to do something nice for Sabira. The girl had refused, thanking him and muttering something he couldn't make out. However, it was clear from the way she had screwed up her nose that the smell of the onions was not to her liking. Yet here she was now, munching away to her heart's content.

Aha, so you no longer hate it now, I see. Your delicate taste buds are no longer what they used to be, Beken thought maliciously.

The old man's sneering look rattled Sabira and she stopped chewing. An elderly neighbour who was sitting next to Beken touched him on the shoulder and said,

'Why are you embarrassing the poor girl? Perhaps she's pregnant.'

Pregnant?! That was really too much! He turned to face the door, resenting Sabira and the woman who had stood up for her.

Would you believe it?! Still not married and already with one on the way! he muttered to himself indignantly.

The torrential rain stopped just as suddenly as it had started. The sound of the gushing water had barely subsided when blinding sunshine burst through the door. Beken stepped outside and was drenched by the last drops of water, falling from the roof. Billions of raindrops had been scattered over the crops, glistening and sparkling as they caught the sun. The wind had plucked them up and thrown them back to the ground. The field had swelled and risen, like dough left to prove. Where streams of foamy water had once rushed, tiny wallows now gleamed with oil.

A man was running across the field, stumbling through the swollen earth and making a great effort to keep his leaden boots on his feet. He slipped and fell, but got up again and continued running. His head was lit up like a red flame and Beken recognised that it was Samat, the tractor driver. He was shouting something, but the wind fragmented his words, blowing them back to the place where he had been running from.

About twenty paces from the hut, he stopped and cried out in desperation,

'It's bad! It's so bad!'

Hearing this, everyone, Beken included had rushed out to meet him. Samat fell to his knees and, shaking his head, he said,

'Oh, Serik, oh, Serik! Why you? D'you hear, people, Serik's been struck by lightning!'

'Oh, no!' the people cried and everyone who had been sheltering in the hut ran out across the field.

Beken leapt onto his chestnut horse and was the first to reach the site of the accident. Beken had ridden this land many years, but he had never seen anything like this. A monstrous force had swept the horse and rider across the field. The horse had fallen onto its back, its stiff legs frozen and pointing skywards. Serik lay several feet away, his incredibly tall frame was stretched over the ground. The red spots that betrayed the sign of death had already covered his face.

Beken dismounted and, reciting a short prayer, leaned forward to close the dead man's eyes, to ensure poor Serik could finally rest in peace. However, Serik's right eyelid shuddered, evidently from a muscle spasm, and he seemed to look at Beken with an unseeing eye. The old man staggered back, wiped his palms over his face and whispered a prayer.

By that time, the others had run up, weeping and wailing, and they surrounded Serik's body. Something made Beken turn around. He saw Sabira, who had lagged behind the others, come running. She looked dreadful.

The crowd made way for her. Sabira collapsed to her knees before Serik's body and spoke in a heart-rending voice,

'Oh, Se-rik, why have you left me?!'

Quite unashamed in the presence of all the people, she moaned like a woman who has lost her husband.

The dead man's body was brought to the farm estate and he was buried the following day. When her lover's coffin was brought to the graveyard, Sabira violated the ancient custom and walked after it with the men. It was painful to look at her; she was not herself at all and she fainted numerous times, held up by those escorting her, but she nevertheless remained alongside her Serik until the end.

Grief had transformed Sabira. She had become quite dark and her cheeks, sunken. People told Beken that Serik and Sabira had been lovers for a long time and their marriage had already been decided upon. They had only been waiting for the sowing to end.

Learning this, Beken took pity on Sabira and forgave her her offence, although, in his heart of hearts, he suspected that it had been no accident that Sabira had lost her betrothed. His proud ancestors had not stood for the young agronomist's blasphemous mistake and had struck back at her. Beken shuddered. Great heavens, he had been extremely resentful of Sabira's behaviour himself, but he found this vengeance terribly cruel.

Could the ghosts of my ancestors really be so merciless? he asked himself in sorrowful bewilderment. *The young are ever foolish and, perhaps, they could have been handed a more lenient punishment. As a warning of sorts, for then they could perhaps have come to their senses.*

He thought about this and then was startled by his own flippancy.

What am I thinking? Am I mad? Who is it I am judging here – my glorious, wise ancestors? he said to himself.

One Friday he said to his old wife,

'Balsary, go and bake seven flatbreads! I'll go and read the Koran.'

Later, tucking into the hot bread, coated in fat, and drinking it down with tea, he racked his brains again and concluded that he had to pull himself together.

There's no going against the will of the Almighty and that's all there is to it. The sacred ghosts of my ancestors know what they're doing and they do not forgive trespasses. I have now come to see this with my own eyes. It would be easy to say that the lad was done for in one fell swoop. He was so young and had yet to see life. They say he was a decent dzhigit, *too. Yes, I have got myself thinking sinful thoughts again. I had better stop there.*

239

Having completed his arduous duty, he sighed deeply and, from that moment on, he tried not to recall the graves where his ancient and excessively vengeful ancestors had laid.

It rained all summer. Hot moisture rose from the earth like steam. The spears of wheat shone with an oily shimmer and flowed like hairs on a dense mane. The green spring wheat began to ear in early June; the ears grew firm and long. The stalks thinned and stretched upwards like a skinny adolescent. An immense storm and wind raged across the field, almost making one's head spin.

At dawn, Beken was already on his horse and he circled the wheat fields until dusk. He was now just existing rather than living, only emptying warm, living grains into the palm of his hand and looking at them tenderly as he carefully sorted through them, whispering, *you are still so soft. It's probably from all that heavy rain. Can't be from anything else.*

However, the grains began to grow and harden, and a rich aroma floated over the field as if from a kneading trough, Beken had thought.

The seasons of the grain on the collective farm fields passed under his vigilant eye, the only blank spot for him being the Uizhygylgan sector. He had no idea what passed there, for he avoided it, justifying himself by saying, *that land is far off and the livestock won't reach those parts.*

July had commenced with searing heat. The hot sky drew nearer to the earth and, from the moment it rose above the horizon, the sun would bake the fields.

When the sun had reached its zenith, its red-hot rays would beat down with such ferocity that it seemed that the dry stalks might begin to smoke at any moment, sending flames creeping across the steppe. The harvest became heavier and the wheat drooped, unable to support the engorged ears. *What a Godsend that heat is,* Beken thought fondly. This was a time when he had lots to worry about and he would race about in excitement on his chestnut horse, though plagued by the midges. At times drowsiness would slowly but surely topple him from his mount.

One day, he took to his horse in the early morning and set off on his customary rounds. The night's chill still lingered in the air. It was damp as if water had been sprinkled over the steppe; the aqueous dust fell in clusters onto the vegetation and hung in the sky. The long, fenced enclosure shimmered as if it had been wiped clean with a damp cloth. Usually, it was used to hold cattle caught damaging the crops out in the fields, but on that day it stood empty. Not a single witless calf had ventured out there, which had not happened once that year. Either the cattle had grown more intelligent and kept away from the crops, or Beken hadn't spotted any. In any case, that summer was a blessed one for the watchman.

However, riding past the enclosure that day, he heard a horse snort and turned his chestnut steed. A heavy black lock hung as it should have on the door. The old man rode along the length of the wall and looked in through a tiny window set into its side. His gaze was met from out of the dark by the enormous, emerald eyes of several horses. He counted four. On closer inspection, he realised he didn't know these horses; at least they were not from this farm.

Wondering who they might belong to, Beken headed to the farm estate. The first person he saw as he approached the main office was Sabira. She was hovering by her little horse, removing a sheaf of wheat that had fastened itself to her saddle. The sheaf was so heavy that it hung beneath the stomach of the horse, almost scraping the ground. The ears of wheat were at least as long as a man's hand.

'Hey there!' Beken called out in surprise. 'Is that sheaf you've got there from an exhibition or something?'

'Of course not! I've brought it back from Uizhygylgan,' Sabira replied wearily.

'From Uizhygylgan? Well now, that is a fine sheaf, for sure!' exclaimed Beken in amazement.

He had nothing else to say. Then he became a bit embarrassed for having expressed his delight and incredulity quite so rashly. After all, he was convinced his relationship with Sabira was a complex one and required a certain degree of restraint.

Sabira, however, behaved as if nothing had happened. It was if it had not been she who had razed his ancestors' graves from the face of the earth, that those spirits had not meted out their terrible vengeance on her, but on someone else and that it had not been Beken who had judged her back in the hut for her clearly frivolous behaviour. He had no doubts that she had read his thoughts.

All the same, Sabira behaved as if there had been nothing untoward. She praised the harvest at Uizhygylgan and then retrieved some keys from her trouser pocket, handing them to Beken.

'Grandfather, you see, there are some horses in your enclosure. I think they are from the neighbouring farm. I saw them trampling the wheat and I had to herd them into the enclosure. Best you look for their owners.'

Beken travelled from the farm office direct to Uizhygylgan. He was itching to learn if the wonders Sabira had spoken of there were indeed true. At the bottom of his heart, he hoped that Sabira had somehow been mistaken. He didn't want to give this woman any quarter.

The harvest was actually more impressive than he had imagined. The woman clearly lacked the eloquence to describe it properly.

Forgetting himself completely, Beken revelled in the wonder that he now saw. He led the chestnut horse along the edge of the field and the ears of wheat stretched out to him, brushing his dusty boots. The stalks were as strong and pliable as his whip; they would only sway gently when the yellow-breasted tits came to settle on them. Beken stopped his horse and searched for the place where the remains of his ancestors should have been. It seemed, however, that this sea of wheat had buried this secret forever in its depths. Still on his horse, he recited a heartfelt prayer.

With his prayer complete, he went straight back to work. Assuming a preoccupied appearance, he got to thinking about the sector that those unknown horses had trampled.

I'd like to know the slacker who left his horses untended, Beken thought angrily.

He recalled that he had not once visited Uizhygylgan that entire summer and he justly reproached himself.

Unhurriedly, he rode along the path and internally passed judgement on the horses' negligent owners. Riding towards him was another wizened old man in a crumpled hat, much like himself.

'Hey there!' the man called out. 'Some of our horses have escaped. You haven't seen them by any chance, have you?' he said, mentioning the neighbouring collective farm.

And so it happened that the very man he had been upbraiding in his head had fallen right into his hands and Beken instantly unleashed all his pent-up anger at him.

'Ah, so I've found you! What devil's induced you to let your horses go wandering off like that? And now, you have the damned nerve to come looking for them right under the noses of honest, hard-working folk?' he said, letting the dumbfounded old man feel the full force of his tirade.

Though the man tried to speak up in his own defence, he couldn't get a word in edgeways. Beken dragged him around after him so that the dullard who had let his horses go wandering off could see the trampled crops with his own eyes, and he didn't let go of him until they had circled the entire plot.

244

After Beken had finally vented his spleen, the unfortunate old man from the neighbouring farm finally managed to speak:

'All right, I think you've made your point. That'll do. I hold nothing against you, I've got what I deserved. But answer me this one thing. I remember, a long time back now, there was an ancient burial ground here. Perhaps, you can tell me where it's gone? It was here and now it's gone! Incredible!'

'It was sown with wheat,' Beken muttered, disheartened.

'God forgive us!' exclaimed the old man and clutched his heart, seemingly protecting it. 'Yes, a real sinner, you are. God protect us, you really are a sinner! Just think: himself with one foot in the grave and there he goes and plants wheat in a grave and then dares to stand watch over this desecrated land.'

The old man, it turned out, was a fast talker and now tore a strip off Beken as well he might, while the latter bowed his head in silence, their roles now reversed.

'I didn't plant the wheat for myself, but for the people, for everyone,' Beken whispered in explanation. 'Decent land shouldn't be left unused, now should it?'

The feisty old man calmed down, sensing Beken's humility. They rode side by side along the path to the enclosure and Beken related everything that had taken place just recently.

'Why do you think Serik got killed?' he asked in conclusion.

The old man gave the question serious thought and then sighed as he said,

'The will of the Almighty!'

'Yes, I also think that that must have played a part,' Beken said and then asked, 'And what about the rich harvest at Uizhygylgan? What have you to say about that? Is that not a good sign? Don't you think that our ancestors are happy now?'

'Yes, I do think that is a good thing. Otherwise, nothing but weeds would have sprung up at Uizhygylgan,' the old man agreed.

The first thing Beken did when he returned home that evening was to sing the praises of the harvest at Uizhygylgan.

'I'd say,' said his wife, listening intently to him. 'The land at Uizhygylgan is blessed.'

The sheaf of wheat that Sabira had brought from Uizhygylgan adorned the chairman's office and this wonder was now the first thing the officials from the district centre noticed the moment they walked through the door. The officials shook their heads and clicked their tongues in admiration; they could not help themselves and measured the length of the ears and counted the grains. When they left, each of them took a couple of ears with them. Just a couple of ears each, but a week later all that was left in the corner was a heap of dry straw. The chairman then called for Beken and asked him to deliver a new sheaf.

And so Beken paid another visit to Uizhygylgan. The wheat had turned yellow by this time and when

Beken shelled a firm grain from the ear, it resonated under his fingers with some hidden force, ready to burst its casing at any moment. He cleaned the grain from its husk, placed it in his mouth and bit down. It stuck instantly to his teeth.

'God be praised,' thought Beken, pleased with his test, 'just a little longer and it will be perfectly ripe.'

Having gathered a decent sheaf of wheat, the old man tied it to the back of his saddle and surveyed the field once more with his experienced gaze, as if making sure one last time that he was leaving it in perfect order. It was then that he caught sight of a young man in glasses, who was climbing the slope of Uizhygylgan, leaning on a stick. The lad greeted Beken and introduced himself as the new agronomist from the neighbouring Birlik collective farm. He had come to see Uizhygylgan's much-lauded harvest for himself. Beken noted with pride how far word had spread.

He couldn't resist the satisfaction of observing the visiting agronomist's admiring the harvest. The young lad counted the grains in an ear, measured its length and rubbed a clod of earth between his fingers. His face displayed real admiration.

'That's what the rain can do! And the rain in these parts has fallen most generously,' he said, wiping his fingers on his trousers.

This lad knows what he's talking about, Beken thought. Not wanting to lose face and demonstrate his own knowledge, he said,

'This is the land of my ancestors. They were famed for their bravery. Their graves were over there,' and he pointed vaguely with his whip. 'This harvest has grown on sacred land.'

'Ah,' replied the young lad politely.

He removed his glasses, squinted his short-sighted eyes and looked closely at Beken. *You've probably got plenty of tales to tell. So, how about it? Go on and tell me one!* he appeared to demand.

Beken was sorry he didn't have the time to chat for an hour or so with such an inquisitive person but he had to get the sheaf over to the office. So, the old man turned his horse towards the lowland, climbed up into the saddle and only then did he say,

'Yes, son. I do have something, and perhaps several interesting tales to tell.'

'Right, then we'll bring in the harvest and I'll definitely come over and hear what you have to say. I'll write down your stories, too. You know, I collect old stories and legends,' the lad replied.

Beken was pleased to hear that the young man intended to write down his stories, but, as becoming of a seasoned, old man, he didn't let on.

'All the best to you, son,' Beken said in farewell and touched his chestnut horse with his heel.

I really could tell him many wonderful things. I didn't have the need before but now I really could. I just never found the right pair of ears, the old man mused, now in a good mood.

The horse flies droned monotonously and the irritated horse danced about, stumbling from side to side. Once he lurched to such an extent that Beken was almost thrown from the saddle. A little ground squirrel

248

had startled the chestnut steed. It was digging a burrow right in the middle of the path and a vulture was circling high up above, ready to pounce on the little creature.

Everything in life is all in a muddle and everything is tied together, Beken concluded with a sigh.

First, he dropped by at his house, for he wanted to surprise his wife with the harvest from Uizhygylgan. He found her busy with the housework. With her hem hitched up, the old woman was treading down the dung into patties for fuel.

'Oh, Beke[15], at first I thought that was saltbush or something. It's so long. Now I see the ears. I don't know if I can believe my eyes,' Balsary chattered as she walked over to her husband.

'You are looking at wheat from Uizhygylgan,' Beken said importantly.

Balsary was about to touch the sheaf, drooping low because of the weight, but Beken cut her off abruptly,

'You'd better wash your hands first!'

Balsary had never been lost for something to say and she would often grumble at her old man for no reason but, on this occasion, she kept her peace.

'Perhaps you'd like some tea? The chairman can wait, no doubt,' she suggested in a most cordial tone.

Then she looked out into the distance, her hand shielding her gaze from the sun. Catching sight of something, she asked,

---

[15] *A diminutive form of 'Beken'*

'What's that smoke out there? Do you know what it is, Beke?'

Beken turned and saw a grey column of smoke rising and twirling above Uizhygylgan.

'Fire! Fire! Hey, rouse everyone!' he screamed with a croak. His face had completely transformed and he set out for Uizhygylgan on his chestnut horse, lashing it with his whip and digging in his boots. 'Hey! Get up!'

The wind stood like a wall before him, bringing tears to his eyes. Beken shielded his eyes and strained his gaze forwards: clouds of black smoke were now rising over Uizhygylgan. Beken could imagine a sea of raging fire and he reckoned that only wheat could burn like that. For a moment, he pictured a terrible picture: the flames were devouring the helpless, golden ears of wheat, crackling and rumbling like an insatiable belly.

He whipped his horse mercilessly until a single hill remained between him and the burning field. The chestnut steed flew flat-out to the top of the hill; all of Uizhygylgan now lay before Beken. The old man ran his palm over his eyes and burst out laughing, rocking in the saddle as he did so. The field was still gleaming before him, untouched and golden. A haystack stood burning to one side, cordoned off from the rest of the world by a broad furrow. The bespectacled *dzhigit* Beken had spoken with was running around the haystack, trying to put out the fire with his jacket.

Noticing Beken, the lad rushed over, dragging his jacket behind him like an old rag. His face was a picture of genuine terror.

'Water! Water!' he cried in panic.

'But what happened?' asked Beken, leaning down from his horse.

'You see, I had a smoke and then... I fell asleep. It was in the shade, you see. And then it, the fire I mean... You have to help me,' he spluttered.

'Calm down, son. There's nothing you can do. The hay is a goner anyway. Let's go and make sure the fire won't spread to the wheat field, okay?' Beken said, getting off his horse.

The fire had destroyed the hay and, having had its fill of destruction, died down. Where there had once stood a beautiful, fragrant hayrick, now lay a pile of light ash. Above it, the remains of the hay were smouldering away.

'What a pea brain! Why did I go and do that?' the young man moaned, still shaking with terror.

Beken had been about to give him a good dressing down and teach him a lesson, but he stopped himself and pitied the lad, who was scared witless as it was.

'I'm not going to get far with you, now am I?! You obviously won't even manage to write down my tales coherently,' he grumbled good-naturedly.

The time had come to gather the harvest. The wheat had taken on an almost scarlet hue and the ears now seemed to ring in the wind. Once again, vehicles would speed through the villages, churning up the grass that had managed to grow on the road and throwing up clouds of dust that had long since laid undisturbed. Now it would hang in the air for days at a time, filling the nostrils and crunching under one's teeth. Beken's face had blackened and dried out from the heat; his lips had cracked and his throat was parched.

That day, he had left for Uizhygylgan earlier than usual. He had been told that the first combine harvester had been brought over and Beken had decided to be there as the harvest started. In an attempt to distract himself from the heat, he immediately turned to the combine harvester. His old acquaintance Samat was sitting at the wheel. Samat was thrilled to see him; he jumped down from the cab and cried out, waving his long arms above his head.

'Hey, old man! Come quick! God Himself must have sent you to me! Well, what's the matter with you – get yourself down from your horse! Hey, Kairat,' he said, turning to his assistant, 'bring the bottle of *kefir*, would you? Come on, hurry up! Can't you see our guest is parched? Let him whet his whistle! Ha-ha!'

Beken brought the bottle to his lips and took a long glug of the cold, fermented milk, as satisfying as water from a mountain stream, and he even failed to notice he had let go of the harness. This was all his horse had been waiting for. He had been tormented by the flies and had been beating about with his tail and shaking his head. Gaining his freedom, he shot off, galloping over the hill.

'Don't you worry, old man, in the age of space travel, you won't have to walk. A truck will be along at any moment. For now, you can get out your tobacco,' boomed Samat in his deep voice and, taking half the contents of the tobacco pouch in his hand, he added, 'Don't you be angry, old man. You're probably thinking: *where did he get such an appetite?* Well, I deserve it. Who do you think this harvest at Uizhygylgan is down to, eh? Me, old man, that's who! Before spring, no one had even thought of ploughing over Uizhygylgan. So much land had been lying here, going to waste. And some land it is, too! Thankfully, though, there is one clear head at the collective farm and that's yours truly! One fine night, I went out and ploughed this Uizhygylgan. *You're bull-headed*, the management told me. Now, though, they say nothing of the sort and only tut and mutter, *how come we never thought of this ourselves? He's a fine bloke is that Samat!* And I tell them, *Well, bosses, you wanted a record, so here you are! Just don't go making me a Hero of Labour. I can't be doing with all that honour and ceremony. I've done all this in the name of love for my art!* That's what I told them, old man.'

He threw some tobacco under his tongue and concluded indistinctly,

'And thank you, grandad! You did a great job keeping watch.'

Beken looked at Samat as if he had never set eyes on his before. His head was in a muddle and his thoughts were swarming. *So, he's the one who's guilty for all that's happened?!* Beken finally got to thinking. *It was this cursed fellow who planned all this! But why, then, is he all happy and still in one piece? Surely, the ancestors should have punished him?*

'Hey, Samat, do you know there used to be a burial ground here?' he asked cautiously.

'What burial ground? What's that got to do with anything?'

'Oh, you wretch, Samat. Are you trying to tell me you didn't see any graves when you were ploughing up Uizhygylgan? Where were you looking?'

'What are you on about, old man?' Samat burst out. 'Who're you calling a wretch? Do you mean me? I, Samat am a Hero of Labour! That's who I am! And you can get right out of here. Go on, clear off!'

With that, Samat ran to his cab, shaking his fist as he went.

'Oh, what a wretch,' muttered Beken, now quite angry. Although, he had to confess that he still feared Samat a little.

Samat drove past, baring his teeth in a terrible grin, and this turned the old man incandescent.

And what about my ancestors?! Where are their vengeful ghosts?! Can it really be that they are unable to teach this snotnosed punk a lesson?! he thought in desperation.

Beken heard the rumble of an engine from over the hill and soon a three-tonne truck came into view. The truck drew up level with the combine harvester and slowly trundled along by its side to receive the grain. Sabira emerged with difficulty from the cab and walked over the strip of field that had just been cut. It was clear that she was finding it difficult to walk.

She returned to the truck and the driver called out to Beken,

'Granddad, come over here! We'll give you a lift.'

Sabira got out of the cab and awkwardly began making her way to the back.

'There's no need for that, my girl. I would have ridden up top,' Beken said in a scolding tone, though he was pleased with the respect he had been shown. 'I'm just not used to riding in such a little box, that's all.'

With the driver's help, Beken too climbed into the back of the truck.

'It really is more comfortable back here. I think I'll stay where I am,' Sabira announced.

It was indeed better in the back and the truck rocked them gently as it travelled over the stubble. The grain gave off a thick, mouth-watering aroma like freshly-drawn milk.

'Are you still mad at me, grandfather?' Sabira asked after a while.

Beken was embarrassed. The direct way in which Sabira had turned the conversation had caught him unawares.

'What on earth should I be angry about, my dear?' he mumbled helplessly.

'Someone told me about the graves. Only afterwards. And you probably believe me to be the guilty party in all this. I was the one who ordered the ploughing, you see.'

255

'My dear, I know you had nothing to do with it. I found that out today,' he said and looked at Sabira with guilty eyes as if begging forgiveness.

'And where were those graves?' Sabira asked.

'Let's leave it. Nobody knows that now. Once they were here and now, they're not,' Beken replied.

'Samat put the wind up you, didn't he? He's got to you as they say,' said Sabira with an ironic smile.

'How could he not have got to me? It's not by chance that they say, *If the mallet is strong, you'll even drive a felt peg home*,' Beken said placably and he even wanted to relate a family parable to Sabira. He was about to start, *back in the old days, one of our forefathers...* but Sabira had already fallen deep into thoughts of her own. Deep furrows had gathered on her forehead. Grabbing a handful of grain, she poured it pensively from one hand to the other.

'This wheat will be used for seed,' she said, for some reason with a sad smile on her face. 'Next year, it'll be buried in darkness, so that the sun might see a new, different life. So, there you have it, grandfather.'

Big, fluffy clouds hung in the grey sun-bleached sky. The speed of the truck gave the impression that they were motionless. Or, perhaps, the truck was standing still and it was the clouds that were racing somewhere? Who was to know?

THE HOUSE OF THE NEWLY-WEDS

What will Father say? Uzak fretted. This thought had plagued him the entire way from the farm garage to his father's house.

Indeed, how *would* he inform his father that he and Tana would suddenly gather their things together and begin a separate life, without even warning him in advance? This would go against the old Kazakh tradition, when the father informs all the relatives in good time that his son is planning to make his own family home. Traditionally, his father would then have slaughtered an animal and thrown a modest party for the whole village to mark the special occasion, because every parent dreams of seeing their youngsters in their own home to continue the family line.

Today, Uzak was going to deprive his father of this joy. His anger had already subsided, giving way to a feeling of embarrassment and guilt before his father. Despite all this, he was not going to change his decision; it was quite impossible for him to continue living under his parents' roof.

The talkative young driver had tried to start a conversation with Uzak but soon thought better of it. All he asked was:

'So, you're going to live in Zhappas's old house?'

Uzak nodded absent-mindedly, too engrossed in his own thoughts.

'But the place is falling apart!'

'It'll do for now. It's warm enough and I'll build a new home in the summer. The chairman promised to help with the materials.'

'You could do that' agreed the driver. 'You'd only need to call the *dzhigits* to help a couple of times and the house'll be done by the end of the summer.'

The conversation dried up, for Zhappas's old house and the construction of its replacement were very much secondary in Uzak's thoughts at that moment. What he would say to his father and how his father would react – these were the most important questions.

There was also his mother. However, he didn't much care how his mother would react to his departure because it had been because of her victimisation of Tana that he had planned to leave the family home early. He only had to recall his mother and his earlier grievances all returned to the surface. Of course, his mother had given him the gift of life and had nurtured him with her milk, and he had no right to oppose her. At the same time, however, no one had the right to force him to continue living within the same four walls as her. He had waited all through the long winter for his mother's heart to melt and change her attitude to Tana. However, the winter passed, the snow melted and the sun warmed the earth, but his mother's heart remained like ice, devoid of all feeling.

Tana had not slept a wink all night, complaining of stomach pains, and she had only dropped off as morning approached. Uzak's mother had already risen

258

by that time and all it took was for Tana to close her eyes and she would emit a piercing scream:

'Tana-a! Hey, Tana! Are you going to tell me you didn't know we had no water in the house?!'

Tana, meanwhile, who had been curled up in a ball, pressed up to him as if she had finally found her protection from all her suffering. Her tender, long-drawn face had become thinner these past days and was cast in bluish shadows from the grey morning light. Tana was sleeping like a child who had finally cried herself to sleep; she sniffled occasionally, sighed intermittently and frowned. Uzak pitied his wife so much it hurt. The poor thing had recently been through a tough time. Their future child was already showing signs of restlessness, making itself known and, to add insult to injury, she had all the household chores on her shoulders, turning in late and rising at the crack of dawn.

'Tana-a, quit your dawdling! Get up this minute!' Uzak's mother screamed, drumming on the door as if the entire world was on fire.

Tana leapt up with a jolt and grabbed her dress.

'I'll be right there, Mama, one moment,' she muttered, shaking with fright and struggling with the dress.

'You stay there, Tana. I'll go for the water,' Uzak said and, getting up, he gently placed Tana back on the bed.

Then he quickly dressed, pulling on his trousers, shoving his bare feet into his boots and throwing his wadded jacket over his singlet, before emerging into the hall.

'Mama, give me the bucket. I'll be right back.'

What was to unfold! The mother quite lost it, as if she had stepped on hot coals, torn the heavens to shreds and laid waste to the mountains. She had buried poor Tana under layers of family soil, dragged her out into the light of day and then buried her again. In his mother's eyes, she was nothing but an idle shirker who had no respect for her elders. Her words whistled like bullets, pitiless and crushing.

She had always been gentle and thoughtful towards her son but appeared blind and unable to see that every coarse word towards Tana caused her son great pain. She couldn't care less that Tana had also been someone else's darling child, raised with care and tenderness.

After her antics that day, Uzak said to himself, *I've had enough of all this. I am leaving today. Whatever happens, we are moving out today.*

He walked out without even drinking his tea. He spent half a day looking for an apartment, but was turned down at every corner; either the people didn't want to share cramped spaces, or they wanted to avoid falling out with Uzak's father. The place on offer was Zhappas's dilapidated old house, where he had previously lived with his old wife. It didn't look particularly joyful, but at least they'd have a roof over their heads and Uzak had made his mind up.

He had headed straight to see the chairman of the collective farm to ask about a truck. Now he was travelling to collect Tana and their things.

So, what on earth will I say to Father? he asked himself for what must have been the twentieth time.

'We're here!' the driver announced. 'Only, Uzak, don't hang about, alright? I'm really pushed for time.'

He remained in the cab, yawning broadly and looking with interest over at Uzak's house, waiting for the performance to begin.

Uzak entered the house, his heart racing.

'Uzak, dear, where on earth have you been? We were expecting you for lunch,' his mother said with a gentle reproach.

She rolled up the wool she had been kneading, evidently intending to feed him.

'Where's Father?' Uzak asked, already fearful.

'I don't know. He was here a minute ago and then he went out for something.'

His mother approached the stove and felt the kettle. It was still warm.

'Here, have a wash in some warm water, dear. Let me pour.' She took the kettle and then cried out in quite a different voice: 'Tana! Get in here and heat up the soup. And be quick about it! Can't you see your husband's hungry?!'

'There's no need, mama, I won't have any dinner,' Uzak declared. He had made his way to a chair by the window and slumped down onto it as if the decision he had made had taken away his last ounce of strength. He looked past his mother and said quietly,

'Mama, we are leaving you.'

He had wanted to add the customary 'if that's alright', but thought it was now meaningless.

'What do you mean, you're leaving? Where to?' she replied, taken aback.

She stared at him, stupefied, and then looked over at Tana, who had appeared in the room. However, his wife was just as much in the dark as to what was going on. She only sensed that something important in their lives was taking place; she turned pale, her eyes open wide.

'Yes, we are leaving you,' Uzak repeated, gaining in confidence, as the highest barrier had been overcome. 'Anyway, we're moving, mama. I am an independent man and I want to live separately. I have my own family. And now a house has come my way. Zhappas has offered me temporary accommodation.' He turned to his wife: 'Tana, hurry up and gather your things. The truck's outside.'

'You could at least drink some tea,' Tana suggested in bewilderment.

'There's no time! The driver won't wait!'

Uzak stepped over to the bed, rolled up the mattress and began to strap it up. He hid his eyes from his mother; he hadn't the courage to face her pleading eyes. He could hear her quietly sniffling and saying,

'Son, and what about your father? Your father: you could have waited for him...'

He tried to suppress his pity and cried out to his wife, who was standing indecisively, glancing over in fright at her mother-in-law.

'Get a move on, come on! I told you: the truck is waiting! You could at least put some clothes on!'

He called the driver over and they took the bed down and took it to the truck in pieces. Then, he loaded the bedding.

'That's it, I think,' he said to the driver.

'Huh, you got a truck over for just that? Couldn't you have carried it on your back?' the driver joked good-naturedly.

Tana finally got herself ready and came out of the house. Uzak sat her in the cab while he climbed into the back. The driver started the engine and the truck shuddered into life, ready to pull away. At that moment, Uzak's father appeared, as if from under the ground. Uzak seemed to turn to stone, while the driver looked out of the cab and killed the engine.

'How's the stove at Zhappas's place? It's fallen to pieces, no doubt?' his father asked.

'It's nothing, we'll light the primus,' Uzak muttered.

'You just make sure that Tana of yours doesn't catch a cold,' his father said with his characteristic reserve.

Uzak's father was completely calm as if he had long been ready for the day when his son would leave without the slightest warning. He approached the truck, checked to ensure the bedhead was properly secured to the side, and then said, 'Wait a moment.' He went to the shed, brought out an old piece of felt and placed it between the side of the truck and the head of the bed, to prevent the paint from scratching.

No one would ever know, thought Uzak, what was going on inside his heart and how much bitterness would now reside deep down. It wouldn't be easy for him. Word would now spread that he was the man who had driven his own son from his family home. Uzak's father, however, was a proud man. He stepped away, turned and straightened a stake in the fence in a business-like manner. He simply made it look as if nothing out of the ordinary was taking place, nothing worth worrying about. And yet, however hard one might try, when you see off a truck, taking your son away from you, your eyes will always give you away.

The driver started the engine once again. The mother, who had pulled herself together at the sight of her husband, couldn't stop herself and said,

'Son! I'm your own mother, why...' but his father stopped her dead, barking,

'Quiet, woman!'

The father's usually grey, deep-set eyes had turned red, like two crystals of red-hot salt, and they were fixed angrily on the mother's face.

The truck pulled away and trundled down the street past the neighbours who, old and young, had poured onto the streets as if to watch a wedding procession. They stood by their fences, whispering to one another and pointing fingers.

Uzak felt hurt, both for himself and, especially, for his father. He had dishonoured his father and muddied his name. He had left his father's house forever; the house where he had been born and where he had grown up. He pitied his good-for-nothing mother. For some reason, all four of them, it turned out, were unhappy, unfortunate people. A bitter lump rose in his throat and Uzak wanted to burst into tears. Endeavouring to suppress his imminent sobs, he grasped the side of the truck, stood up and faced the biting wind that was blowing towards him.

The day was overcast and inclement. There was still dirt out on the road. The manure and rubbish that had lain under the snow throughout the winter had now thawed, giving out an acrid, unpleasant smell.

Bumps in the road rocked the truck from side to side. Uzak recomposed himself a little from the shaking of the truck and the penetrating wind.

One by one, homes with walls, flaking and soaked-through after the winter and spring, flashed by and were left behind. Then, Zhappas's new house with its metal roof came into view. In front of it was his old, lop-sided, tumble-down house, built back in the first year of the collective farm's existence. Its new occupants were greeted with grubby walls of crumbling plaster and a subsiding roof; its only window looked out at the world like the eye of a man, tormented by disease.

No matter, it will do for now. We'll make do for the time being. We'll be fine and later we'll build ourselves a real home, Uzak thought, in an attempt to raise his spirits, for the appearance of this run-down hovel would have been enough to bring anyone to despair.

'Your palace awaits,' the driver said, stopping the truck and climbing out of the cab.

Uzak jumped to the ground and helped Tana down. She still seemed half asleep and was quite unable to make head nor tail of what was going on. Zhappas and his wife were the last to appear on the scene. The old man congratulated Uzak and Tana on the start of their independent life. The old woman, though, suddenly grew angry:

'How could your father and mother allow their children out to fend for themselves? Oh, how helpless they are!'

'Don't listen to her, kids. You know what they say: the camel train only builds as it goes along. The time will come and you'll have it all: a roof over your heads and all the rest,' Zhappas assured them, in an attempt to lighten the depressing tone of the old woman's words.

They brought their things into the house. They set the bed in the second room and the meagre array of cooking utensils in the first. When Tana had made the bed, Zhappas's wife spoke up once more:

'Consider the hearth lit, daughter, dear. Now, live in happiness!'

Having blessed the new occupants, the old couple departed. The driver also wished them all the best, climbed up behind the wheel and set off for the farm office. The young couple, for probably the first time in their lives, were left genuinely alone. This was a feeling neither of them had experienced before: Uzak on the only chair and Tana, standing by the window.

They remained in silence, cautiously listening out at the unaccustomed silence that surrounded them after breaking away from their noisy, crowded world. Had this silence prepared something for them?

At last, Tana appeared to free herself from her invisible fetters and she quietly came up to Uzak. She sank her fingers into his thick thatch of hair, combing his tangled locks. Then, she embraced her husband's head and held him to her chest. Uzak let out a sigh as if he had just woken up and he drew Tana closer. He thought he could hear the beating of both his wife and child's hearts, even though they were beating in a single rhythm.

Uzak raised his head, looked into his wife's eyes and smiled. She responded with a tender smile of her own and he suddenly felt a wave of immeasurable happiness come crashing down on him. Tana sensed this in his eyes, grew bashful and blushed; laughing with embarrassment, she hid her face in her hands.

'Don't look at me like that. I'm ashamed,' she whispered, faintly touching her burning lips on his ear.

Whenever she would caress him, she would speak in whispers, as if her own words made her feel awkward.

'Oh, but you must be hungry!' Tana recalled. 'I'll go and prepare something to eat.'

Uzak laughed and shook his head, holding onto Tana. He had forgotten both about their leaving home and the recent bitterness he had felt. All of this had been washed away by this deluge of happiness.

He took her hand tenderly and brought it to his face. To think what had happened to his wife's hands in just one year! Tana's once soft, slender fingers were now cracked, blistered and swollen.

Abashed, Tana whispered guiltily,

'I really don't know how my hands came to be like this.'

She released herself from his embrace and went out into the hall. He could hear her lighting the primus and rattling a frying pan. The aroma of melting fat soon crept into the room, followed by the head-spinning smell of fried meat.

So, our independent life has begun, Uzak said to himself.

He cast a thrifty eye over the walls that Zhappas's wife had hurriedly whitewashed. Her thin solution of bluish lime had not covered the spider's web of cracks on the walls. The ceiling had sagged over the course of time and the beams protruded like ribs. The plastering had crumbled away in places and the ceiling looked like the hide of a mangy horse. Yellow streaks ran from the ceiling to the floor. Clearly, living beneath this roof when it rained was not going to be a load of fun. And everything was wreathed in the deep-rooted, rotten smell of a deserted home.

'Uzak, go and wash your hands!' Tana called.

They laid a cloth over their suitcase and sat down to eat. Uzak thought he had never tasted a dinner so delicious.

'Don't you go far away from now on,' Tana said. 'I'm afraid on my own.'

'I'm going nowhere,' Uzak reassured her while shovelling down the meat. 'The chairman has promised not to send me away on long trips. Until you've given birth.' He scraped his spoon over the bottom of the aluminium bowl and concluded: 'Delicious. I've never eaten anything like it.'

'I didn't make enough, clearly. You're still hungry, I bet.'

'Not at all! I am quite full! Up to here, in fact,' and he brought a flat palm up to his throat.

'Then I'll prepare more for supper.'

'Dinner *and* supper?! It'd be best if you rested. You must be tired after today. Let's go to bed early today.'

'Well, I will have a rest. There's so much to do in this house; I've fed you and that'll do for now,' Tana sighed.

Outside, it had slowly begun to turn dark, but they had remained at home until the evening, sitting knee to knee and discussing what needed to be done. To anyone else, their worries may have appeared minor and insignificant, but, to them, there was nothing more important at that time and Uzak was prepared to sit there forever by Tana's side, talking and talking.

'I'll buy a simple gown for the May holiday. A loose one that won't cost too much,' Tana said.

'But why buy a cheap one? We'll get a decent, expensive one,' Uzak objected.

'Why spend the money? I only need one to wear for now, while I'm expecting.'

'We'll still buy an expensive one! You've got to let people think we're doing alright,' Uzak declared adamantly.

It had turned dark in the room and the darkness had hidden his wife's face from view. Now he made her out by her voice and her warm breath. Tana had been about to get up and light a lamp, but Uzak held her back. He liked sitting with his wife in the dark and knowing that she was there by his side.

'Aren't you cold?' he asked and, embracing Tana around the waist, he drew her near.

Only the day before, Tana would have offered some resistance, whispering something like, *Don't, Uzak. What if mama were to come in; imagine the shame!*

Now, though, she pressed herself up to him, enveloping herself in his embraces. Uzak tickled her neck, kissed her prominent, clean forehead and buried his nose in her hair, breathing in her fragrance.

'Uzak, Uzak!' she called out, suddenly overcome with alarm.

'Tana, what is it?' he responded reluctantly; he had not wanted to interrupt the enchantment of that evening.

'Uzak, mama is really cross with us.'

Uzak flinched as if someone had poured icy water down the back of his neck.

'Uzak, we've rushed into this, haven't we? You have always been so patient. We could have said what we wanted to do and then waited a few days before moving. You know, so as not to offend anyone.'

Uzak remained silent, trying to suppress the pain that had begun to return.

'Father didn't even let on. But it must have really hurt him, mustn't it, Uzak?'

'Yes,' Uzak said with a heavy sigh.

A swishing sound could be heard outside and then an invisible someone began drumming on the glass, barely audible. The couple listened intently and realised that it had started raining.

'Your poor parents. Now they're all alone,' Tana said sadly.

Uzak rose from his chair, stretched his numb muscles and attempted to laugh it off:

'Why *poor*? Maybe, they're sitting in each other's arms just like we are and having a good time.'

He decided that it would be better to joke, chat in a loud voice and move about more and with more spirit, than become overcome with anguish for, otherwise, he'd be done for, what with that bitter lump catching again in his throat.

'Uzak. Hey, Uzak,' Tana went on. 'We'll have children and they'll grow up. Surely, we won't experience the same thing; surely, they won't desert us and leave, right?'

'And rightly so!' Uzak declared, almost joyfully. 'My love, the most important thing is that we are together, always together!'

He found her in the darkness and lifted her gently in his arms.

We really will have children. And let them leave us to live with their own families. I will have my Tana, Uzak thought and placed his wife back on the ground.

'You can light the lamp.'

Tana rummaged around until she found the matches. She struck one and then another, and then lit the kerosene lamp, before hanging it on a nail by the doorpost.

A dull, yellow ball of light appeared in the room. Beyond its reach, everything was pitch black and mysterious; the walls disappeared and the room appeared as large and unwelcoming as the deserted steppe in the twilight. *It would've been better to sit in the dark*, Uzak thought.

Tana wandered about the room, not knowing what to do with herself. Usually, at this time, she would be sieving flour, mixing dough to make bread the next day, handing her father-in-law a jug of warm water to wash with and generally busying herself around the house. Now, though, there was nothing to do. The only thing she could do would be to look over at her lanky, awkward-looking husband. He was amusing himself, creating the appearance that he was enjoying himself, although his cheekbones had become more pronounced and his eyes were sad.

Uzak paced over the earth floor, approached the window a couple of times and tried to peer out into the darkness as if anything could be seen in that rain; he turned up the wick on the lamp. However, this had no effect; the light was still just as dim and silent, just as unfamiliar and depressing.

Tana finally found herself something to do: she picked up a sagebrush broom that Zhappas's wife had left and began sweeping the floor, which had actually been clean. She was evidently doing her best to escape from her thoughts.

It was not difficult to guess what she was thinking about. She was probably thinking about how long she had waited for them to leave Uzak's parents and that she would become the lady of the house in her own right. Her dream had come true and yet she sensed no joy. She felt pity for the old couple they had left to live alone. They were no doubt weeping and cursing her. Perhaps her father-in-law would not judge her, but her mother-in-law would most certainly say something like, *She's tricked our son, she has, that crafty daughter-in-law. She set him at odds with us and disgraced us before the entire aul.* The only thing she was guilty of was that she had never once shown defiance nor even laughed heartily since she had crossed the threshold of her husband's house.

At that moment, it was if her name had been mentioned; she dropped the broom and burst into tears. She buried her teary face into his chest when he embraced her in his attempt to offer comfort.

'Uzak, take me home to my folks. Just take me! I can't go on like this, Uzak, dear,' she asked through her sniffling.

'You silly thing, what have you got into your head? As if I've offended you over something. Everything will work out fine, just have patience,' Uzak muttered, calming his wife.

Tana seemed to quieten down; she wiped her eyes on her apron and repeated,

'Really, Uzak, take me away. I am not in the least offended. You've had a row with your father and mother, and it's all because of me.'

'Stop it!' Uzak cried and picked up a knife from the suitcase. 'Just try and say that again!'

Tana fell silent and turned away.

He embraced her from behind.

'Don't be angry.'

'Wait a moment, I'll cover the window,' Tana said, checking herself. She removed her apron and blocked out the window with it.

'Don't look at me like that. Close your eyes,' Tana asked.

'You're not still shy, are you?'

Tana nodded affirmatively. She went to the lamp and put it out, then approached her husband, sat on his lap and put her arms around his neck.

'Uzak, can I tell you something?'

'Of course.'

'I am really afraid of death. Really and truly. I have these terrible nightmares. I fear that I will die in childbirth.'

'You do talk nonsense, sometimes,' Uzak reproached her softly and ran his hand over her pointed shoulder blades, thinking painfully: *My poor thing, how thin you've grown! You really will find it hard!*

'Time for bed! Come on,' Uzak announced.

Tana fell asleep immediately, having warmed up by his side. Uzak, however, lay on his back, his long legs against the foot of the bed, as if he was trying to stretch out their cramped nest.

So, what happens now? Where do we start? he asked himself, listening to the murmur on the other side of the window.

In the meantime, the rain had begun to fall more heavily. The drops fell more frequently on the glass, transforming into a monotonous, rhythmic noise. This spring rain would now set in for the entire night and would fall unhurriedly, soaking the earth to the last fertile layer and, by morning, it would wash away all the roads.

Someone's late-night cart rattled outside and the earthen floor in their house began to shudder.

'Who is it?' Tana asked, frightened, raising her head from the pillow.

That meant her sleep had only been light and anxious.

'Sleep, my brave one! It's only a cart going by. Why don't you lie against the wall? It'll be quieter for you there.'

They changed places. Uzak looked out into the impenetrable darkness and once more became lost in thought. The caustic aroma of sagebrush from the corner where the switch broom stood filled his nostrils. Yes, it was the sagebrush with its bitter smell.

He remembered the day he had first met Tana. It had been last summer; he had taken grain to the elevator and was returning to the village.

A girl in a white dress stopped him by the barrier at the railway crossing. She raised her hand and he pulled to a halt. The girl's face seemed familiar and he recalled that he had indeed seen her several times clearing dirty dishes from the tables at the station canteen. Judging by appearances, she had been standing there for some time, because soft grey dust

275

had managed to settle in the corners of her eyes and slender nose.

Blushing coyly, the girl asked if she could get in. She needed to get to her relatives who lived at Uzak's collective farm and asked if he wouldn't mind. He opened the door for her in an instant and she sprang up into the cab, light and supple as a flame and radiating joy. Uzak looked at her in surprise. Back in the canteen, she had seemed nothing but a clumsy adolescent unworthy of his attention. *When on earth had she managed to blossom like that?* he asked himself, clucking his tongue in amazement. He continually looked over at her out of the corner of his eye, laughing to himself: yes, that's how life goes sometimes.

He was in such excellent spirits that, halfway through the journey, he fumbled around under his seat and retrieved a bottle of red wine that he had been taking home. Then, he stopped his truck, opened the bottle and offered it to the girl.

'Here, beautiful, have a drink!'

But the girl flushed a crimson colour, shook her head and refused.

'Well, don't you go saying I never offered you any.'

He threw back his head, brought the bottle to his lips and took a swig. The wine went straight to his head and he began to flirt with the girl, trying to find out how obliging she might be.

'You have really grown into a genuine beauty.'

However, the girl remained silent and sat with her back to him. He looked at her deep red neck, her small ears and the thick plaits on the back of her head. *What a perfect neck; A swan's neck, they call it,* he thought and then tried once more to bring her out of her shell.

'I suppose you have a young man, right? Some gallant *dzhigit*, eh?'

The girl remained silent and blushed; he was astonished at how she could blush all the time.

'Speak up, or has the cat got your tongue?' he added, even more amused.

The girl shrunk back shyly and said nothing.

'It's not good, you not saying anything. You know, it's not very polite,' he added haughtily.

He started the engine and they pulled away, but two or so kilometres down the road, he stopped again, in the middle of a road that was as smooth as the palm of the hand.

'The engine has overheated,' he explained, looking around.

Sagebrush was growing waist-high along both sides of the road. It stood like a thick, grey forest, covered and coated with the summer dust. The air, too, was impregnated with the strong aroma of sagebrush and dust.

The girl finally turned her head, looked at him enquiringly, as if to ask, *are we going to sit here long?* The lad smirked and took her hand. The girl shuddered and began to fumble for the door handle with her free hand.

'Don't be frightened. I'm only mucking about,' he said, continuing to hold her hand. In desperation, the girl flapped her arms, like a dying bird flaps its wings, slapped him across the face and began to shed silent tears.

She looked so unhappy that he sobered up in an instant and came to his senses.

'Sorry... I'm sorry, alright? I really am sorry, do you understand?' he muttered.

She didn't believe him; he would never forget her eyes at that unfortunate moment. They contained such desperation.

They travelled the rest of the journey in silence. When they entered the village, the girl asked him to stop the truck and he had barely helped her open the cab door than she jumped out like a rabbit, sensing an opportunity for escape.

He sat in the cab and watched her go with a sense of eternal guilt. You could say that that was the moment he had fallen in love with Tana.

His wife stirred. Uzak heard her voice:

'You're not sleeping?'

'No, I just remembered something. You remember, the first time we travelled from the station?'

Tana laughed sleepily.

'Oh, you frightened me then and no mistake. You scoundrel!'

She poked him with her elbow, feigning anger.

'You could do in my lungs like that,' Uzak joked and then became serious: 'You know, I may have frightened you, but I would never have done anything bad. I even repented after that.' Then, after a pause, he added, 'I can only imagine how you must have hated me back then.'

'For what?'

'Come off it, I stopped the truck in the middle of the steppe, without a soul to be seen, and I started hitting on you. What girl would go for a lad like that?'

'I always liked you. You may have scared me, but there was no hatred. I don't know why, but there was none.'

'And if I had... you know... then what?'

'I probably knew that you wouldn't take it that far. Perhaps, deep inside, that's what I believed. Otherwise, I wouldn't have waited for you and taken the bus. And everything would have been fine if you hadn't had that wine. That's what caused it all.'

'Hold on a minute,' Uzak said in surprise. 'So, you were waiting there for me on purpose? Just for me? Especially for me?'

'Well, yes. I had long had my eye on you. Ever since that time you came into the canteen, all covered in oil, I think it was. I don't know why, but there was something about you I liked. And if I hadn't liked you, I would never have agreed to marry you,' Tana went on, a little embarrassed.

Only then did it occur to Uzak that, despite that event, Tana had indeed agreed too quickly to become his wife.

That evening, he had met her at the club. He caught sight of her white dress the moment he crossed the threshold. Either the village lads had not yet noticed her, or they were still shy in coming forward, but she was dancing alone with the other girls. Nevertheless, her face still radiated happiness; the music and the dance itself seemed to fill her with joy. It was only when she lifted her eyes to meet his dogged gaze that a flash of fear flared up in them.

He wanted to atone for his guilt once and for all, repent once again, to ensure she realised that the lad standing before her was wholly respectable. Twice, he tried to approach her, but each time she hid from him in the crowd of dancers. Then she slipped away from the club, quite unnoticed.

The next day, he visited the barn again, loaded his truck with grain and set off for the station. A familiar figure in white stood at the end of the village. He braked quickly and the truck came to a halt in front of Tana, as if striking an invisible wall.

'Are you going home? Hop in, I'll give you a lift,' he offered with feigned bravado as if nothing at all had happened the day before.

Tana demonstratively turned away.

'I'm sorry about yesterday. Can you really not forgive me?' he asked meekly.

Tana didn't reply. A whirlwind suddenly swirled in from the steppe and launched into the folds of her dress. The girl held down her hem, but remained silent. But Uzak waited. He didn't really register how much time had gone by. Then another farm truck drove up, filled with grain, and Tana climbed in.

Uzak spent the entire journey utterly incensed: *Just look at that princess, behaving like the devil knows what! How many times do I need to say I'm sorry?! But not any more,* and he drove his truck on like a madman, barely paying attention to the road, his wheels slipping into the potholes and the ditches on either side.

However, when the vehicle up ahead pulled into the side before the barrier and came to a halt, Uzak pulled his own truck to a stop.

Tana got out of the cab; Uzak could not restrain himself, leaned out of the window and cried out,

'Hey, are you still upset, is that it?'

The girl turned around and waved her hand as if to say, *No, I'm not upset,* and she ran off towards the canteen.

Several days went by and he had returned to the station when his truck began to feel sorry for itself, leaking oil and much more besides. He laboured the entire day and, having more or less patched the truck up, he trudged to the canteen, weary and hungry. He opened the door and almost knocked Tana clean off her feet as she carried a pile of dirty dishes.

'I'm really sorry!' he said in desperation.

For the first time, the girl looked him square in the face and laughed merrily. She put the dishes down onto a free table and ran to the kitchen with her hand over her mouth. Uzak sat down and she busied herself with her chores, but the moment their eyes met, she would instantly burst into fits of laughter. When she walked past him, he asked her in a hurt tone,

'What's so funny?'

'Oh, I just remembered something from *The Death of a Clerk*'

'Chekhov, isn't it?' he queried cautiously, quite unable to comprehend what she was hinting at.

281

'Aha, that's right,' she replied with a smile. 'He, too was forever asking forgiveness, much like you. And I'm laughing, but you'll get home and take to your bed and pine away...'

He had not even managed to take offence when she changed her tone and looked concerned:

'Is there something wrong with your truck?'

'It was playing up a little, yes.'

'Is it all sorted now? Have you fixed it?'

'Of course. And do you have any further plans to come over our way?'

The girl replied with a vague shrug of the shoulders.

'When do you finish work?'

'Very soon; about fifteen minutes.'

'I'll wait for you outside, alright?' he suggested with his final shred of hope.

She did not reply, mentioned something about the work she still had to do and that she had been standing talking too long. She disappeared into the room where they washed the dishes. Nevertheless, he waited for her to finish. After a brief hesitation, she climbed into his cab and they drove all the way to her house.

'Tana, don't take offence, but just hear me out,' he began to say hurriedly, while the girl was still in the truck.

Tana nodded as if consenting for him to continue.

'Come to our village with me!' he blurted out.

'What on earth for?'

'You see, I love you. I want to take you away with me, you see! Forever!'

282

Uzak spoke passionately and at length and afterwards could not remember exactly what he had said. That was because he had quite lost his head for fear that she might not believe him.

A month later, they were married. Tana moved to Uzak'sparents' house, leaving behind her widowed mother and two brothers.

From the very first day, Uzak's mother tormented the poor girl. She had had plans to marry off Uzak to the daughter of a friend who lived nearby. However, that girl had been too young for marriage and she would have had to wait and be patient. A year or two down the line and everything would have worked out as planned, only this demure little thing had come along, bewitched and enchanted Uzak and his mother's plans had gone up in smoke.

'Uzak, are you asleep?'

'No, I just can't seem to drop off.'

'I'm wide awake too. I think that everything, even my head, is spinning... Why is it that a person grows and their sadness grows with them? There were times in childhood when I was hurt, but I thought to myself: *Not to worry. Just wait: you'll grow up and then everything will be alright.* I grew up and started telling myself: *Not to worry. You'll get yourself a home, a family and everything will fall into place.* Now I have a home and a family. Don't be upset; I *am* happy. I am just saying that I am happy; it's just that the sadness doesn't seem to diminish.'

283

'This is all temporary. Why are you talking like that? We'll build ourselves a real home and things will be as they should be.'

'That's not what I'm talking about, Uzak. Do you know what I mean? Look, a boy and a girl marry out of love. What else, you would think. But then they start to offend and hurt one another. Well, they live together a month, or five, or ten, but then they still end up arguing. So, I've been thinking: what's it all down to? It's probably because love turns cold.'

'Well, there's life for you, I suppose,' he replied vaguely, but fell into thought: *Indeed, why can't people live in peace and harmony?*

'So, what we have is the strong ordering the weak. But life isn't easy for the strong either, is it?'

'I don't know. What is love at the end of the day? What do you think?'

'Well, it's probably about walking, breathing and doing something every day,' she said pensively.

'Tana, but that's what we're doing, isn't it? So, life is all about you and me!'

'That's what I'm saying: if life is all about us, then why are we doing bad things to ourselves and others? Why can't everyone just be happy?'

'Clearly, there is no one who can answer that. Although, perhaps there is,' Uzak said with a sigh.

They fell silent, each wrapped up in their own thoughts. Then, he heard his wife's even breathing. She was sleeping. Having warmed up, Tana continually threw off the blanket. He sat up, replaced the blanket and tucked it under her side. She slept fitfully, crying out from time to time.

He recalled how beautiful Tana had become in the first weeks of their marriage; a little plump with rosy cheeks. It seemed that the slightest knock would ignite the inner flame she hid within. Back then, it didn't even occur to him to pity her. She seemed so wonderful and independent that at times he couldn't believe that this woman could have married him, Uzak. It was then that he had begun to see some scheming calculation in Tana's affections.

Uzak was plagued by a sense that Tana didn't entirely belong to him. He wanted to bring his wife to heel, whatever the cost. About two months later, he raised his hand to her for no apparent reason. On that late summer's day, he had been taking hay to the winter camps out in the sands and he returned only deep into the night, tired and in a foul mood. By that time, Tana, also weary from the daily drudge, had fallen asleep and Uzak's mother opened the door.

'The husband returns from his journey, barely able to stand on his feet, but his shameless wife just stretches her legs out like some lady of the manor. She is clearly taking advantage of her placid husband,' she declared.

On that occasion, she achieved her goal. Bristling with rage, Uzak burst into the room, lifted the curled-up Tana by the shoulders and slapped her across the face twice.

At that moment, he didn't realise that the only thing Tana had been guilty of was to have grown weary from her household chores; she had fallen asleep, sitting up waiting for her husband. She was still little more than a child and was indeed able to handle work about the house from morning till late at night? Tana didn't even ask why her husband was beating her. She simply cowered and covered her face with her hand to protect herself from the man who, on their wedding night, had vowed never to strike her and carry her on his palm like a delicate plume.

Uzak moaned with shame when he remembered this.

Something rustled in the corner. He strained his ears and his acute hearing discerned the squeaking of mice. Their feet scuttled along the floor and over the dishes, emitting a ringing sound. The mice seemed to be racing after each other, filling the silence with their frantic scurrying.

That's all we need, Uzak muttered resentfully and, trying not to disturb his wife, he reached down from the bed, picked up a boot and hurled it into the corner. The mice fell silent but, after a short while, they continued scurrying about again, this time with double the effort. Uzak launched the second boot, only this time he missed the mark and the sound of smashing dishes rang out.

'What was that?' said Tana with a start.

'It's me... Rather, it's mice... We have mice in the house.'

'Oh, you really gave me a fright. As if you'd fired a gun. Don't go making any more noises like that, Uzak.'

She pressed up close to him. It seemed that her heart was beating right up in her throat.

'Relax and sleep. I'll be quiet now, I promise.'

Uzak rose from the bed, walked across the room barefoot, lit a match and put the boots back in their place.

'I broke a bowl. That's a shame,' he reported, getting back under the covers.

'Not to worry. We'll share the bowl in the morning and then I'll buy another,' Tana said soothingly.

They chatted a little longer. Uzak had wanted to light a lamp to ward off the mice, but Tana told him she wouldn't be able to sleep with the light on.

The rain fell in a melancholic drone, as if it had set its mind on slowly washing everything, including the old, dilapidated wattle-and-daub house.

'Uzak!'

'What is it, my dear?'

'Give me your hand. Can you hear how restless he is? He's kicking away like nobody's business! Before you know it, he'll force his way out of my side. Oh, this one's going to be a right rascal.'

'That's good! We'll have a boy and I'll teach him how to be a proper rascal. He'll never give anyone any peace! All people will hear is *Uzak's son did that*, or *That son of Uzak's is a right mischievous imp*.'

'What's so good about that?'

'Oh, I'm just talking away. You'll need to give birth to him first.'

'If only everything ends up alright!'

'Come on, don't cry. There's no need for that! You'll see: there's nothing to fear.'

'I'm not crying any more.'

Sleep had finally got the better of Tana. Again, though, Uzak's thoughts scattered in forty different directions. He reckoned he'd get down to repairing the house the next day. *Even if we only live here until the summer in this dump*, he said to himself stubbornly. Then he would set poison for the mice, for they couldn't afford the crockery if he were to chuck his boots around the place every night. And they couldn't do without a stove, either. They only had to make it through till the summer and, heaven forbid, Tana wouldn't catch a cold. At the same time, he would have to start getting the materials together for their future home.

He realised only at this point how hard it was to be the independent master of your own house and what responsibility he had taken onto his shoulders.

Tana groaned quietly in her sleep. Their little one was eager to emerge into the world and kicked out from inside. Uzak imagined that this kick reached him as well. *A rascal indeed, and no mistake*, he marvelled.

He firmly resolved that, once Tana had given birth, he would remain by her side, until both his wife and child had grown stronger. The farm chairman would have to wait with his long trips; he'd have to count on finding someone else. He wasn't going to step a foot beyond the village. Heaven forbid, anything should happen to Tana when he wasn't around. *Best not think about it; I don't want to tempt fate,'* Uzak said to himself.

He no longer paid any attention to the scurrying of the mice. He recalled his former life with Tana, one day after the other. And it had held little joy for her. One day, she had almost left him after one particular affront.

That day, Uzak had been paid his salary for three months' work and had gone out with his friends. He returned only at dusk, swaying this way and that, leaning his shoulder against the fence. His father was driving the cow into the shed at the time. His mother's irritated voice reached him from the doorway. As always, she was finding fault with his wife.

'What's up?' Uzak queried, holding onto the door.

'What are you asking me for? You should ask that wife of yours. She does whatever she pleases in the house.'

'What's happened?' he asked, staring at Tana who was crouching down, lighting the stove.

'My dress was growing tight on me, so I bought four metres of material to make a new one,' Tana explained with a guilty smile.

'Buy ten metres, for all I care. But why didn't you consult with me? Do I not count for anything in this house?' his mother snivelled, tears welling up in her eyes.

The confused smile remained on Tana's face and this put Uzak out of temper. He flew into a rage.

'Oh, so you think you can make fun of my mother, do you?' he screamed wildly.

Tana said something by way of justification, but her every word seemed to add further fuel to his fire. He showered her with the most terrible language and then cried out:

'Get out of this house this instant! I don't care if you are carrying ten children in there; get out right now! I'll find myself a better wife, you'll see! You suggested getting married yourself and you're still laughing at our expense. Just look at you, you wretch!'

Tana ran out of the house in what she was wearing – nothing but a flimsy dress. Uzak rushed out after her, but in the yard, he came face to face with his father. His father slapped him with the back of his hand and cried out,

'I'd have been better off without a son!'

Uzak crouched down where he was and clutched his shoulder. Returning to his senses, he looked around and imagined he could see something dark like a large owl out in the twilight, rising up above the top of the hill beyond the village. He realised that Tana was now running straight out across the steppe towards the station.

What is she doing? he thought fearfully. *It must be thirty kilometres to the station from here. She can't do that, doesn't she know?*

Uzak rushed off along the path that Tana had taken, his feet slipping in the dirt that had become coated in frost. The dusk soon became impenetrable darkness and he was running almost blind. The darkness had seemed to swallow Tana up and Uzak lost hope of ever seeing her again.

The pathway wound its way around the plain, shot up into the hills and spiralled down into the ravines.

'Tana-a! Tana-a!' he screamed in a heart-rending voice.

His cry filled the vale with its echo and spluttered across the plain, but Tana did not respond. The path circled the next hill and, up ahead, Uzak caught sight of a tall bonfire. Tana was sitting by the flames, her knees up by her chest.

He ran up to the bonfire and stopped to catch his breath. Tana didn't stir and continued to stare at the flickering flames. Uzak took her under her arms and tried to lift her, but Tana wouldn't let him. They remained there until the morning, throwing what was left of the hay from the rick onto the fire. Uzak begged forgiveness and pleaded with Tana, but his wife offered no response. Then he wept and she also shed tears, but it appeared she had no intention of forgiving him. She was not aggrieved at him or her mother-in-law; rather, she judged herself for having rushed into her marriage. And it was this that tormented Uzak more than anything.

At dawn, his father came to them on his dray. The old man got down from the cart, sat down beside Tana, embraced her and said,

'Tana, my dear daughter, let's go home. I've come for you.'

If his father had not come that morning, Uzak would probably have lost Tana for good. However, she returned home a different person. From that day on,

Uzak often noticed the indifference that haunted her face. Not a trace was left of her customary gaiety and chattiness. There were times when she would remain silent for days on end. When he caressed her as he did on this day, her response no longer emanated the same warmth as before.

Uzak shed a secret tear and he felt better for it, as if his heartstrings, which had been hitherto tense to the point of pain, had slackened a little. He realised that tears degrade a man but no one would ever know that he had wept that night.

The cockerels crowed in the yards but Uzak had not closed his eyes the entire night. He raised himself on an elbow and looked out the window. It was dark as night and the rain was still falling incessantly.

Uzak had already grown accustomed to the noise of the downpour and the scurrying of the mice, but he also discerned some new sounds. The drip, drip of water coming through the corner nearest to him. Uzak carefully sat at the end of the bed, lit a match and purveyed the ceiling. Droplets were hanging like grain in a colander. The droplets swelled and then fell before his very eyes. He would only have to touch that part of the ceiling and a small waterfall would have deluged the bed from above.

Uzak put on his boots and went over to the lamp, struck a match and, finding an empty bucket, he placed it under the largest of the holes. The drops drummed a dull beat on the bottom of the zinc pail.

Right at that very moment, a large piece of sodden plasterwork came away from the wall. Uzak grabbed the kettle and placed it under the new opening. Soon he had set out all the pots and pans in the house and an orchestra of droplets rang out.

Uzak then devoted all his efforts to saving the bed. He gently moved it away from the wall and laid his canvas raincoat on top of the blanket.

All thoughts of sleep had deserted him. Like a besieged animal, he listened attentively in the darkness, guessing where the next onslaught would come from, covering his wife's face with his hand just in case.

The concert refused to end. The kettle rang shrilly and the bucket tapped dully.

Tana turned over onto her other side but, thankfully, did not wake up. The shrill and dull sounds continued. Tana suddenly let out a groan. Then the raincoat rustled and that meant she was hot; she tried to throw off the coat and the blanket with her foot.

'What are you doing? You'll catch a cold,' Uzak whispered and set about covering his wife up again.

However, she struck Uzak on the arm and with some force, as if she had wanted to strike off his desire to care for her once and for all. He hesitated but then looked closely at Tana's face and saw that she was still in a deep slumber.

Sodden plasterwork crumbled from the walls and the ceiling. There weren't enough pots and pans and the water now fell freely onto the floor in shrill, dull and sharp succession.

No matter, we'll survive. Tomorrow, I'll sprinkle ash over the roof and then get hold of some roofing felt. Then you can fall as much as you want, Uzak addressed the rain.

Tana turned and snuggled up to him. Uzak was happy and calmed by the thought that, as before, his wife sought protection in him.

He fell asleep without realising. His eyelids had become heavy and closed of their own accord. Uzak whirled into the darkness. When he awoke, he felt full of energy; he laughed and sat up in bed. It was light in the room; outside, the clouds had cleared to reveal patches of blue sky. He looked up at the ceiling. No droplets were falling but it had become dark and wet.

His wife was not by his side.

Now we're an independent family. A house of newly-weds, you could say, he uttered happily.

Voices could be heard from the doorway. Uzak listened in; his wife and mother were discussing something.

'We'll lay this matting on the floor. The floor must still be cold,' his mother said.

The dull thud of an axe and the voice of his father reached him from the yard.

'Listen, Zhalpas, would it not be better to place this pillar in the room?'

His father's boots stamped in the entranceway and he said,

'But where's that Uzak? Is he planning to sleep in until dinnertime?'

Uzak woke up, stretched and leapt from the bed as if he had been launched by a metal spring.

294

Printed in Poland
by Amazon Fulfillment
Poland Sp. z o.o., Wrocław

65326766R00168